rec'd 1/20/23

DATE DUE

3/20/23	283

Secrets of the Nile

A LADY EMILY MYSTERY

SECRETS OF THE NILE

TASHA ALEXANDER

WHEELER PUBLISHING
A part of Gale, a Cengage Company

GALE
A Cengage Company

**LIBRARY OF CONGRESS CIP DATA ON FILE.
CATALOGUING IN PUBLICATION FOR THIS BOOK
IS AVAILABLE FROM THE LIBRARY OF CONGRESS.**

ISBN-13: 979-8-8857-8550-1 (hardcover alk. paper)

Published in 2023 by arrangement with St. Martin's Publishing Group.

Printed in Mexico
Print Number: 1   Print Year: 2023

For Jonathan Boulton, Peggy Emery,
Dolores Frese, Mary Peters,
Richard Sisti, Jeannine Garrard, and
Jane Syburg: extraordinary teachers
who enriched my life beyond measure.

Our sins, like to our shadows, when our day was in its glory, scarce appeared; toward our evening, how great and monstrous!

— *John Suckling*

1904

1

Colossal ancient monuments. Azure skies. Desert sunsets. The endless romance of the Nile. That was my vision of travel in Egypt, a vision sadly incongruous with reality. Perhaps that's not quite fair. Monuments, skies, and sunsets we had in abundance, but my imperious mother-in-law and petulant stepdaughter presented a significant barrier to romance, endless or otherwise. And then there was the matter of violent death at the dinner table.

When Colin first broached the subject of taking a holiday with his mother, Ann Hargreaves, I beseeched all the gods I could think of — Christian, Jewish, Muslim, Hindu, ancient Greek — to bring me serenity. One or more of them proving effective, I found it in me to take my husband's hand, bestow upon him a radiant smile, and tell him I could think of nothing that would bring me better pleasure.

"You're a terrible liar," he said, raising my hand to his lips before retreating to sit on the chair across from me, its leather softened by generations of use. We were in the library of our country estate, Anglemore Park, situated in the most beautiful part of Derbyshire, all peaks and glorious moors. "We'd be doing Mother an enormous favor. She's been invited by an old family friend, Lord Bertram Deeley."

"Lord Deeley . . . I seem to recall him from an exhausting dinner party some years ago. Relentlessly cheerful and has all the wrong ideas about politics?"

"That's the one. His wife suffered from consumption, and as a result, they started wintering in Egypt decades ago. He kept up the habit after she died. Dabbled at excavation, but found he prefers buying antiquities to getting dusty finding them. Still, not the worst bloke I've ever met. Terribly fond of Mother. Tended to folly-largesse in his youth, but reined in his worst excesses once he inherited his title."

"Presumably at the same time his politics took a turn for the worse?"

"Quite right, my dear," he said, stretching his long legs in front of him and crossing them at the ankle. There was the slightest hint of silver in his dark hair, near the temples, but he was even handsomer than he'd been the first day I met him. My dear friend Cécile du Lac insisted that no man could be interesting before forty, and while I didn't subscribe to her opinion, I could not deny that Colin's features — more chiseled than they'd been in his youth — only improved with age. He would still make the perfect model for a Praxiteles sculpture. "Deeley's of a different generation, so I try not to hold it too much against him."

I raised an eyebrow; Colin was not ordinarily so generous when it came to politics. "So your mother requires us as reinforcements?"

He shifted in his chair. "Every year, Deeley puts together a party to join him for a leisurely cruise up the Nile and a stay at his house in Luxor. Now that he's invited her, she doesn't feel that she can refuse."

"No doubt she balks at the idea of finding herself trapped on a boat for week after week in limited company." If that were the case, I wouldn't blame her. I didn't like the sound of it, either.

"I'm sure she does, but that's not what's stopped her. You know she met Father in Egypt —"

"Halfway up the Great Pyramid at Giza," I said. "They were engaged by the time they

11

returned to the bottom and married three days later." The story had endeared his mother to me from the first moment I'd heard it. It was the culmination of nearly two decades during which, with her delightfully eccentric father's support, she'd steadfastly avoided marriage in favor of exotic travel. I had expected we'd get along famously, but our relationship had a tendency to run from moderately strained to openly hostile. Still, we respected each other — begrudgingly — and had more in common than either of us was likely to admit in public. I had no illusions that traveling together would bring us closer.

"They went back every winter after that until he died, but she hasn't returned since," Colin said. "She couldn't bear to go without him."

"What changed?"

He shrugged. "She told me I was impertinent when I asked. Presumably Deeley knew going there might be challenging for her and that's why he hasn't proffered the invitation until now, after so many years have passed. I think we ought to accompany her as it may prove an emotionally difficult journey. We won't be alone in offering support. Kat's agreed to come as well."

Colin's nearly grown daughter, Katharina

von Lange, was unknown to him until two years ago. His work as an agent of the Crown took him around the globe, securing the interests of the Empire. It was frequently dangerous. Long before we met, he'd had a relationship with an Austrian countess and longtime colleague. Kat was the product of their involvement. The countess had hidden their daughter's existence from him, fearing that if he were known to be her father, the child could be used to get to him. Such are the ways of covert agents, or so I'm told. I long ago decided not to argue the point; it made for a more peaceful home. Obviously, Colin had no such fears — he did not hesitate to marry me and start a family — yet apparently the countess felt differently. Theirs had been a passionate and tumultuous affair, but Colin had ended it the moment he fell in love with me. That he had adored her I'd never doubted; a dozen years ago I'd seen the pain her death in the line of duty had caused him. Now, I was content to relegate the past to where it belonged. Most of the time, that is. Kat did her best to keep it front and center.

"She can afford to take the time away from her studies?" I asked.

He scowled, not an expression he pulled often while discussing his daughter. When it came to his children, he had a tendency toward overindulgence. "I haven't managed to convince her to continue at Oxford. She explained she prefers the world as classroom."

The countess had settled upon Kat a significant fortune that, until she turned twenty-five, Colin would manage on her behalf. Even so, her generous allowance enabled her to do nearly anything she wanted. Any father would worry, but Colin had no stomach for controlling her by tugging purse strings. He was wise enough to recognize that would only cause longer-term problems.

"Better that she come to Egypt with us than go on her own and meet someone halfway up the Great Pyramid," I said.

"I doubt our presence would stop her."

If anything, it might encourage her, and I doubted marriage would be the outcome. Kat was a very modern girl. There was no imperative to say it out loud. I could see in his dark eyes that my husband shared my concerns.

The sublime difference between a cold, wet English winter and Egypt's golden sun cannot be overstated. Snow fell at Anglemore over Christmas, but it turned to rain soon after the turn of the new year, when we set off on our journey. Egypt was a wholly different world. It's always a bit shocking how quickly the damp that settles into one's bones on a wet island can be eroded. Colin's mother had set off in advance in order to prepare a boat for our journey, unwilling to leave the arrangements to anyone else. Lord Deeley owned one of the finest private steamers on the Nile, but she refused to travel on it. She wanted to see Egypt as she had on her first trip there: from the deck of a dahabiya. These elegant boats, direct descendants of those that glided along the river in antiquity, relied on two large sails for propulsion — backed up by the strong arms of a crew of rowers. The wind was not always favorable, especially when traveling against the current upstream to Luxor.

I will forever be grateful to her for insisting on this mode of transportation. The *Timsah* — Arabic for crocodile — our floating home, was perfectly appointed. A spacious saloon at the stern contained a long oak dining table and bookshelves teeming with volumes about Egypt, among them a complete set of *Description de l'Égypte,* the monumental work produced by the scholars in Napoleon's expedition to Egypt; Wilkinson's *The Manners and Customs of the*

15

Ancient Egyptians; Murray's *Handbook for Travellers in Egypt;* and Amelia Edwards's remarkable *A Thousand Miles up the Nile.* Most interesting to me was Adolf Erman's *Egyptian Grammar,* translated into English by his former student James Breasted, an American affiliated with the University of Chicago and the head of their Haskell Oriental Museum. As an amateur linguist, I'd long been impressed with the value the ancient Egyptians placed on the written word — every ship that docked in Alexandria was required to turn over all the books on board so they could be copied and placed in the city's famous library. I relished the idea of taking up the study of hieroglyphs, particularly now, when I had the opportunity to put the work to use at the monuments we visited.

Beyond the boat's saloon, four cabins lined the sides of a narrow central passage. They were small, but adequate for sleeping. As we only required three, Mrs. Hargreaves had one converted into a study, replete with reference books, a desk, and writing supplies. Above, on the quarterdeck, a navy and white striped awning covered a lovely open-air lounge. Comfortable settees and chairs were arranged to best take in the view of the villages, temples, and tamarisk trees that dotted the emerald green strip along the bank. We had tea there every afternoon. It was bliss.

Lord Deeley's boat made far better time than ours, but I wouldn't have traded those quiet hours on the Nile for anything. The rumble of a steamer was intolerable compared to the sound of the breeze filling our sails. The weeks we spent making our way up the river, stopping to explore ruins and admire the local wildlife, were some of the most pleasant of my life. We stood on the barren desert plateau at Amarna, where the heretic pharaoh, Akhenaten, had built a new capital city in the fourteenth century BC. He (temporarily) revolutionized Egyptian religion, insisting his people worship only the sun god Aten. This did not win him supporters among the powerful priests who served other gods, and, after his death, his son brought back the old religion, abandoned his father's city, and returned to Thebes. We visited every pyramid we could find, from those at Giza to Djoser's step pyramid at Saqqara and the red and bent pyramids at Dahshur. Whenever I found hieroglyphic inscriptions, I copied them into a notebook and, back on board the boat, did my best to puzzle out reasonable translations. The language was a trial and a

17

delight: a perfect challenge. The entire journey was spectacular. Even Kat refrained from her usual peevishness. She taught her grandmother how to use her prized Brownie camera. The four of us got along shockingly well, despite the cramped quarters.

Thoroughly enchanted and relaxed, we at last — and too soon — came around a curve and saw Luxor before us. We had all gathered on the upper deck to watch as the town rose from the eastern bank of the river, a jumble of modern buildings that gave way to the ruins of the ancient temples of Luxor and Karnak. To the west, green fields, fertilized with the rich silt left by the annual inundation, stretched to the desert and the Valley of the Kings, where looming cliffs were still bathed rose gold by the last remnants of the sunrise.

Lord Deeley met us when we docked, waving with such enthusiasm that he nearly tripped as he crossed the gangplank. He'd brought with him a bottle of champagne to celebrate our arrival.

"I'm afraid it won't have stayed cold, but that shan't stop us." He handed it to one of the crew to open. "Now, if I may be rather cheeky, may I take a peek inside? There's something I must check." He disappeared down the stairs and into the saloon below where we were, only to reappear a moment later. "I ought not be surprised, but it's a crushing disappointment nonetheless. I'd tried to arrange to have flowers delivered to you last night, but I see my efforts were in vain. Never fear, I'll send some over posthaste."

His mood was so jovial we couldn't help but adopt it as our own. We drank the champagne and told him about our trip. All the while, he sat across from Mrs. Hargreaves, beaming.

"Truly, Ann, it is good to see you. I'm glad we shall have this time together. It's been far too long."

"You did visit me in France not long ago," she said.

"Yes, but for so few days it hardly counts." He had been tall and wiry in his youth; now he was just wiry, having started to lose some of his height. His hair had turned bright white, with no hint of silver in it, but was still thick and luxurious. He tapped tapered fingers on the arm of his chair. "Now we can settle in for a long catch-up. I can't think when I've so looked forward to something."

She smiled. "Nor can I, Bertram."

"I'll leave you now, but look forward to seeing you for dinner. I've quite a feast planned and promise it shall be the most unforgettable evening you've ever experienced. Take the day to recover from your travels. I'll send the carriage for you later, but have the wagon with me now to take your luggage. Is it still only you, Ann, who plans to stay at the house? I truly believe you'd all be more comfortable there than on the boat."

Nothing could have made me happier than him convincing Kat to take the room he offered her. Colin and I were desperate for privacy; that was why we planned to stay on the *Timsah.* However, once Kat had learned this, she, too, determined to remain, no doubt specifically to prevent us from being alone. Alas, she still — ever so politely — refused his hospitality. I was disappointed, but not surprised.

The day stretched before us. Mrs. Hargreaves went to her cabin to pack, not planning to leave the boat until it was time to set off for dinner. Colin wanted to send the boys a telegram so they'd know we had reached our destination. I was eager to start exploring Luxor's ruins and, although there wasn't time to do the site justice, decided to make a preliminary visit to the enormous temple complex at Karnak. Kat offered to join me, and we spent the afternoon there, marveling at the sprawling collection of temples, chapels, obelisks, statues, a sacred lake, and more columns than I could fathom. It was to the latter that the Greeks referred when calling the city Hundred-Gated Thebes. Even Homer was impressed. To the ancient Egyptians, Karnak was Ipet-isut: the Most Privileged of Seats. I was extremely pleased to be able to translate some hieroglyphs for Kat. It was nothing extraordinary, just a date from the reign of Ramses II.

"This" — I pointed to a group of signs — "indicates the second year of the pharaoh's reign. They weren't interested in a dating system that covered all of time, or all of their history. The pharaoh mattered above everything, so it made sense for the calendar to reflect that. Each year was divided into three seasons, corresponding to agriculture: inundation, planting, and harvest. The last was when the water from the annual flood receded. So when you see a date, it will generally tell you what number day in which month of a particular year in the king's reign."

Kat shook her head. "I'm more interested in the fact that it looks beautiful." She had taken countless photographs, raising her camera every few feet. It was an astonishing place. We hardly managed to tear ourselves away in time to dress for dinner.

But tear ourselves away we did, and before long, Lord Deeley's carriage — gleaming black, with the family crest painted on the side — pulled by a gorgeous pair of perfectly matched black Friesians, their coats brushed until they shone, collected us from the *Timsah*. Lord Deeley resided across the Nile from Luxor, so we had docked on the same side. Now, we drove along the river until we reached the gates of his house, which was called Per Ma'at — the House of Justice or Truth, depending on how one translated it. Carved into the arched stone gate at the front of the estate were hieroglyphs.

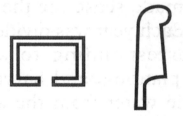

They were enclosed in an elaborate cartouche, which even my brief study of hieroglyphs taught me ought to have been reserved for royal names. Lord Deeley was more concerned with style than substance. His family crest was displayed on either side of the cartouche, a mingling of the two cultures to which he was devoted. Beyond the gates stood the villa. Ancient designs inspired the building's architecture, with rooms arranged around a lush central courtyard brimming with palms, jasmine, and a riot of vines climbing artfully placed trellises. It was here that we gathered for predinner drinks with Lord Deeley's other guests, English footmen in stiff livery filling our glasses with champagne.

Because our little group had traveled separately, we had not met the others en route. They had little interest in the ancient sites beyond mullocking about, while we preferred a more careful examination of the ruins. Hence, the difference in the speeds of our boats worked to everyone's advantage. They could rush up the Nile, while we lingered. Our host, eager to make the requisite introductions, clinked the side of his glass with something that looked like a tuning fork.

"Right, now I don't want to spend hours on this, so I'll keep it short. At my side this evening is Mrs. Ann Hargreaves, dearest friend of my youth, and a force of nature. Mr. Caspian Troubridge" — he pointed to each guest as he named them — "typically describes himself as a man of no distinction, but is endlessly amusing. As a result, one must forgive all his faults. Mr. Inigo Granard and his delightful wife, Adelaide, have long been my closest political counterparts."

Colin leaned down to whisper to me. "We shall avoid them like the plague."

Lord Deeley continued. "I can't think of anyone more in need of a winter in Egypt than Lady Wilona Bestwick." Lady Wilona nodded her head, looking very grave. I assumed we were meant to draw the appropriate conclusions about her health. "Her companion, Miss Pandora Evans, has surprised us all with her skill as an artist."

The young woman must have been only a few years older than Kat, but her appearance was so unremarkable that she might have been any age between twenty and forty. *Gray* is the only word that could describe her.

"I lured Dr. Oliver Rockley away from the Harley Street practice he was about to open in order to have a physician round out our party. So essential in this part of the world. Sanitation is not what it ought to be, although I assure you every facility in my home is the equal — if not the better — of any you could find in Britain. I've invited Mr. Tristan McLeod to join us this evening. He's a cracking archaeologist who can hold the attention of even the most hopeless philistine with tales of his excavations in the Valley of the Kings. Finally, we have the rest of Mrs. Hargreaves's party: her son Colin; his wife, Lady Emily; and Mr. Hargreaves's daughter, Katharina von Lange. Clearly there's a story there. I do hope they can be persuaded to share it."

His direct reference to Kat's parentage shocked me, and my face must have shown it. "There, there, Lady Emily, no need to fret," our host said. "It's better to have these things out in the open from the beginning. Keeps the rabble from imagining the worst."

Kat grinned. "I admire your audacity, Lord Deeley, and will happily explain." Her recounting was rather too enthusiastic, but accurate. When she was done, we all stood silent for a moment and then the manners instilled in us since birth took over. We descended into harmless chitchat.

The stars hung bright in the inky blue sky, mirroring the flickering torches in the courtyard below. The moon, a slim waning crescent, provided little additional illumination. Jasmine scented the air. Dotted around the garden were smooth wooden benches, perfectly suited for more intimate conversation. Kat headed straight for Mr. Troubridge, a dazzling smile on her face. Although I suspected he was vaguely middle-aged, he looked more vibrant than most of the rest of the party and had a welcoming glimmer in his eyes. Before long, he was steering her to one of those secluded benches. Colin frowned and set off toward them. Left alone, I surveyed the group and decided to approach Mr. McLeod, who seemed the most interesting of the lot. He spoke before I did.

"So, Lady Emily, have you come to Egypt with the goal of penning your own version of Mrs. Edwards's famous memoir?" he asked.

"Not at all," I said. "I would never claim to be a writer of Mrs. Edwards's caliber. Upon embarking on this trip, I harbored no intention other than immersing myself in history and ruins. Then I found a Middle Egyptian grammar on our boat. I'm now thoroughly engrossed in the study of hiero-glyphs."

"An ambitious pursuit, but a noble one. Which grammar is it? Not the one written by Budge, I hope."

"No, Erman's."

"Excellent. Budge may be beloved by the British Museum, but the man's an absolute scandal. I'll say no more as I ought not insult your fellow countryman so early in our acquaintance."

I knew very little about Mr. Budge but had heard more than one story that cast doubt on his ethics. Yes, he had acquired an astonishing number of stunning objects for the museum, but his methods could only be described as dodgy. "My fellow countryman? Surely yours as well."

"My dear Lady Emily, I am a Scot and shall brook no nonsensical talk about united kingdoms."

His voice revealed no trace of an accent that could identify his nationality. "I shan't argue with you."

He threw back his head and laughed. He was so affable it was impossible not to like him. "Deeley told me you're sharp. He didn't exaggerate. Is it true you translated Homer's *Odyssey*?"

"Yes, but I wouldn't dare claim it was anything but an amateur effort."

"And now you're learning Egyptian. It's quite wonderful. I'm no philologist, but have an adequate knowledge of the language. Turn to me should you require assistance, but don't expect I'll be too much help. I'm far better with the practical applications of learning."

"Hence your work in the Valley of the Kings?" I asked.

"I'm currently focused in a different area, actually — Lord Deeley doesn't have much of an eye for detail, but his intentions are good — the ruins of a village near both the Valley of the Kings and the Valley of the Queens."

"I shouldn't have thought anyone lived so far out in the desert. Surely most pockets of civilization were closer to the river."

"Ordinarily, yes," he said. He was tall — taller even than my husband — and his face burnt. The sun had streaked his chocolate brown hair with gold. All of this, along with broad shoulders and an athletic build, neatly fit the image I had of an archaeologist. "Deir el Medina — that's the modern name — was designed to house the artists and craftsmen who built the pharaohs' tombs. It's not actually all that far from the river, but definitely in the desert. The people who lived there called it Pa Demi — the village — although it was officially known as Set-Ma'at — the Place of Truth. It's an extraordinary site —"

"There's no need to bore the lady." Although this was my first encounter with Lady Wilona, I would soon recognize her as a person from Porlock, with an uncanny ability to interrupt any conversation that might have proved enlightening. "Lady Emily is bound to be far more interested in the floral displays of this magnificent garden than your dusty old ruins. I should be delighted to give her a little tour of the plants surrounding us. You, Mr. McLeod, should know better than to drone on to someone of such fine breeding."

This was just the sort of inane comment I was accustomed to hearing from my mother. Fortunately, the sound of a gong calling us to dinner saved me from having to respond. We all moved inside, eager to dine, not having the slightest inkling that our meal not only would prove unforgettable, as Lord Deeley had promised, but also would lead to a cataclysmic shift in all our lives.

PA DEMI, REGNAL YEAR TWO
2

I wasn't unreasonable. I didn't expect everyone to like me. I didn't expect most people to do more than tolerate me. But I would have preferred it if my twin brother's wife fell short of actually despising me. It would have made many things easier. Sanura wasn't interested in easy; she preferred complication. When you're convinced you're superior to everyone around you, you're also convinced you alone can gracefully navigate complication. I didn't see the point but knew not to comment. It would be better to let myself fade into the background, if I could ever figure out how to do that. Growing up in my family made that all but impossible.

My parents had a simple love. My father, considered by everyone to be the greatest painter in Egypt, took my mother, a priestess of Hathor, as his wife six days after they met. Their house in Pa Demi was one of the finest in the village, and they both wanted to fill it with children. They had seven, but only two of us survived past the age of five: Bek, born three minutes before me, Meryt. Our mother and father tolerated their losses with equanimity, rarely showing the heartbreak that pierced them both. Instead, they doted on us twins, indulging nearly all of our whims, but never spoiling us altogether. My brother and I, acknowledging our good fortune, were careful never to let it taint our characters.

When our father hired a tutor for Bek, I studied alongside him. There was no discussion of whether this would be allowed. Instead, without incident, I sat next to him every day, learning to read and write. We were inseparable, doing everything together until the time came for him to train in our father's art. As a girl, I could not travel with him to the Valley of the Kings and paint Pharaoh's tomb.

This bothered me less than you might expect. I missed Bek when he disappeared into the desert with the other painters, working on-site for eight days before returning home for two, but it gave me time to pursue a craft of my own. I was a sculptor.

Not of the monumental statues found in temples. Not of the exquisite low reliefs carved into the walls of tombs. Not even of the small representations of household gods or of the countless ushabtis every person would need in the afterlife. At least not in the beginning. I fashioned representations of the people and animals around me. I'd started doing this as a child, forming mud in my hands to look like my favorite cat. Then I made a dog and pretended they were friends. Then I decided they needed a girl to look after them. Soon, I had a miniature village, although its residents resembled anonymous mud lumps more than the beings they were meant to represent. I didn't mind. I liked them, regardless.

Soon, however, my father's best friend intervened. He was a sculptor and found my attempts at his craft charming. He brought me clay. Then he brought leftover pieces of limestone, too small to be of use to him, and taught me to carve. I learned so well that soon he gave me bits of alabaster and quartzite. No more did my statues look like lumps.

Bek sometimes painted them for me. Later, he taught me the basics of his art and gave me a set of powdered paints. I preferred working with stone but delighted in the way my creations came to life when I colored their eyes and clothes. My decorations became more elaborate as the years went by.

When I turned fifteen, it was past time to find a husband. A scribe called Kamose started coming to see me, impressed that I could read and write. I didn't mind the attention, but neither did I particularly welcome it. Bek wouldn't have to choose a wife for another five years. Given free rein, I would have stayed in our parents' house as long as he did. Kamose started writing little stories for me to paint onto my statues. This endeared him to me. A few months later, we moved into one of the smaller houses in the village, starting our life as a married couple.

Bek painted our door red to ward off demons and decorated the walls of each of the four rooms with scenes of waterfowl, lotus blooms, and borders of papyrus, fashioning for us an oasis of sorts in the desert. I made a sculpture of Kamose and me, which I placed in a niche in the kitchen, pleased to have it looking over me when I prepared our meals. Our life was happy.

At least until the babies started to come.

Luxor, 1904
3

At the urging of our host, we made our way
from the jasmine-scented courtyard into the
house. The interior was an olio of contemporary and ancient design, with antiquities
everywhere. A heavy stone sarcophagus
greeted us in the entrance hall, which made
it feel as if we were being welcomed into a
tomb rather than a home, but it set the right
tone. Lord Deeley was devoted to all things
Egyptian, particularly those related to
ancient burial practices. Niches in the corridor displayed an astonishing collection of
alabaster canopic jars, used to hold the
organs of the deceased, as well as statues of
animal-headed gods and armies of seemingly identical small mummiform figures.

In the dining room, a massive oak table
stood beneath a ceiling covered with gold
stars against a deep blue background. Each
of the walls was painted to mimic scenes
from the pharaohs' tombs. One side of the

table faced an exquisite rendering of the ceremony that the Egyptians believed they would all face in the afterlife: the weighing of the heart against the feather of Ma'at. Osiris, god of the underworld, led the dead man toward the scales. A just individual who had lived a moral life would have nothing to fear. His heart would balance with the feather and his ba — the rough equivalent of the Christian soul — would enjoy eternity.

Those whose hearts didn't balance faced an ignominious fate. Ammit, a demon whose body was an amalgamation of crocodile, lion, and hippopotamus, stood by, ready to devour their bas. Regardless of the result, Thoth, the ibis-headed god of writing, recorded the judgment while Anubis, the jackal-headed god of the dead, oversaw it all.

"It wouldn't be a pleasant way to go." Lord Deeley, taking notice of me studying the painting, brushed away a footman and held my chair out for me before taking his place at the head of the table. Mr. McLeod, seated on my other side, laughed.

"You're very grim, Lord Deeley. The Egyptians were rather obsessed with the concept of Ma'at, but they were more concerned with it guiding how they chose to live than with the gruesome end they'd face if they didn't succeed at keeping it in balance. The scene you've got here would never have been in a private home, only in a tomb."

"Quite odd that one would choose to decorate one's home with so much pagan imagery," Lady Wilona said, squinting as she removed her pince-nez. I was glad she was seated as far away from me as possible.

Lord Deeley laughed. "Wilona, my dear, you are a battle-axe. It's delightful."

Battleship might be a more appropriate comparison, given the lady's build, with broad shoulders and a thick neck. Colin, across the table and over two seats from me, caught my eye and raised an eyebrow. I pressed my lips together and tried not to laugh. His mother, at the foot of the table, opposite our host, made no such effort.

"Bertram, you are disgracefully amusing and it's far too long since I've spent time with you. Do go easy on your guests, won't you? We're here for another three weeks and must find a way to get along without offending each other's sensibilities."

"My dear Ann, you know I choose my friends carefully and bring them together to expand their horizons, not to offend them. Lady Wilona, I pray you take my comment in the spirit it was made."

"I've known you too long to do otherwise," she said, "and it's decades since I gave up any hope of saving your soul. It was a tedious endeavor at the best of times, full of sound and fury, signifying nothing." Had her tone been even slightly softer, it would have suggested amusement. Sadly, it did not.

Miss Evans paled at her employer's words, then forced a smile onto her face. "Did you know that it's possible to be driven mad by the railway? It's something to do with the motion of the carriage. It can injure one's brain." She turned to Dr. Rockley, seated on her left, looking as if she hoped he might comment on this ridiculous claim. He did not.

The meal was meticulously prepared and one of the most exquisite I have ever had, every course perfection, although the exotic setting was discordant with the food, which seemed more appropriate for Windsor Castle than an Egyptian villa. We started with a perfect consommé à la Monaco, scented with truffles and sweet Spanish peppers. Next came turbot in a mousse-like sauce flavored with butter and lemon.

"And now, one of my absolute favorites," Lord Deeley said, as the footmen served us lamb cutlets à la princesse. "I first had this when I was thirteen and visiting a chum from Eton. His parents were indisposed and he persuaded their cook to make them for us. I'd never tasted anything so delicious, partly because I believed they were meant to be a special treat only for grown-ups. To this day, I can't judge the dish objectively and will forever consider it the best. Does it deserve the accolade? I shall leave that to you all to decide."

No one disagreed with his opinion, biased or not.

Pork, game pie, and roast beef followed. Even the vegetables — asparagus with hollandaise — were perfection. We finished with raspberry soufflés glacés and mince pies. Truly, it was a feast.

"We shall return to the garden for coffee," Lord Deeley said, "but first I'd like to offer a digestif. Alas, it no longer agrees with me, but the scent always reminds me of my youth. I do hope you all enjoy it."

The footmen now brought small glasses filled with ice and a dark brown liquid to all of us save our host, to whom they delivered a steaming tisane instead. He led us in a toast, his voice a singsong chant.

"O table god, you have spat forth Shu from your mouth . . . O table god, may he give to

38

you all that he will have dedicated, since he has become a god who is an emanation, alert, worshipful and powerful. May he dedicate to you every good thing which you will give him, since he has become Heka. May he dedicate to you every good thing, food offerings in abundance. May he set them before you and may you be content with them, may your spirit be content with them and may your heart be content with them forever."

Several of the gentlemen chorused *hear, hear,* and we all drank. I nearly choked on the bitter, herbaceous liquor.

Mr. McLeod grinned and leaned toward me conspiratorially. "It's not the best choice, perhaps, for varied company. As for Lord Deeley's toast, it's an Egyptian spell, intended to be spoken at the beginning of a meal, most likely by the pharaoh, but one could argue —"

A crash diverted his attention — diverted all of our attention — to our host, who lurched to his feet and knocked over his chair, his face stricken with pain. He staggered for a moment and then collapsed onto the floor, his body convulsing. His breath came ragged and hard. Dr. Rockley, sitting at the far end of the table next to my mother-in-law, leapt from his seat and rushed to Lord Deeley. He knelt down and bent over him, feeling for a pulse and trying to revive him. A few minutes later, he rocked back onto his heels and shook his head.

"I'm most dreadfully sorry to deliver such terrible news. He's dead. It's poison. I smell bitter almonds."

Colin, who had reached our host seconds after the doctor, moved closer to the body. "Cyanide. Yes, I smell it, too."

Kat came to her father's side. "I don't. Why not?" Not everyone can smell cyanide. I would explain this to her at a more opportune time. Instead, I went to my mother-in-law, who looked entirely stricken. I took her hand, but she pulled away from me.

"What on earth is the meaning of this?" Lady Wilona barked. "Surely you're not suggesting he's been poisoned, Dr. Rockley? That's ridiculous. No doubt the fish disagreed with him. I never trust fish this far from England. It's unwise. That's why I refused it."

"A sound decision," Miss Evans said, nodding enthusiastically. We were all standing around the body now, but no one seemed more taken with the spectacle than the gray young woman. Her eyes were all but popping out of her head. "I followed your example, Lady Wilona. You've saved me

40

from a hideous death."

"Don't be absurd." Mr. Troubridge winced. "The rest of us had the fish and are perfectly fine. Furthermore, if the dish had been poisoned, Deeley would have been dead before the pork was served. Cyanide acts immediately."

"You seem to know rather a lot about it," Mr. Granard said. He was as portly as Mr. Troubridge was lanky; next to each other, they looked almost like a joke. Or they would have done if they weren't arguing about the details of a hideous death. "Why is that?"

"What are you implying?" Mrs. Hargreaves pulled herself to her full height and glared at Mr. Granard.

"I meant nothing by it. It's simply that —"

Lady Wilona interrupted. "If someone has murdered Lord Deeley, that someone knows about cyanide."

"I've heard quite enough," Colin said, crossing his arms, his tone of voice making it clear he was taking charge of the situation. He motioned to one of the footmen. "Send for the police. Rockley, stay here with me. Emily, take everyone else into the drawing room. No one is to leave until I give permission."

I followed his instructions nearly to the letter. The drawing room was next to the dining room, and I preferred to take my charges further away from the scene of violence. We wound our way along wide corridors until we'd reached the wing of the house opposite the entry, perpendicular to the one where we'd dined. There I found a breezy sitting room, furnished with low couches and inlaid tables. Gauzy curtains fluttered over the windows. More of Lord Deeley's collection of antiquities hung from the walls: limestone reliefs that appeared to have been hacked from tombs. Tables displayed armies of ushabtis, some faience, some limestone, some alabaster, ranging in size from a few inches tall to over a foot. Like all the rooms in the house, this one opened onto the courtyard. Mr. McLeod started to step outside.

"I must insist that you stay here," I said.

"Apologies. It's just that I could use a cigarette."

"You can smoke inside. I'm sure we all understand —"

"I don't understand and, in fact, object vociferously," Lady Wilona said. "It's disgraceful to indulge in such reprehensible habits in the presence of ladies. Pandora, I want you to return to your room at once.

This isn't fit company for a girl like you."

"I'm afraid that won't do," I said. "Miss Evans is to remain here, like the rest of us. The police are on their way and will —"

"If you think I shall subject myself to the interference of the police, you are very much mistaken, Lady Emily, and I shall have words with your mother about it. That anyone of your breeding would dare suggest —"

Now my mother-in-law interrupted. "Sit down and be quiet, Lady Wilona. You, too, Miss Evans. Mr. McLeod, smoke if you'd like, but please do give me one of your cigarettes. We all need our nerves calmed."

"I certainly do." Kat stepped toward Mr. McLeod and held out her hand. He passed her two cigarettes, one of which she gave to Mrs. Hargreaves.

Lady Wilona drew a sharp breath as the archaeologist lit a match and held it first to Mrs. Hargreaves's cigarette and then Kat's. She was more horrified by the idea of ladies smoking than she'd been watching Lord Deeley die. Mrs. Granard, whom I had not yet heard speak, came to my side and placed a gentle hand on my arm.

"It's very good of you to try to keep us organized, Lady Emily. Important, I think, in the circumstances, although Mr.

Hargreaves would better have assigned one of the other gentlemen to assist him. We ladies, you understand . . ." Her voice trailed and she looked up at me, her eyes wide. I could almost see the young lady she'd been, decades ago, her long, dark eyelashes deployed to ensure she would always get what she wanted. I doubted it worked so well now as it had in the past.

"You're very kind to be concerned, Mrs. Granard, but I assure you I have more experience dealing with violent death than anyone else here, save my husband. I've been directly responsible for ensuring that more than a dozen murderers face justice. Our little group isn't any more unruly than others I've taken in hand. You needn't worry."

"I say, Lady Emily, there's no need to speak to my wife like that." Mr. Granard took her firmly by the arm and pulled her away from me. "Not everyone lives in such a coarse world as that you claim to inhabit."

"Thank goodness for that," Mr. Troubridge said, then grinned. "Don't think I'm judging you, Lady Emily. Personally, I prefer a coarse world. Gentility is so tedious, don't you think? Which is not to suggest that any of us came here looking for murder. Might be an idea for me to corral the servants. We

44

all know it's one of them who killed Deeley."

"At the moment, we've not the slightest insight into who poisoned Lord Deeley," I said. "As he was someone I presume you all care about, the best thing we can do is wait for the police."

"We could play The Minister's Cat to pass the time." Miss Evans's voice rose to a higher than usual pitch and I wondered if she was becoming unhinged.

Lady Wilona glared at her. "Not now, girl," she said. "Sometimes you've no more sense than a hedgehog."

No one spoke. Miss Evans picked at her cuticles. Mr. and Mrs. Granard sat still as sculptures. Kat coughed every time she took a drag from her cigarette but soldiered on smoking it. Mr. Troubridge paced. I found myself wondering if it was fair of Lady Wilona to cast aspersions on the sense of hedgehogs. After what felt like a geological era had passed, Colin entered the room with two uniformed police officers and a tall, thin man in a suit. The latter spoke.

"I am most pleased to inform you that we've identified Lord Deeley's killer. He was a member of His Lordship's staff and disappeared shortly after you all sat down to dinner. Have no doubt that I shall use

45

every resource at my disposal to apprehend and capture him. There is no reason to believe that any of you is in the slightest danger, and I do hope this sad event won't adversely color your opinion of my country." With that, he nodded and stalked out of the room, followed by the other officers.

For a moment, no one moved or spoke. We were all stunned.

"Surely you don't accept this?" I asked Colin.

"No, it's far too soon to draw sweeping conclusions about Deeley's death. It's clear that he was poisoned deliberately, but beyond that we know nothing. The police may be content to condemn the first potential suspect, but we must insist on a thorough investigation."

"If the police say this native bloke's done it, that's good enough for me," Mr. Troubridge said. "No business of ours."

"It's the business of anyone who called Bertram a friend," Mrs. Hargreaves said, rising to her feet. "To suggest the matter ought not be given the most serious sort of consideration is not only unacceptable, but outrageous."

"I'm sure the police know more about it than we do," Mrs. Granard said. Her husband gripped her arm, and she fell silent.

Apparently, this was a pattern with them.

"Your friend was the victim of a vicious murderer," I said. "What can be more important than finding out — beyond all doubt — how this came to pass? The only reason to allow the police to brush it aside would be to hide someone else's guilt. Surely none of us have anything to fear on that count?"

A low murmur of strained voices rumbled through the room.

"No, of course we don't," Mr. McLeod said. "I don't know any of you particularly well, but I did know Deeley. He wasn't the sort of man who drew the ire of his friends. Whoever killed him must be —"

"A maniac of some sort." Lady Wilona gave a smug smile, pleased with her observation. "They have them everywhere, you know. It's bound to be an Egyptian, obviously, because we're in Egypt, and one never can be too careful around these native types."

"These native types?" Kat spat the words. "What an outrageous thing to say. Englishmen are native types in their own land, you know, and many of them not so civilized as their Egyptian counterparts."

"You were raised abroad, Miss von Lange, and as a result have not had the opportunity to witness the superior quality of the Englishman," Lady Wilona said. "Had your parents —"

"I've noticed you have no aversion to interrupting others, so I don't see a reason to extend the courtesy to you." Kat's face was turning beet red. "I'm quite certain, Lady Wilona, that you have very little good to say about foreigners. You do realize, I hope, that you are a foreigner here?"

"This is perhaps not the time —" Mr. Granard started, but now it was my turn to interrupt.

"It is always the time to stand up against ignorance and prejudice," I said. "Thank you, Kat, for holding us to a higher moral standard than some segments of society consider necessary."

Shock flashed in her eyes, turning them even more emerald, when she heard me defending her. "Thank you, Lady Emily," she said.

"Are we then to concern ourselves with reforming the Englishman's view of himself and of Egyptian natives rather than trying to ferret out Deeley's murderer?" Mr. Troubridge asked. "I, for one, think we best not tackle more than a single problem at a time."

"Which is precisely why nothing ever

changes," I muttered. Only Kat, standing next to me, heard my words. She squeezed my hand and I wondered if we might be taking a significant step toward becoming friends.

"Right now, it is critical that we gather as much information as we can about Lord Deeley," Colin said. "Aside from myself, my wife, and my daughter, each of you knew him well. As Emily pointed out, none of us have anything to fear from investigation. We would never have wished even the slightest harm on him. I will ask each of you to tell me everything you can about your friend. Somewhere in your stories we will find a clue that leads us to his murderer."

"Not unless one of us is responsible for his death," Dr. Rockley said. "Otherwise, what could we possibly reveal?"

"I don't suggest any of us knows details about the actual crime," Colin said, his tone deliberately nonthreatening. "However, you may have observed something without realizing it — an unexpected letter that Lord Deeley received while you were cruising the Nile, a story he recounted that seemed innocuous at the time but may prove more meaningful now."

"Yes, I see," Mr. Granard said, nodding. "You want to know about him, not us."

"Precisely," Colin said, his voice calm yet commanding. They would believe anything he said. "None of you is under the slightest suspicion. Starting tomorrow, Emily and I will speak with each of you in turn. I've no doubt we'll find someone worthy of the title of detective among you."

"Surely, Mr. Hargreaves, you don't mean to use the professional designation of a tradesman as an inducement?" Lady Wilona asked. "I am horrified merely thinking about it."

"Fear not," Kat said. "No one would ever mistake you for a detective, Lady Wilona."

"I should hope not!" She shuddered, indignant.

"It would be best now for us all to try to get some sleep," Colin said. "The events of the evening have been most trying, and I know you are all shocked and grieving. We will reconvene tomorrow."

As they shuffled out of the room, I leaned toward my husband. "Surely you consider them all suspects?"

"Of course. Ought not to tell them, though, if we've any hope of cooperation."

"So I'm a suspect?" Kat asked. "And your mother? And Lady Emily?" There was a particular note of glee in her voice when she spoke my name. So much for taking steps toward friendship.

"Don't be absurd," Colin said, but I knew what he was thinking. When someone is murdered, everyone in the house where it occurred merits a measure of suspicion, even mothers and daughters.

PA DEMI, REGNAL YEAR TWO
4

Given my parents' difficulties when it came to having healthy children, I ought not have been surprised that Kamose and I would struggle as well. And I wasn't. Surprised, that is. Not by the struggle, at least. The searing heartache and relentless pain that consumed us after our first three babies died within months of their births was worse than I ever could have expected. We muddled through it the best we could. What else was there to do?

Now, after five years of marriage, our grief had pulled us close. I'd always liked Kamose. He was handsome, with well-developed muscles and luminous eyes. Our marital bed was a place of immense pleasure. I felt myself grow warm thinking about it. We got along well. Laughed at each other's jokes. Liked the same poetry. Our house was a happy place, just as many people's are. But it was more than that, more than a superficial — even if well-intentioned — happiness. The losses we suffered bound us together so profoundly that we felt every emotion more keenly. Our joy pulsed with wild abandon. Our sorrow ripped through our souls. We experienced both extremes and everything in between not as individuals, but as a union. Our lives were one.

One bright day — the sun had been unbearably hot but, thankfully, was now slipping below the horizon — my father, back from his eight days in the Valley, came to see me. A few years ago, Eetee had begun construction on his tomb, something to which every conscientious person of means must attend. We ordinary folks would never have houses of eternity that could rival those of our pharaohs, but the artists and craftsmen who lived in Pa Demi were the best in Egypt. And they worked on each other's tombs. The end result might be smaller than Pharaoh's, but no less beautiful.

"Bek is doing the painting, as you know," Eetee said. We had retreated to the roof of my house, where we could just start to feel a cool breeze. "I want you to make the ushabtis."

"Me?"

"Who else? That cat?" He motioned to the

furry ginger heap on my lap.

"Miw might not be the prettiest creature, but she's an excellent mouser and has an appropriately disdainful personality."

"You never did take to cats who pretend to like you." He laughed softly. "Not even when you were a tiny girl. As for the ushabtis, they will be made from alabaster. Bek will see to it that you have whatever paint you need for decoration. I don't want a legion of identical figures, but neither does each have to be unique. Just different enough, you understand? So that I will recognize them."

Ushabtis, an essential part of everyone's funereal equipment, were figures, usually in the shape of a mummy, that would stand in for the deceased when he — or she — was called on to do work in the afterlife. The servants we all wished we had while we were still on earth. Spells carved onto them would spur them into action:

The illuminated one, the Osiris . . . he says: O these ushabtis, if counted upon, the Osiris . . . justified, to do all the works that are to be done there in the realm of the dead — now indeed obstacles are implanted there — as a man at his duties, "Here I am!" you shall say when you are

54

counted upon at any time to serve there, to cultivate the fields, to irrigate the river banks, to ferry the sand of the west to the east and vice-versa, "Here I am," you shall say.

"Here I am," I said. "Like your ever-faithful ushabti, ready to serve."

"Or carve." He laughed again. "I require fifty."

That was more than most people had, but my father was no ordinary man. He was the leader of all the painters and captain of one of the two gangs of workers in the village. Few men garnered more respect than he. He deserved however many ushabtis he wanted.

"Bring me the alabaster and I will get to work."

"You'll have plenty of time to complete the task. I've no intention of dying for many, many years."

I wished he hadn't said the words out loud; speaking them might bring bad luck. "I'd expect nothing less."

"Have you talked to Sanura lately? She and your brother are moving into their house tomorrow. We must be sure to make her feel welcome, even if she's not the wife any of us would have chosen for him."

"Bek probably picked her just for that reason," I said. "He loves being contrary."

"I doubt that was what enticed him. She's a beautiful girl and the daughter of a respectable man."

"Yes, yes, I know. The stonecutter without whom no tomb could be built."

"Stonecutters are the most essential of all of us, and Sanura's father is the best." Eetee was always magnanimous. Stonecutters had the worst jobs of anyone, their work backbreaking and undertaken in unbearably dark and dusty conditions. I wouldn't want to carve my way through all that hard bedrock. But Eetee appreciated them. Respected them. They knew that and loved him for it. "You will make overtures of friendship to Sanura, won't you? Don't make me send your mother to beg."

"I'd never stoop to that," I said. "I'll bring her a gift in the morning."

"Good girl." He mussed my hair — part of him never accepted that I was older than five — and climbed down the steps, making his way out of the house and into the street. I watched him until he disappeared into the inky twilight and then made my own way down and back inside, into the room that in many of our neighbors' houses would have been for sleeping. Kamose had turned it into a workshop for me, insisting that he was perfectly content to put our couch in the living room.

All of the houses in Pa Demi were of similar design: four rooms, one behind another in a row. The front room, the darkest in the house as there were no windows looking into the street, held statues I had made of our household gods in niches carved in the walls. Behind it came the living room and then my workshop. The kitchen was in the rear with a small cellar dug below. Every house's exterior was painted white, but we all decorated the inside walls as we pleased. Everyone in the village retreated to the roof to sleep when it was hot, which was much of the time. No wonder Kamose didn't object to abandoning the bedroom.

He'd hung shelves on the walls of my workshop and bought sturdy chests to hold my tools, doing his best to urge me toward organization. It didn't take. My mind rarely worked in an orderly fashion, but I always knew where to find what I needed. Almost always. Right now, I was at a loss. I searched through my partially finished projects to see if there was anything Sanura might like. I hadn't yet seen Bek's paintings inside his new house; he hadn't allowed anyone but our father so much as a peek, and him only because he sought his advice on the project. He wanted Sanura to be the first to experience their beauty. There could be no doubt his work would be stunning. I had recently completed a series of animal sculptures, each of them oozing personality, but I feared Sanura would find them too unsophisticated for her taste. She was nothing if not elegant.

Which probably accounted for us not getting along. I admit to being more than a little jealous of her. She was younger than I, obviously, or she'd already be married. She was far more sensuous than I could ever hope to be. Kamose did his best to convince me that he preferred reedlike to curvy, but no one could really believe that, could they? That aside, what really mattered — what truly fed my jealousy — was that she took my brother from me. No more would we be inseparable. No more would we work side by side. No more would we . . .

It was obvious I was being unfair. Things had started to change when Bek began working in the Valley and had shifted all the more when I got married and left home. Kamose and I were the inseparable ones now, and I hadn't given a second thought to how that made Bek feel. I hadn't needed to. He encouraged me to go, knowing I would find happiness with Kamose. I loved my husband but had found it hard to leave my family. Life is different for men. Easier. Someday, my parents would move in with Bek. I would never live with them — or Bek — again.

Unless Kamose divorced me. I smiled, contemplating it. No, nothing could ever come between us.

I pulled one of my sculptures down from a shelf. It was a small piece, only about eight inches tall, fashioned from the finest alabaster I'd ever had, a beautiful woman standing with her arms spread wide, like a goddess. I'd had difficulty deciding who she was and had left her face only partially completed. Now I could see Sanura's perfect features in her. I stayed up all night finishing the carving and then painting the details. Finally, I added a verse from a love song on the front of the woman's dress, carefully forming each hieroglyph with a fine brush:

I embrace her,
and her arms open wide,
I am like a man in Punt,
like someone overwhelmed with drugs.
I kiss her,

59

her lips open,
and I am drunk
without a beer.

I was pleased with myself. It was a perfect text, capturing the joy of a happy marriage. Sanura would be flattered. There was no doubt she would recognize herself in the statue's beautiful face. Who would not be pleased by that? As I did on all of my pieces, I stamped in black paint the bottom with hieroglyphs that read *my way is good.*

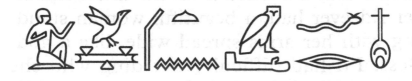

It wasn't customary to mark one's work, but I had always done it. I took the phrase from the tale of the Eloquent Peasant. Khun-Anup, the peasant in question, sought justice after his donkey was taken by a landowner who, claiming the beast ate a small bit of barley from the man's field, seized all of the peasant's donkeys and the goods they were transporting. When Khun-Anup protested and demanded justice, the man laughed at him. No one would listen to a lowly commoner. Undeterred, Khun-Anup pled his case to local officials and magistrates until one, so impressed with the man's eloquence, told Pharaoh about him. Pharaoh wanted to hear more. Who would expect a peasant to be such a skilled rhetorician? Eventually, Pharaoh ordered Khun-Anup's possessions to be returned to him, along with all of the landowner's property, but not before making Khun-Anup give discourse after discourse on Ma'at. That's what happens when you're too smart for your own good. Although, if Khun-Anup had been your typical inarticulate peasant, he wouldn't have seen so much as a hair on his donkey's hide again. As it was, he was put through the ringer, but came out far better off than he ever could have hoped. Anyway, I liked to think of myself taking my own path, my own way, much like Khun-Anup. Only with fewer donkeys.

The sun was rising when I finally dragged myself up to the couch on our roof. Kamose was already awake. He pulled me down next to him and kissed me.

"No more nights apart when I'm home. Promise me."

LUXOR, 1904
5

En route to Luxor aboard the *Timsah,* Colin and I had engaged in lengthy discussions with his mother and Kat about what we would do when we got there. Not regarding sites to visit, but where to sleep. Lord Deeley had offered rooms in his house, and Mrs. Hargreaves had accepted on our behalf. Colin, however, had no desire to stay in the house of a stranger. At least that's what he claimed in front of his mother and Kat. I knew the truth: he could not resist the temptation of remaining alone on our dahabiya, away from everyone else. It was too small for us to have much privacy when the others were there, but perfect for a couple alone. We so rarely had time to ourselves. At home, our houses were full of servants. And then there were the boys.

Henry and Richard, our twins, were a few months younger than Tom, technically our ward, but as dear to us as any son could be.

Each of them had pleaded — Henry, violently — to be allowed to come to Egypt. Both Colin and I looked forward to showing them the world, but the idea of three nearly-eight-year-olds on a boat in the Nile did not inspire confidence. Quite the contrary. I dared not imagine the trouble Henry alone could cause. Richard and Tom were far better behaved, but either of them might fall overboard and be eaten by a crocodile.

"There haven't been crocodiles in this part of the Nile since the completion of the Aswan dam two years ago," Colin said, "although I wouldn't put it past Henry to find a way of having some installed."

We had returned to the *Timsah,* still reeling from Lord Deeley's untimely demise. In the aftermath of the murder, Kat had decided to stay at the house. She assured us she would be in hog heaven (a phrase she claimed to have learned from my American friend Margaret) and was convinced she was better positioned there to solve the crime. Erroneous though her belief might be, I happily supported it, or rather, the privacy it would bring Colin and me.

"Don't utter the words aloud," I said. "Henry will hear them, somehow, and before you know it, there will be crocodiles."

"I shouldn't think so, at least not until

63

he's in Egypt himself. He wouldn't waste the effort if it didn't benefit him in some way."

"He's not that awful."

"He's not awful in the least," Colin said, protesting. "A delightful young chap, all the way around. Exuberant, but he'll grow out of that. When he does, we'll miss it." The night was fine and after the shocking events of the evening, we were too agitated to sleep, so we decided we would have a drink on deck. First, though, we went to our cabin below so I could change from my elegant but uncomfortable evening gown (made by the House of Worth, creamy satin brocade decorated with golden appliqué stars and silver embroidery) to a much less restrictive yet still lovely tea gown (also Worth, rose-colored chiff on with a charming little lace bolero jacket). Once Colin had freed me from dress and corset — I hadn't brought my maid with me — he went up to pull the awning back from the sitting area. When I joined him, he was stretched out on a chaise longue staring up at the stars, his dinner jacket lying in a crumpled heap on the deck. Two glasses, a bottle of whisky, and a decanter of vintage port were on the table next to him.

"What do you make of Deeley's death?"

he asked, picking up the bottle of port and filling a glass.

I lowered myself onto a chair and slouched down as far as I could, relieved to be free of my corset. "Lord Deeley comes to Egypt every winter without fail. I imagine the average Englishman would believe it simpler to commit a crime of this sort without getting caught here than in London. Which is not to say that I subscribe to the notion that it is easier to get away with murder far from our scepter'd isle."

He passed me the port. "I agree with your sentiment. Why kill him in England if you believe you're at less risk doing so in Luxor? The sad truth is that it's easy enough for tourists here to blame any number of crimes on the locals. The police accept it more often than they should. They don't want trouble."

"What do you know about Lord Deeley?" I asked. "Does he have children?"

"No children, but someone's going to inherit his fortune."

"And his title. Pity my mother isn't here; she'd know the details." My mother owned every edition of *Burke's Peerage* but never had the need to consult them. They were the only books she sought actively for purchase. She displayed them in her favorite

65

sitting room in my parents' London house so that visitors would notice the spines were not broken. She wanted everyone to see that, for her, they were unnecessary. I gave up trying to convince her of the inanity of this years ago.

"She is useful on occasion, you know," he said.

"You wouldn't look so favorably upon her if she'd seen Kat with that cigarette tonight. There would have been more than one murder at Per Ma'at."

"I've given myself permission not to worry about my daughter's bad habits until at least lunchtime tomorrow." He sighed, sat up, and poured another splash of whisky.

"That's reasonable." I put my untouched port on the table. My stomach was unsettled. I could not stop thinking about what had happened: Lord Deeley's struggle to breathe, the sight of his muscles contorting, the harsh smell of bitter almonds. It was horrific, nightmarish, impossible to accept. "The only thing that will get me through this is finding whoever is responsible."

"Let's start with what we know about the crime," Colin said. "There's no doubt it was cyanide — interesting that Kat couldn't smell it, isn't it? — there will be an inquest, of course, but we know what the outcome will be. The murderer chose his timing deliberately, waiting until we were all gathered together at the end of what was a truly extraordinary meal."

"Do we know the timing was deliberate? It appears so, but what if the murderer had no opportunity to slip the cyanide into anything Lord Deeley was going to ingest until the digestifs were being served?"

"According to his butler, Deeley has that tisane every night after dinner — he's a man of strict routine. It's some concoction he apparently gets from Constantinople and is quite expensive. He was a generous man in nearly every other circumstance, but the servants insist he never once offered to share it. I pressed them on it, and none of them budged. It was for Deeley and Deeley alone."

"Where is it stored?" I asked.

"In an ordinary tin in the butler's pantry. Anyone in the house could access it easily enough."

"But it would have to be someone familiar with his routines. Even better if it were someone who had once asked to try the famous tisane and was denied it."

"Not an impossible scenario. You're right about the routine; however, I'd argue that anyone traveling with him up the Nile would have noticed he always had the tisane."

"Which leaves us out of the suspect pool. And your mother and Kat."

"I know you and Kat have had your difficulties, but surely you don't think she would murder someone?"

I laughed. "Only if I were her victim. I think we're safe excluding the Hargreaves party from suspicion."

"Are you quite sure? We ought to consider everyone."

"We only reached Luxor this morning," I said. "You went to collect our mail and send a telegram to the boys letting them know we'd arrived while Kat and I went for a quick visit to Karnak."

"You never can resist ruins, can you?"

"I make no apology for it. If I had been the victim tonight instead of Lord Deeley and hadn't gone, I would have died without seeing one of antiquity's greatest sites."

"What's left of it."

"Stop teasing."

"Forgive me. I wish I'd gone with you."

"If you had, you'd have an alibi. As it stands, instead of seeing to the errands you claimed to have done, you might have surreptitiously gone to Per Ma'at, tossed some cyanide into the tisane — although how were you to know Lord Deeley's habits at that point? — and returned to the boat without any of us being the wiser. Your mother, who tells us she stayed on the *Timsah* all day, could have slipped away to do the evil deed. The crew are far too frightened of her to tell us otherwise."

"They're not afraid of her," Colin said. "She runs a tight ship, but she's never unfair."

"Quite right, although I'm not sure her reis likes her running his ship, tight or otherwise. Captains are the same everywhere."

"She would have known about Deeley's tisane. They've been friends for ages."

"When did he first start drinking it?" I asked.

"Decades ago."

"I think it highly unlikely that she murdered her childhood friend."

He pulled a face. "You're generosity itself."

"You can question her if you'd like. And I shall question you." I stood up, planted myself in front of him, crossed my arms, and gave my best impression of a police inspector. "Mr. Hargreaves, where, exactly, did you go when you left the boat today? What time did you leave? When did you return? Can anyone vouch for your claims?"

"You're rather fierce," he said. "Do you suspect me of the worst?"

"No. Or rather, yes, but not in this instance."

He raised his eyebrows.

"I know enough about your work not to ask too many questions. Some answers are better left unheard."

"I would never do something unethical."

"The definition of *unethical* might vary based on whose side you're on." I held his gaze for three beats longer than was comfortable. "Yet I know there's no one with higher moral standards. Except perhaps Tom. He's nearly-eight-going-on-forty and would make an excellent Lord Chief Justice."

Colin reached for me, pulled me down onto his lap, and kissed me. I knew it was half intended to distract me from thinking about his work. He'd formed the habit early in our marriage when I was far less understanding than I was now about what his role as agent of the Crown entailed. I did not object. Habits are hard to break, and when they result in the most pleasant of experiences, why should one try?

The next morning, we returned to Per

Ma'at before the assembled party had finished breakfasting. Only Mrs. Hargreaves was not present; upset by her friend's death, she had stayed in her room. Colin had eaten on the boat, but that did not stop him from filling a plate from the heaping dishes on the sideboard. I shall not comment beyond acknowledging that he'd exerted himself a fair deal the night before. Lord Deeley's butler, Jones, a man of sense, set up the meal in a bright room far away from where the murder had occurred. Otherwise, I don't think anyone could have eaten. Like the others in the house, the chamber was full of antiquities, its collection focusing on ceramic vessels in various sizes and shapes. I wished Mr. McLeod were there, so I could ask him about them.

Colin and I had discussed our strategy before we arrived and decided to take a subtle approach with our suspects. Most of them had revealed themselves as the sort of people who felt themselves above suspicion, and the less we offended them, the more likely we were to glean useful information. As a result, we would focus on conversation rather than interrogation.

"I say, Hargreaves, are we allowed to play tourist despite this murder?" Mr. Trou-bridge asked. "I mean no disrespect to Deeley, but I don't think he'd want us to go home without seeing the sites. We've not done much since arriving in Luxor other than go shopping yesterday morning followed by luncheon at the Luxor Hotel. Deeley wanted us to wait to explore until Mrs. Hargreaves joined us."

"There is no reason any of you should refrain from exploring the area," Colin said.

"Surely you're not planning to go out today? Waiting a decent interval out of respect for the loss of our friend is the decent thing to do." Mr. Granard tossed his napkin onto the table. "Adelaide and I want to go to Karnak, but not until a suitable period has passed."

"I'd prefer to start in the Valley of the Kings." Lady Wilona sniffed. "One does want to pay one's respects, both to the pharaohs and dear Lord Deeley."

"I'm not sure that a trip to the tombs of the pharaohs is a way to pay respects to Lord Deeley," I said.

She sniffed again. "Well, he did dabble in pagan religion. Just look at all the statues of false idols in this house. It's shocking, really. One can't consider them art when they're meant to be worshipped. You can be as pedantic as you want, Lady Emily, but I do think calling in at the tombs is a mark of respect to Lord Deeley's eccentricities."

"We'll have to hire donkeys," Kat said, "unless Lord Deeley kept some in his stables."

"He has enough donkeys for us all," Mr. Troubridge said, "and some bloody fine horses as well, although donkeys are the preferred method of reaching the ancient sites."

"I have no intention of debasing myself by riding a donkey," Lady Wilona said. "I brought a sedan chair."

Kat rolled her eyes and muttered something; Lady Wilona took no notice.

"Had Lord Deeley planned an itinerary for our trip?" I asked. "It would be a mark of respect to follow it, even with him gone."

"He did," Mr. Granard said. "I've no doubt Jones will know the details. Quite a reliable man. Started as a footman when Deeley's father was still alive and proved himself indispensable."

So Lord Deeley was a man who inspired loyalty in his staff, at least his butler. I went off in search of Jones, who led me into a good-sized room that his master had used as his study. The walls and ceiling were covered with paint that, like that in the dining room, mimicked the decoration of Egyptian tombs. The furniture was sparse: a desk and chair, some bookcases, and, in front of the fireplace, four sturdy folding stools copied from ancient designs. It was all very beautiful, but there was something claustrophobic about the space. Jones directed me to a sheaf of papers on the desk.

"These were the plans, madam," he said. "His Lordship broadly followed the same route every year, having spent decades homing in on what he felt was the best way to see Egypt. He had a certain amount of experience in the field — digging, that is — although it's decades since he funded or participated in excavation."

"Why did he stop?" I asked.

"It's not for me to say, madam." His voice was grave.

"I understand. It's only that I'd very much like to get to know the man he was as much as possible. He was so dear to my mother-in-law — they were friends from childhood, you know — and she was thrilled that at last her son and I would have the opportunity to spend time with him. I assume, as his friend, she had supported his move away from the academic side of Egyptology."

"Quite right," Jones said. "Lord Deeley never considered himself more than a well-educated dilettante, but he'd hoped that the archaeologists working around Luxor would accept him as a colleague of sorts. He's hardly the only Englishman who asks for that courtesy, and generally it's given."

"But it wasn't for him?"

"It was initially, but I understand there was a squabble of some sort over a group of small statues."

"What was the squabble about?"

"Upon that point, madam, I am not wholly clear. It happened when we were in England, some twenty years ago — not long before Miss Ann's — excuse me, Mrs. Hargreaves's — husband died."

"You knew her before her marriage?"

"Yes, madam, I worked for the old Lord Deeley before his son inherited. Miss Ann's father was the old lord's closest friend and the families frequently socialized together."

I would have loved to hear his uncensored thoughts on the young Ann but knew a butler of his standing would never be so indiscreet. "You were not in the house when the falling-out over the statues occurred?"

"No, madam. My mother had taken ill and died shortly thereafter. I was away seeing to things for several weeks. Lord Deeley was always generous about giving me time when I needed it."

Generous indeed. Few masters would do

half as much. "Nonetheless, you learned of the feud?"

"Only because it led to the destruction of an antique lamp. I was given the job of finding someone who could adequately repair it."

"How did it come to be broken?" I asked.

"I understand there was a bitter argument and one of the individuals involved flung a book across the room. It collided with the lamp."

"Do you know who did it?"

"That, madam, I do." He very nearly let a smile escape. "It was Miss Ann's husband."

"Nicholas Hargreaves?"

"Yes, madam."

This sent me reeling. I had never met Colin's father, but none of the myriad stories I'd heard about him suggested he was the sort of man who might fling a book across a room during a heated argument about antiquities. Thinking about it, I'd never heard anything to suggest he had an interest in — let alone a passion for — antiquities, Egyptian or other wise. "Mr. Hargreaves wasn't an archaeologist."

"No, madam, perhaps he was there representing the interests of someone else. Unfortunately, the details eluded me. By the time I returned to work, the incident had all but been forgotten."

"Other than the lamp."

"As you say, madam."

"Yet somehow this led to Lord Deeley no longer being a welcome associate of the Egyptologists near Luxor?"

"Yes. They stopped coming to the house here and he did what he could to arrange his visits to the Valley of the Kings so as to avoid them as much as possible."

"Except for Mr. McLeod," I said. "He was at dinner last night."

"Mr. McLeod is of the newer generation, Lady Emily. That set has never troubled Lord Deeley. If there's nothing further, I ought to return to my duties."

I thanked him for his assistance and, once he was gone, sat down at Lord Deeley's desk. I made a quick search of the drawers — there was nothing of particular note. A cigar cutter, a stash of Bryant & May's matchboxes, bottles of ink, reams of paper. I spread out the pages of the itinerary in front of me. It was perfectly ordinary — so ordinary, in fact, that one could believe it had been taken straight out of Baedeker's, surprising given that its author not only wintered in Egypt every year but had built a home there. I had expected something more insightful, more significant, guided by specialized knowledge of the place and its history, especially from a dilettante. In my experience, they tended to be overly impressed with their own standing, convinced they knew more than the academic authorities. Evidently, Lord Deeley had less of an ego than I'd guessed.

PA DEMI, REGNAL YEAR TWO
6

The next day, Kamose and I joined my parents — as well as Sanura's family — cheering the happy couple as they entered their house together as man and wife. That was all they had to do to be married. Declare it and move in together. The families had signed some sort of contract, but the details of such things were of no interest to me; I preferred the celebration. We followed Bek and Sanura inside, complimented them on their beautifully decorated rooms — my brother had outdone himself — and accepted the beer and food they offered. It was a jovial morning. The mothers were getting on famously and the fathers soon settled into a comfortable corner to talk about Pharaoh's tomb. When they called Kamose over to discuss something, I took the opportunity to go to Sanura.

"I wish you endless happiness and hope you will accept this small gift that I made,"

I said. "No statue could be as beautiful as you, but I hope I've succeeded in coming close." I'd taken extra time lining my eyes with kohl that morning, using my favorite green malachite, my hand steady as I held the blue and gold glass wand my mother had given me as a gift. I colored my lips with red ochre and applied lotus flower perfume. I'd never be as beautiful as Sanura, but I wanted her to see I was making an effort. Cosmetics were one of the few things over which I'd ever seen her wax rhapsodic.

She took the alabaster figure from me and smiled. "It is pretty. You have some talent. What does it say?"

I forgot that she wasn't literate — most girls weren't — and read the verse out loud to her.

She cringed. "What do you mean by this? Does some harmful magic inhabit this sculpture? Do you cast a spell on me?"

"It's not a spell, it's from a love song. I hoped it would —"

"It is undignified and unseemly. What sort of woman do you take me for? I dare not let Bek see this. He'd be outraged and insulted."

"He wouldn't — he knows the song as well as I. It's meant to be sweet."

"Not when you say it to me, it isn't."

I was getting frustrated. She was determined to find fault. "I'm not saying it. It's being said to the figure —"

"By whom? My husband? Hardly." She dropped the statue onto the ground and stepped on it, but it did not break beneath her sandaled foot. Alabaster was fragile, but not that fragile. She picked it up and thrust it back at me. "I've heard stories about you, about the strange work you do. I will not have you use this kind of magic in my house. Take this away. I never want to see it again."

Why did she think I was involved in magic? I'd had no training in that art and showed no aptitude for it. She backed away from me and then grouped her three closest friends around her. They watched me and laughed, which made me think they were harmless. Cruel, but not dangerous.

How wrong I was.

I did not mention the incident to Kamose until we were lying on our rooftop couch that night, watching the stars prick through the sky as the light around the cliffs and the mountain faded. I told him what happened and asked him if I should share it with Bek.

"That is hard to say." He spoke the words slowly, contemplating. "On the one hand,

81

he should know you tried to give her a gift. He thinks you don't like Sanura, you know."

"He's right."

"That's a separate problem and we'll discuss it later. On the other hand, why stir up trouble? What's Bek supposed to do about it? Force his wife to be friends with you?"

"No, I wouldn't want that any more than she would."

"Then why bother? Give them something else — something innocuous, something impersonal. Present it to them both and forget about the rest. And you can give me the evil magical sculpture because when I kiss you, it is like I am drunk without beer." He moved closer to me, but I pushed him away.

"Why is she doing this?"

"You and Bek are a formidable pair. Your closeness to him threatens her."

"It doesn't."

"She believes it does, and I understand that. I wondered if I would ever mean half as much to you as your brother does."

"That's absurd."

"Yes, but the newly in love are often absurd. She'll feel more secure as she comes to realize that she is the center of her husband's world."

I laughed. "Sanura? I can't imagine her as the center of anyone's world. But I suppose you're right. He must like her."

"Every man likes her. Except me. I'm immune to all of her charms."

"You think she has charms?"

"All women have charms and they all pale in comparison to yours. Bring the happy couple another present and then let them be. Sanura will see soon enough you've no interest in running her household."

"I barely have interest in running my own household."

"Which is just as it should be. Your time is better spent on your art. Sleep now and give this ridiculous situation no further thought. You won't even remember it happened in another year."

Another year? It would take far longer than that.

LUXOR, 1904
7

Breakfast was long since cleared away when I returned from Lord Deeley's study. The day was hot, but the flowers in the courtyard thrived in the sun. Not all of us humans fared so well. Mr. and Mrs. Granard had retired to their rooms, Lady Wilona and Miss Evans following their example.

"I don't think it will be useful to speak to the Granards together," Colin said. He'd retreated to the courtyard, as the heat never bothered him. His face was already starting to tan in the sun and, with a gentle breeze mussing his curls, he looked the image of a Greek god, although Apollo would pale next to him. "He doesn't appear to like letting his wife talk. Troubridge, whose idea of mourning is soldiering on, wants to go to Luxor Temple today. Dr. Rockley seems fairly desperate to get out of the house, and Kat is quite keen on the idea as well. Troubridge has attached himself to her in a most alarming manner."

From what I had witnessed, it seemed more like Kat was the one doing the attaching. "I could go with them," I said. "If you stay behind, you might have the opportunity to speak with Mr. Granard. He's unlikely to remain holed up in his room all day."

Colin agreed this was the best way forward, so I gathered up everyone interested in playing tourist. Mr. Troubridge helped me into the carriage first and then Kat. She sat across from me and scowled when he did not take the seat next to her. It was clear she had no interest in Dr. Rockley, whom she pointedly ignored on the drive after she made a show of placing her Brownie camera between them. It didn't make for much of a barrier. We made quick time, alighting to cross the river on a small boat when we reached Luxor.

In many ways, Luxor bore little resemblance to the Thebes of ancient days. Humans had lived at this place for a quarter of a million years, building new structures over the ruins of earlier ones. Luxor's draw today is the same as it was when Julius Caesar sailed up the Nile with Cleopatra: the spectacular monuments constructed by the pharaohs of the New Kingdom. All those years of civilization, yet few people care about any of it outside a period of five centuries or so, fifteen hundred years before the birth of Christ.

The temples at Luxor and Karnak weren't simple buildings, but rather complexes that included places of worship as well as housing for the priests who ran them, storage for their enormous wealth, and space for the bureaucracy required to support it all. Each pharaoh left his mark, adding new chapels, statuary, and more. As the years passed and Christianity took over from the ancient cults, the buildings were repurposed and used as villages, a practice that caused immense damage to the structures and their decorations.

We had decided to visit Luxor Temple, the site closer to the center of the modern town. The temple was dedicated to Amun, the ancient Egyptian god of the sun and the air, and its construction began during the reign of Amenhotep III. Ramses II constructed the eighty-foot-high twin towers of the entrance pylon, which were flanked by enormous statues of himself — two seated, four standing — and two pink granite obelisks. Sadly, only three of the statues and one of the obelisks remain in situ; the second obelisk now stands in the Place de la Concorde in Paris.

The imposing walls of the pylon felt utterly different from a Greek or Roman temple, as did the stolid columns beyond it. The complex in its entirety projected might. The Parthenon, with its elegant lines and perfect proportions, did not force upon one the notion that the Greeks were very firmly in charge. The Greeks were content to let one draw that conclusion, obvious to anyone paying attention. The Egyptians, however, left no one in doubt as to their strength. This impressed even Alexander the Great, who renovated a chapel of Amun to include an image of himself.

We wove our way through a seemingly endless forest of columns, plunging into cool shadows and then back into the hot sun, birdsong our constant companion. Perhaps because I was less familiar with Egyptian culture than Greek, I struggled to get a sense of the place. It all felt like a jumble, albeit a stunningly beautiful one. When we reached Amenhotep III's solar court, built in a radical design that allowed for open space and sunlight, I asked Mr. Troubridge to give me his arm. Kat wasn't best pleased and stalked off, no doubt trying to lose Dr. Rockley, who trailed behind her.

I let my companion lead me to the processional colonnade, where we stood in front of a hulking double statue showing Amun sitting next to his wife, the goddess Mut. It was still early in the day, but the sun was blistering hot and I was grateful for my parasol. I envied the ancients, dressed only in thin linen sheaths and sandals. They were far better equipped to survive in this environment than the contemporary Englishman.

"What a spectacular place," Mr. Troubridge said. He was nearly as tall as Colin, but lankier, all arms and legs, more like an adolescent than a middle-aged man. Neither his hair — thin and mousey brown — nor his eyes — a mundane shade of gray — were particularly notable, and his other features were utterly forgettable. No single part of his physical appearance could be described as attractive, yet somehow, in combination, they worked. His eyes danced when he talked, sparkled when he didn't. His narrow mouth frequently split into an eager grin, and his voice, a pleasing tenor, teased and enticed. "I've never been much for history or art or, well, anything that has cultural merit, but now I begin to see the error of my ways. I ought to have paid better attention in school."

"Have you traveled much?" I asked.

"The usual Grand Tour after university — I was sent down from Oxford after my second year, as were my two best mates. We thought we might as well make the trip regardless. Can't say we distinguished ourselves, although it is quite possible we consumed all of the beer in Bavaria. We certainly sowed scandal and disgrace everywhere we went. I have a vague memory of a few of the sculptures in Florence. Who would they have been by? That Degas fellow who likes ballet? No, they weren't dancers." He tossed his head and then adjusted his hat, a straw boater with a striped band. "It doesn't matter."

I suspected this bluster was all veneer. I shouldn't be surprised if Mr. Troubridge had not only graduated from Oxford but distinguished himself in the process. Jeremy Sheffield, Duke of Bainbridge and one of my dearest friends, was a man who liked to believe he had spent his youth sowing scandal and disgrace. I recognized in Mr. Troubridge a similar desire for wanting to be worse than one was.

"How did you come to know Lord Deeley?" I asked.

"It's a funny story, that. We met about ten years ago at a shooting party thrown for the then Prince of Wales. You know Bertie? Er,

His Majesty?"

"All too well."

"Then I shall leave it to you to fill in the details of the festivities. I made the acquaintance of a lady there. Her husband — a violent and vicious man — was abominable to her. I found her weeping in a corner the second morning of the party and did what I could to offer her comfort. Unfortunately, within another year, he was suing her for divorce and named me as co-respondent. You can imagine the scandal. Deeley was one of the few people who stood by me through it all. Said I was too amusing to abandon."

No doubt, that explained — at least partially — why Mr. Troubridge was so bent on playing the role of profligate now. "Fear not. I shan't breathe a word of your past to Lady Wilona."

"I've never met a person so perfectly named. Wilona," he said. "It's Anglo-Saxon, you know, and I'm convinced it's an old family moniker, going back to the days of brutal warrior queens."

Just as I suspected, he was smarter than he meant to let on. "Were you acquainted with Lady Deeley?"

He prickled, just a bit. "I was, though not so well as I would have liked. I'm not the

90

sort wives take to."

"Come now, Mr. Troubridge, you're precisely the sort wives take to. Their husbands perhaps not so much."

He clasped a hand to his chest. "You wound me, Lady Emily. I suppose I'm charming enough to be appreciated in some company."

I laughed, stopping when I noticed a man wearing an absurdly large pith helmet standing some feet behind my companion, close enough to hear our conversation. He was making a show of pretending to be engrossed in the copy of Baedeker's he was holding; it was upside down. I'd seen him earlier, hovering nearby. For him to do so twice could not be a coincidence. I moved away, Mr. Troubridge following. "What was she like, Lady Deeley?" I asked, once we were out of the other man's earshot.

"Reserved. Obsessed with all things orchidaceous. I hadn't the slightest idea one could feel so strongly about plants of any sort, let alone orchids, before I met her. I've always thought them rather odd looking, but she taught me to appreciate their beauty. She had little interest in fashion or frivolities. Had she, she might have been one of the greatest beauties of her generation. Of course, she was ill — consumption — but that only made her complexion lovelier. Byron would have adored her."

"Did Lord Deeley adore her?"

"That's not the sort of question I expected from a lady of your breeding." He paused. "Did he adore her? In his way, I suppose. Theirs certainly wasn't a grand passion, but that's the case for most married couples, wouldn't you agree?"

"I can only speak for my own experience and based on that, I could never agree."

He looked into my eyes. His ability to pull one in was astonishing, but I was not the sort to fall for such things. "Your husband is most fortunate." He laughed. "Forgive me. I struggle to rein in my lascivious tendencies."

He was a flirt, of that there was no question, but he seemed largely harmless. I doubted he was the sort who seduced innocents, but it would not surprise me to learn he could have been named co-respondent in more than just one divorce. "I imagine you're quite adept at keeping them in control unless you encounter a lady — a married, experienced lady — in need of consolation."

"Dear Lord, am I so transparent?" Beads of sweat started to drip down his face. It might have been the heat, or it might have been me making him uncomfortable.

"Forgive me, Mr. Troubridge, I ought not tease you. Tell me more about Lord Deeley. He must have been devastated to lose his wife."

"Absolutely gutted. Whatever their relationship lacked in passion, it made up for in mutual understanding. They were very close in many ways. We all knew when her time was coming — at least I did; it seemed heartbreakingly obvious — but I'm not certain Deeley saw what the rest of us did. When she passed, it was almost as if it took him by surprise."

"Perhaps it wasn't her death, but his reaction to it that he did not anticipate," I said. "Or maybe there was more passion than he led you to believe."

"No, there's absolutely no chance of that. I knew him too well for it to be hidden. He didn't appreciate her as much as he ought to have." His voice almost cracked. I wondered at this. Just how close had he been to Lady Deeley?

"Why did he lose interest in excavation? Was that before or after his wife died?"

"Before — in fact, before I'd ever met him. As to the reason, I couldn't say. Frankly, I never understood why he concerned himself with it in the first place.

Many blokes like him enjoy funding a dig and playing king while they do it, but that wasn't Deeley's style. He was the lord of the manor; he didn't need to pretend. He took his first trip to Egypt long before I met him. I know it made a significant impression on him, but I don't believe he returned until his wife's health required it. Of course, that was only a few years after they married. Five, perhaps, but don't take me at my word."

"He never talked about why he abandoned excavation?" I asked.

"Not that I can recall. Do you think it's important?"

"I've heard rumors of a rather spectacular falling-out with the archaeologists in Luxor, but no one admits to knowing details."

"McLeod must, although they haven't known each other more than a few years. Still, he's in with that lot and they're bound to have told him the story. I'm not sure I'd give this gossip much credence, though. Deeley was never the sort to fall out with anyone. If anything, he tolerated people's bad behavior with far too much equanimity. I can't recall ever seeing him angry. Still waters, I suppose, and all that, but it doesn't ring true. Not to me."

"Who do you believe should have made

him angry?"

"What a fascinating question, Lady Emily. You do make a gentleman think. Let's see . . . surely there are any number of people from his years in politics that ought to have enraged him. There was a time — long before I knew him — that it looked as if he might gain a ministerial position, the sort that might have led eventually to his becoming prime minister. Of course he never speaks about it. I'm only aware of it because an acquaintance mentioned it. Party wrangling is decidedly uncivilized and I shouldn't doubt that whoever was responsible for thwarting his chances ought to have raised his ire."

"When was this?"

"Ages ago, most likely long before you were born. Beyond that, I've not the slightest idea."

"People are far more fascinating than we give them credit for, aren't they?" I asked. "I should love to know more."

"Your mother-in-law is likely in possession of all the facts. They've always been thick as thieves. Her husband was in politics, too, although different parties, obviously. I'm not sure their views could have been further apart. Still, she always had a soft spot for old Deeley and I know he relied on her advice."

"I shall have to prod her for details."

Our meandering brought us to the peri-style court of Ramses II, where double rows of thirty-seven heavy columns each towered around the perimeter. We saw Kat and Dr. Rockley standing in front of one of the gargantuan statues of Ramses at the south-ern end of the space. My stepdaughter lifted the hat from her head and waved it as she hailed us. They closed the distance between us in almost no time, and Kat pulled me away from Mr. Troubridge so that we might speak privately.

"Lady Emily, I shall be eternally in your debt if you free me from the dear doctor. He gets in the way nearly every time I try to take a photograph and is the most boring man I've ever met."

"Is he? Or only in comparison to Mr. Troubridge?"

Her eyes opened wide, turning a deeper green than usual. She was a beautiful girl, with hair as dark as a raven's wing and perfect features that came alive when she spoke. She knew it and didn't shy away from using her looks to her advantage. I didn't blame her. We ladies would be foolish not to deploy all of our resources and, like it or not, many gentlemen could be swayed to do any number of things by a pretty face. If they chose not to look further, why should we refrain from exploiting their shallowness? She shook her head. "No, in comparison to everyone, including that awful gasbag you and Father forced me to take tea with in Alexandria who talked about nothing but mining for some mineral I'd never heard of."

"He was no friend of mine. Your father was trying to be polite." The man in question was a guest at the same hotel as us and all but insisted on sitting at our table.

"It was unbearable, was it not?"

"It was," I admitted.

"The doctor is worse."

I didn't necessarily believe her. How could I when she kept glancing over my shoulder to look at Mr. Troubridge? No one could deny he exuded charm, but after our conversation, I felt confident that he would not make any inappropriate advances toward Kat. She was too young, too inexperienced, and too unmarried. He wouldn't run the risk of saddling himself with a wife.

"I'm very rich, you know," she said. "I'll pay you for the inconvenience."

"I'm richer." I turned around and walked back to the gentleman. "Dr. Rockley, might I steal you away for a little conversation?

I'm rather desperate for your insight into a medical matter."

Kat pressed her hands together as if she were praying, mouthed *thank you,* and looped her arm through Mr. Troubridge's. "If it's all the same to you, I'd prefer to avoid all conversations on the medical front." Her companion gave me a jaunty little salute and they walked off.

Dr. Rockley awkwardly offered his arm and then pulled it back. "It might be better if I saw you in my surgery at the house. It's state-of-the-art and —"

"Oh, Dr. Rockley, you misunderstand. Not a medical matter concerning my own health. I'd like your opinion of what happened to Lord Deeley."

"Well, I'm afraid there's not much to be said about it, Lady Emily." He tugged at his collar. "Cyanide works quickly — as we all saw — and causes a brutal death."

"Why would so deadly a substance be in Lord Deeley's house? Is there any medical use for it? Do you keep it on hand?"

"Heavens, no, I wouldn't dream of having it around. There's no medical reason to. It's not inordinately difficult to obtain — one could use it for any number of legitimate causes, I suppose — poisoning rats, perhaps. I believe it has something to do with a paint color as well — Prussian blue? — but there is no good use for it ordinarily, if you understand my meaning."

"No one pops round to the shops to pick up a little to improve their complexion?"

"No, that's arsenic. There have been a rather shocking number of poisons used as beauty remedies. It likely comes from the rage for looking consumptive in the last century. Something I've never understood, but perhaps that's because I've seen the actual effects of consumption too many times. I can't count the number of women I've encountered who put drops of belladonna into their eyes to make their pupils appear larger. Can you imagine?" He posed the question but didn't pause for me to answer. "Belladonna does have medical benefits. It can be used to treat several conditions. Asthma. Arthritis. Heart difficulties. But in the eyes? Repeated use can cause blindness. Blindness. One shudders at the thought of gullible young ladies applying such a thing. This fixation on appearance that plagues our society tries me greatly."

"It would anyone," I said. "But as for the cyanide, clearly no one brought it to Per Ma'at as a beauty treatment. Was Lord Deeley in good health before he died?"

"The rudest good health," Dr. Rockley

said. "I can't claim to be his long-term personal physician — that's Dr. Claydon in Harley Street — but I've kept an eye on him since we left London. He brought me on this trip not because he requires treatment, but due to his concern for Lady Wilona. She suffers a great deal."

"Yes, so it seems. What, exactly, is her condition?"

The doctor gave a crooked smile. "Boredom, mainly, so far as I can tell. She's reached the age where some people decide the only way they can get attention is by falling victim to some sort of vague illness that brings them sympathy from others without actually impeding their lives."

Dr. Rockley was more insightful than I'd given him credit for. "A common affliction."

"Sadly so. I believe it's not wholly unconnected to the urge to cover one's face with lead or risk blindness with belladonna. Many people believe no one will look beyond the superficial to see who they are inside."

I wonder if the doctor included himself among those people. He was an ordinary-looking man, with spectacles that gave him an air of intelligence, but nothing about him particularly drew one's eye. Most likely, he was frequently overlooked. "Where did you study medicine?"

"Edinburgh. I had only recently earned my qualifications when Lord Deeley's solicitor got in touch and offered me this position. I thought it an excellent opportunity. Not medically speaking, I'm ashamed to say, but when else would I have the chance to go to Egypt? Once my practice is established, it shall be quite difficult to leave for any extended period of time. Pausing before I get entrenched seemed an excellent idea."

"How did you meet Lord Deeley? Do you have mutual acquaintances?"

"Not at all. I was a grammar school boy and earned a scholarship to Edinburgh. I'd always planned to open a practice in Harley Street, but feared the cost of setting one up was beyond my reach."

We had been walking along a row of columns that stood nearly forty-five feet high, close enough together that one could hide in their shadows. The man with the ridiculous pith helmet was lurking in the darkness, following us, using the columns to keep us from noticing. It did not work. I sped up, moving to the other side of the temple before turning to speak again to Dr. Rockley. "How, exactly, did Lord Deeley come to choose you?"

He removed his spectacles and wiped

them with a handkerchief. "He's long respected the medical training provided at Edinburgh and contacted the medical school for advice about whom he should hire. They recommended a handful of recent graduates and he selected me. I can't say I know precisely why. I recognize that I'm beyond fortunate. The salary Lord Deeley offered will make it possible for me to have a Harley Street practice when I return to London."

"He was a generous man."

"Indeed. I cannot claim to have known him well, but enough to wish I knew him better. We'd never met until I reached Cairo, although we did correspond before then, briefly, concerning the details of what he expected from me."

"Did anything about him take you aback when you did meet?" I asked.

"Not precisely, though I can't say he matched the image I'd constructed. I imagined him a combination of Zeus, Beethoven, and Henry V. No one can entirely live up to that."

"Certainly not." What an interesting collection of idols, and how odd to have compared Lord Deeley to them after so little contact. The financial compensation for his position must truly have been life-changing for the young doctor.

"Obviously, I'm not of his class, but he included me with his guests at every stage of this trip, never treating me with the slightest condescension."

"I imagine you can't say the same about Lady Wilona. Forgive me. I shouldn't be unkind."

"It's hard to be anything else when it comes to her. She's quite frightening, isn't she? I despair for poor Miss Evans. She's browbeaten at every turn."

I detected a slight change in his tone when he mentioned Miss Evans and suspected an attachment. At least on his part. I very much doubted the object of his affection noticed much beyond her employer. "Aside from Lady Wilona, has anyone suffered ill health on their journey?"

"Most of the party have struggled with the usual stomach troubles encountered in this part of the world. Fortunately, Lord Deeley demands — demanded — high standards of cleanliness in his kitchens, so we've all suffered less than the ordinary traveler would."

"What inspired his standards?"

"So many years in Egypt, I would think," Dr. Rockley said. "It doesn't take long to notice the correlation between clean water, well-prepared food, and a lack of ill health. An ounce of prevention goes a long way. Is that how it's said? I always confuse these proverbial sayings."

"An ounce of prevention is worth a pound of cure."

"Quite. You'd think I'd remember that one. Please don't hold it against me. I promise I'm much more capable when it comes to medical matters."

Pa Demi, Regnal Year Two
8

I respected Kamose's opinion about most things and decided to take his advice about Sanura. Three days after she and my brother moved in together, I returned to their house with a pair of statues, cats carved from limestone. Innocuous and impersonal. Sanura cooed over them and Bek smiled.

"Thank you," he said. "My baby sister is so talented."

"You're barely three minutes older than I am."

"Three minutes wiser. You'll never catch up."

"I'd never bother to try." We were in their living room, where Bek had painted a glorious scene of the Nile. The river, lapis blue, crossed all four walls. Lush greenery bordered the water along with reeds, papyrus, and lotus flowers. Birds filled the sky and there were myriad animals: hippopotami, crocodiles, baboons, donkeys, and more.

On one wall, he'd depicted himself and Sanura, holding hands, the picture of beauty and love. When I saw the care with which he'd painted his wife's face, I knew he adored her. I decided then to do whatever I could to befriend her. He deserved that.

And so I tried.

I asked her to show me how she made the bread Bek liked. I invited her to sit on the roof with me to watch the sunset. I let her borrow our servant girl one day a week. I gave her a bolt of the finest linen I could find and a kitten from Miw's latest litter.

I felt I'd made a decent effort. But is that how friends are made? By giving gifts and pretending to show interest in someone? Far better to feel a connection, to share common interests, to make each other laugh. My best friend, Tey, mocked me.

"It's pathetic, Meryt. You can't force her to be your friend. You probably can't even get there with gentle persuasion. Sanura is not like us. She's one of the beautiful people, who knows she deserves more than the rest of us."

"She most certainly doesn't," I said. We were walking through the village on our way to collect the water supplied daily for every household. Pa Demi was not like other places in Egypt. We didn't live near the river, didn't benefit from the silt left behind by the annual flood that made the soil so rich foreign travelers believed it was the source of life. The Greeks claimed a woman could get pregnant just by drinking the Nile water. That was ridiculous, of course, but no one argued that our fertile fields proved the gods favored us Egyptians above all others.

But I didn't live in that Egypt, not exactly. The pharaohs wanted our village here because the location was near the Valley of the Kings. Sustaining it was no simple task. There were no easily accessible natural resources near us. Water had to be brought in daily, and the government supplied us with food as well. This was why I loved going to Thebes, where I could wade in the river, feel the cooling effect, bask in the shade of the trees along its banks. There I could watch countless species of birds and pick fruit. Yes, I'm idealizing it. That's what we do with places we don't know well. It feeds our fantasies, and who wants reality all the time?

"That's the thing with the beautiful people," Tey said. "They believe they're better and have no interest in what anyone else thinks. They reside in an extremely pleasant bubble of their own invention and admit no one who challenges their suppositions."

"But they're completely misguided."

"Which only matters if you care." Tey knew something about this. She was even more lovely than Sanura, but their characters could not have been more different. Tey was magnanimous, insightful, open, and smart. She was aware of her beauty, but never showed it. Never traded on it. Never used it. "We all decide how to live. You, Meryt, notice the entire world around you — good and bad, kind and cruel — and feel things keenly. It's that sensitivity that makes you such a gifted artist. Sanura and her pals prefer a narrower view. All that matters is their own little world. When they're forced to acknowledge others, they tear them down. It solidifies their belief that they alone are worthy."

"A belief that depends upon a limited sphere," I said, swatting away a fly.

"You and I would find it intolerable, but fortunately, we don't have to live in their world. You must maintain a certain civility with Sanura, but that doesn't need to be difficult. Avoid her. You'll both be happier."

"I can't avoid her if I want to see Bek."

"Bek is her husband. You must accept that you're no longer the closest person to him. He's twenty years old. It would be odd if you were."

I sighed. We'd reached the spot near one of the guarded gates in the thick village wall where we collected our water. I picked up a jug — they were always heavier than I remembered — and considered Tey's words. "You're right, of course. But Bek and I are twins. We grew in our mother's womb together. We've never existed separately. It's different for us than it is for other siblings. I feel his pain. I know when he is lonely. I hear his voice in my heart when we are not together. I hear thoughts he will not let himself hear."

"Don't tell Sanura any of that. She'll be more convinced than ever that you're dabbling in evil magic."

"There's no magic involved," I said.

"You've always held on to things too tightly, Meryt. Now it's time to let go. Bek will always be your brother. Your twin. But what that means as adults is different from what it meant when you were children."

"If I had children of my own, it would be easier."

"If you had children of your own, nothing would be easier." Tey had five, so she would know. "You'd be eternally exhausted, fat, and cranky. And your loving husband would morph into someone unrecognizable."

"Surely it's not that bad."

"No, it's not that bad. Not all the time, anyway. I'm told romance can return when the children are grown."

"I see how Raneb looks at you. There's plenty of romance still there."

"You're right about that. Otherwise the babies wouldn't keep coming, would they?" We both laughed. The hurt of not having children had long since dulled for me, but it would never disappear altogether.

"I know I'm overreacting to Bek's marriage. Sometimes it's so hard to keep my emotions neatly boxed the way I want them to be."

"Focus on your art, Meryt. That's where all your outsized emotions will flourish. It will purge from you the pain of feeling them. They'll leave your heart and become embedded in your work, which will give other people, who feel these things almost without knowing it, the gift of beginning to recognize their own sensations when they look at your sculptures."

"That sounds an awful lot like evil magic."

"Perhaps we're looking at this all wrong," Tey said. "What exactly can a person accomplish with evil magic? I may have been too quick to dismiss the possibilities. I have many questions. Do you think the Wise

110

Woman could help us?"

We relied on the Wise Woman, one of the most important people in the village, for medicine and magic. She could cure nearly any ill, physical or spiritual, but wouldn't tolerate being called upon for something so trivial. Tey and I laughed, thinking about it, still unaware of just how serious this situation would come to be.

LUXOR, 1904
9

Following our excursion to Luxor, I returned to the *Timsah* while the gentlemen accompanied Kat to Per Ma'at. The walk was a pleasant one, although the heat of the sun couldn't be mitigated even by proximity to the river. I loved the sound of the language — Arabic seemed wholly exotic to me — and was not aggravated in the least by the ever-present children begging for baksheesh. I gave them what coins I had. When I reached the boat, no sooner had I stepped onto the gangplank than the man who had been following me at the temple appeared on the riverbank, shouting.

"Lady Emily! Lady Emily Hargreaves! May I please have a word?" He was clutching his too-large pith helmet to his head as he ran toward the boat. He was young, probably not much older than twenty-two or so, dressed in shambolic fashion, the hat capping off a disastrously tailored dusty

112

tweed suit. However, he was in possession of a face handsome enough that Kat would take notice.

I stopped, turned around, and went back to the bottom of the gangplank so he could not cross onto the boat. "I am not accustomed to being shouted at by strangers," I said, holding my parasol at the ready. I could poke him with its tip should it become necessary.

"Forgive me, madam," he said. "I am Jamie Mallaby, from the *Daily Yell,* a paper which reports —"

"That's quite enough, Mr. Mallaby. I don't make a habit of speaking to reporters. Certainly not reporters from less-than-respectable tabloids."

"You have no comment on your friend's murder? I should have thought you'd want to set the record straight."

"Good day, Mr. Mallaby," I said. "If you don't voluntarily remove yourself at once, my husband will do so in what I can promise will be a decidedly unpleasant fashion."

He looked as if he was considering the options, but not for long. "I shall persuade you eventually, but shan't force the matter at present." He skulked away.

Colin, back from Per Ma'at, came up to the deck. "A reporter? Already?" He shook his head. "I thought we'd have a longer respite before they descended. It's inevitable, though. A mysterious death in Egypt makes for good copy — no doubt he's already trying to claim it's the result of a pharaoh's curse." Few things were more popular with the readers of tabloids than a pharaoh's curse. I still remembered the lurid accounts published some years back — before I was married to Colin — about an English lord who died soon after opening a tomb near Luxor. A number of other deaths occurred, and, naturally, they were all attributed to a curse, until — if I remember correctly — the wife of a well-known English archaeologist managed to identify the individual behind the crime.

Rid of the reporter, we looked forward to a few hours of solitude before Mr. McLeod would join us for dinner. On my way from the temple, I'd paused to collect our mail. An egregiously thick envelope had arrived from Anglemore Park; the boys had a tendency to verbosity. Colin called for tea, and we settled in to read.

Tom started the letter. He explained that he'd decided to write a novel set in ancient Egypt and included an excerpt: a lively account of a pharaoh's hunting party. It was not strictly fact-based — the pharaoh (named Thomasmose) was after bears — but the young author did an admirable job of describing the scene and the weapons used. Richard wrote next, concerned not with Egypt, but with having seen what he believed — firmly believed; he'd underlined *firmly* seven times — to be Jenny Greenteeth in a stream. One of the under-footmen had told him about the mythical river hag who pulled unsuspecting children down to a watery grave. It didn't take much to get Richard's imagination going, particularly when it came to mythical creatures. He attempted to reassure us by explaining that he'd directed his brothers to keep a wide berth from all water on the estate. Finally, Henry added to the missive. His section was somewhat alarming:

As you know, I requested that Grandmama bring us to Egypt with you all. It is wholly unfair to include Kat and not us. Everyone knows boys are better suited to the Nile than girls and Kat doesn't even have a proper bow and arrow for hunting crocodiles. Grandmama agreed — naturally, she is rather intelligent — but said there was no sense in us coming as they don't allow anyone under ten years of age into the tombs. No one wants to go to Egypt if they

115

can't see tombs, so I argued no further. I have since learned that this age restriction is entirely fictious and have started to make plans for us to join you. I don't know if Nanny shall agree to accompany us and may need supplemental funds to hire a more willing companion.

Fortunately, Nanny had written as well, to assure us that no such trip would take place. Had anyone other than Henry suggested it, I would have found it amusing, but he was the sort of child who just might figure out how to get himself — and his brothers — to Egypt. Colin laughed. He had less faith in Henry's abilities than I.

Mr. McLeod arrived soon after the sun started to disappear below the horizon. It looked as if he'd arrived straight from his dig. His hair was rumpled, his tweed suit dusty, and he clutched a pith helmet to his chest.

"Apologies for my appearance," he said as Colin pressed a glass of whisky into his hand. "I've had a rather exciting day and was at the dig longer than I meant to be. I had to choose between changing clothes and arriving on time."

"It doesn't matter in the least, I assure you," Colin said. "What have you found?

Rock cut steps?" Even the least interested tourists in Egypt knew what rock cut steps meant: a tomb. Preferably, royal.

"Not quite, but you're not altogether off base. I explained to your wife that my work isn't in the Valley of the Kings, but in a workers' village nearby."

"Deir el Medina?" Colin asked.

"You know it?"

"I recall reading once about some papyrus discovered there."

"It's a phenomenal site, but as of yet no one's undertaken a thorough, systematic excavation. The pharaoh's government built and funded the village in order to house the craftsmen who worked on the construction of royal tombs in the Valley. As such, it's likely to provide a trove of information about daily life."

"So what have you found?" I asked. "Not a royal tomb, obviously, but a tomb of some sort?"

His eyes shone and his voice took on a tone of awe. "Imagine a place populated exclusively by the best artists in the land — painters, sculptors, stonemasons. They're handpicked to ensure that the pharaoh's house of eternity is nothing short of spectacular. What do you think their houses would be like? Well-decorated, I suspect, but we're unlikely to ever know, as the Egyptians didn't build them to last. Stone was reserved for tombs and temples, not ordinary homes or even palaces, which they constructed with mud brick. But what about the tombs of these villagers? If your best friend is Egypt's greatest sculptor, wouldn't you ask him to work on your own — admittedly, far more modest than Pharaoh's — house of eternity?" His enthusiasm was contagious. I found myself wanting to pick up whatever were the appropriate tools and dive into helping him discover the answers to these questions.

Selim, our crew member who served as footman/valet/man-who-could-do-just-about-anything, interrupted, telling us dinner was served. We went down to the saloon and sat at the table, placing Mr. McLeod across from us. We wanted intimate conversation, not to be shouting at each other. I had instructed our cook — the son of Lord Deeley's cook — to prepare for us Egyptian dishes. I loved nothing better than immersing myself in a new culture. Tonight, we would dine on bamia, a lamb stew with tomatoes and a strange-looking vegetable called okra, all seasoned with garlic, coriander, cardamom, and onion.

"I'm not the first to excavate at Deir el

Medina, nor the first to locate a tomb. But if early indications bear fruit, the one I have discovered will prove an extraordinary find."

"How soon will you know?" Colin asked.

"Excavation moves at a slow pace, at least if it's done properly. It will easily be weeks before I enter the burial chamber. Or chambers. More than one family member could be interred in the same tomb."

"We ought to be drinking champagne to celebrate," I said.

"A very kind thought, Lady Emily, but celebration would be premature. I do appreciate being able to share this first bit of encouraging news with friends — if I may be so bold as to call you that — of intelligent sensibilities. Most tourists lose interest the moment you confess to not having uncovered hoards of gold."

"Gold is what the people funding the digs are after," Colin said. "I doubt most of them have any interest in ordinary houses or papyri."

"Too right," Mr. McLeod said. "The situation is improving — there are more serious scholars of Egyptology than ever — but I fear archaeology will always attract fortune hunters."

"Was that what drew Lord Deeley to it?" I asked.

Mr. McLeod scrunched his forehead. "I didn't know him in those days, so I can't speak with any authority. I understand he was quite keen on the subject for some time, but eventually lost interest."

"Did he fund digs?" Colin asked.

"He did, but only once or twice. A great many aristocrats with archaeological urges find themselves frustrated when the work turns out to be less glamorous than they'd expected. Lots of sand to be sifted, little gold to be found."

"Was he bored or was it something else?" I asked. "I've heard stories about a spectacular falling-out with the Egyptological community."

"There's some truth to them. He never spoke about it to me — I think he viewed our friendship as possible only because I didn't know him or anyone working in the field in those days. I was still at school when it happened."

"What was the truth in the rumors?" Colin asked.

"It had to do with the sale of some sculptures," Mr. McLeod said.

"I believe it all came to a head in London," I said. "There was a fairly violent altercation."

This made our guest laugh. "Insofar as

Egyptologists become violent, I suppose that's true. My understanding is that a gentleman from outside of the discipline objected to some of Deeley's methods. An argument ensued and a lamp was broken. Or maybe it was a vase. Either way, the accusations stuck, and Deeley was never quite accepted by anyone in the field after that."

"What was the nature of the accusations?" Colin asked.

"The usual sorts of things: illegal excavation, illegal sales of artifacts, questions about forgeries. I never quite understood why he was so pilloried, given that most of those things were indulged in by any number of early explorers in Egypt. I suppose we all like to think we're better than the last lot. We're scientists, they were treasure hunters."

"Even up to the time of his death, his reputation hadn't recovered?" I asked.

"Well . . ." He paused. "I can't say that I've ever known my colleagues to care about it one way or another. They were outraged at the time, but they're outraged whenever someone engages in unethical behavior. As I said, such things weren't uncommon in the past. By the time I met Deeley, I don't think any of the professional archaeologists gave much thought to the incident, if they even remembered it. Deeley's pride was wounded, and I suspect it was he who didn't want to move on. Even if he did, he'd developed a routine when he was in Egypt that didn't include those of us working here. He was happy with that, so why change?"

"How did you become acquainted with him?" Colin asked.

"At a diabolical drinks party thrown by some American heiress. I'd been invited for her friends to gawk at. They weren't accustomed to associating with the working class."

"Yes, you university-educated archaeologists are the perfect embodiment of the working class," Colin said. "Although I suppose one could argue that the air quality in a deep tomb isn't much better than that in a coal mine."

"Quite. I did have some fun with it. Horrified them by not wearing evening dress. I came in tweeds. Figured why not give them what they wanted? I half suspect they thought I was stuffing my pockets with bread so that I'd have something to eat the next day. I will say that I've never seen so many diamonds in one place before. I shouldn't have thought traveling with large quantities of jewelry the wisest course of action."

"I shouldn't think it appropriate for desert excursions," I said, "but then tourists aren't often known for sensible decisions. On the subject of excursions, desert and otherwise, I had an interesting conversation with Dr. Rockley at Luxor Temple today."

"I find it difficult to give that statement credit," Mr. McLeod said. "Rockley's a bloody bore."

"My daughter agrees," Colin said.

"Miss von Lange is too intelligent to want to waste her time pretending to be interested in his ramblings. What, pray tell, did the good doctor share with you?"

"First I must defend him," I said. "He's not so bad as either of you is making him out to be. He studied in Edinburgh — a city I assume you, as a Scot, know well."

"Aye." Despite the choice of word, he sounded as English as I.

"After qualifying as a physician, someone from the university recommended him as a candidate for his current job. Does that seem odd?"

"You expect me to have insider knowledge due to my nationality?"

"No, it's only that your being Scottish reminded me of what he said. I wasn't posing the question only to you, Mr. McLeod. My husband might answer as well."

123

Colin looked thoughtful for a moment before replying. "No, I don't find it strange. Deeley wanted a physician to travel with him for several months. Anyone already engaged in his own practice would have difficulty abandoning his patients for so long. It's reasonable to recruit a new graduate, particularly given that there's no one in Deeley's party who requires serious medical care. It's sensible to have a doctor on hand to deal with whatever small problems crop up, but beyond that, his only responsibility is keeping Lady Wilona content."

"Not an easy job, Hargreaves," Mr. McLeod said. "Not at all."

"Quite. Not easy, but not a job that requires decades of practice in the medical arts. A young man, new to his profession, is more likely to have the patience necessary for dealing with her than someone of more experience."

"A fair point," I said. "Do you know if Lord Deeley always had a doctor with him on his trips?"

"Now that you ask, I don't believe he did," Mr. McLeod said. "I certainly never met one before. Perhaps he never had a guest who suffers like Lady Wilona."

"Why did he invite her?" I asked. "She doesn't seem the sort who would want to travel beyond the Channel Islands."

"Her husband was a great friend of his," Colin said. "They were in Parliament together — along with Granard — and were something of a force to be reckoned with. When she was widowed, it became clear that he wasn't as good with money as he was with politics. She wasn't destitute, but she wasn't comfortable. Deeley made a habit of lending a hand without drawing attention to what he was doing. Settled accounts with merchants, that sort of thing. He told my mother. Said Lady Wilona has never given any indication that she's aware of his help."

"Was this the first time he invited her to join him in Egypt?" I asked.

"That I don't know," Colin said. "It's certainly the first time she accepted the offer."

"What do you make of Miss Evans?" Mr. McLeod asked. "I don't think anyone could have invented a better companion for Lady Wilona."

"Too right," Colin said. "I'd bet anything the old girl has a knack for hiring staff. She can see right through anyone."

"Can she?" I asked. "She apparently hasn't noticed the assistance Lord Deeley's given her over the years, and she doesn't seem to have twigged that no one else believes she's ill."

"There is such a thing as willful ignorance, my dear," Colin said. "She might be a philistine, but she doesn't lack intelligence. Or at least cunning. She's not the sort to do anything that would cause herself discomfort."

I turned to Mr. McLeod. "I should warn you that she plans to visit the Valley of the Kings in a sedan chair."

"She won't be the first or the last," he said. "It's appalling the way tourists behave. You wouldn't believe how many of them don't even go to most of the sites. They come only for the weather. Deeley had a good bit of fun tormenting them."

"You two were quite close, weren't you?" I asked.

"We had enough in common to enjoy each other's company, but enough differences between us that we didn't wind up always in each other's pockets. I shall miss the old boy."

"Forgive me if this is an impertinent question, but did he ever offer to fund your work?" I asked.

"Dear me, that is quite impertinent!" He shifted uncomfortably. "No, he didn't. As I said, he'd long since abandoned involving himself with archaeology."

"I shall be even more impertinent than my wife. How do you fund your work?"

"Blimey, you're direct. I thought you're supposed to be English?" He drained his glass of claret in a single gulp. "Right. My work. I had a small inheritance when my mother died some years back. I'll have just about run through it by the end of this season and shall have to start campaigning for support. If this tomb pans out, I shall be beating them off."

"Anyone in particular you've set your cap for?" Colin asked.

"Just your ordinary toff: someone with more money than sense who likes the idea of swanning around Luxor bragging about the treasure he's dug up. They always act as if they're the ones doing the work. Even better is if the toff's married to someone who fancies herself as the reincarnation of Cleopatra. That sort of *lady* — I use the term loosely — can be strung along indefinitely by the barest hope of uncovering jewelry. Mind you, I don't like taking advantage of ladies, so I'd never seek funding from one on her own. I prefer skewering the husbands. They're easier to despise."

"I like you, McLeod, very, very much," Colin said.

From that evening, we fell into an easy friendship with Mr. McLeod. He was smart, engaging, and funny. I hoped very much that he was not responsible for Lord Deeley's death.

"I don't see why he would be," Colin said, when we'd retired to our cabin. We'd stayed up longer than we intended, returning to the deck with our friend for hours after dinner, where a certain amount of whisky had been consumed by the gentlemen. Neither of them showed the slightest sign of having overindulged, but I did notice that Mr. McLeod slipped into a pronounced Scottish accent when he was drinking.

"He's an archaeologist in need of funds. Lord Deeley wasn't offering to help him."

"Killing him wouldn't have changed the situation. There's no reason to think Deeley was planning to leave him a legacy. At any rate, we'll know for certain soon. I've asked the solicitors to inform me of any pertinent information."

"Someone will benefit, there's no doubt of that," I said. "I wonder who? No children, no family. Heavens, what if he's left it all to your mother?"

"What on earth would have motivated him to do that?"

"They've known each other forever. Who

else does he have?"

"I'm certain the loyal Jones will receive a generous sum," he said.

"Not enough to kill for, surely?"

"My dear, I don't believe the idea would ever occur to Jones. He's the sort of butler who is loyal to the end and beyond."

"I quite agree. Davis is the same. He would never murder me, even if I planned to leave him a fortune." I frowned. "Unless my insistence on drinking port starts to wear him down. He's a very traditional sort. It's possible my habits could send him over the edge of reason."

"Your habits could send many people over the edge of reason. Fortunately, we have no interest in associating with any of them. Davis has accepted the port. It's the cigars that cause him to struggle."

"I shall have to be gentler with him."

"That would horrify him even more than the cigars."

"I suppose it's a hopeless business, then. So, we will know soon who benefits financially from Lord Deeley's death. Does anyone stand to profit in other ways? Has someone long coveted his house in Egypt? His antiquities? The loyal Jones?"

"I doubt very much anyone has ever committed murder in order to steal someone's butler," Colin said, "although it wouldn't be the most outrageous motive I've ever encountered. Davis, certainly, is worth his weight in gold. Some might argue I married you simply to have him in my service."

"It wouldn't be the most outrageous motive I've ever heard for marriage," I said. "Now that you've raised the possibility, I'm afraid you shall have to convince me — thoroughly — that it's not the case."

"Thoroughness is my specialty."

It did not take long before he had me well and truly convinced.

Pa Demi, Regnal Year Two
10

Tey and I might joke about using magic for evil purposes, but the fact was, hardly anyone in Egypt used spells and amulets in that sort of way other than the government, who of course would deploy any useful means against traitors and enemies. Magic was a part of all of our lives, intricately tied to religion. It was how we harnessed the powers of the universe. Or at least how wise women and priests did it for us. Frankly, it was strange that Sanura seemed so focused on it.

I slipped back into my normal routine, spending most of my time working on the ushabtis for my father's tomb. To start, I studied the alabaster he'd brought me, looking for faults in the stone and deciding how best to divide it into smaller pieces. I lifted each block to the light, to judge how translucent it was, then lowered it and closed my eyes, focusing on the coolness of the stone while running my fingers over every inch of its surface, mapping its rough edges. Still, I was not ready for my chisel.

Next, I pulled out a large wooden drawing board over which I'd skimmed a fine layer of plaster. It was time to think about design. The mummy form the statues would take was simple, but I wanted to make each face distinct. Our art tended to be symbolic. Representation did not necessarily require individual portraiture, but the individual was what interested me, what fueled my passion. The slight variations in noses, eyes, lips, cheekbones, and chins were my alphabet. Even the smallest tweaks made profound differences. Narrow eyes versus wide ones. Aquiline noses versus turned-up ones. There were endless combinations.

I mixed black paint in my wooden palette, picked up my finest reed brush, and started drawing. I needed fifty unique faces, fifty unique personalities. The task would not be a quick one, but it would take me a step closer to beginning to carve. That first morning, I finished only one sketch and then went for a walk, out of the village and into the desert. Pa Demi was surrounded by the Theban hills. The highest of them, called the Peak, was shaped like a pyramid and was the home of the cobra-headed goddess Meretseger. She guarded the royal necropolis and also watched over those of us living in the village. I climbed her mountain, stood at the top, and drew in a deep breath of hot, dry air. Nothing broke the view; it was as if I could see to the very ends of the earth. The sky, pale blue, caressed me. Heat radiated from the golden sand. A lone bird circled overhead. I had carried with me a statue I had made of Ptah, patron of sculptors, and held it up while I recited a hymn to the god. He would ensure I had the inspiration and the skills needed to complete my father's ushabtis.

I followed a narrow path partway down the slope and then turned off it to make my way along a steep scree field until I reached the entrance to a small cave. I ducked inside, lit an oil lamp, placed the statue into a niche I'd carved into the wall years ago, and chanted another prayer. No one knew of this place but me. It was where I came when I needed space for contemplation. There was nowhere I felt safer. I stayed long into the afternoon, praying and meditating, returning home — taking Ptah with me, to return to his place in our front room — only once the sun had started to sink in the sky. I had three more faces for Eetee's ushabtis clear in my mind.

Kamose had waited for me to eat. He knew my habits. He'd sent our servant home and laid out a feast of melons, pomegranates, dates, and nuts, along with good bread and beer. We ate on the roof, both of us savoring the feel of the cool evening air on our faces.

"I wonder sometimes if we really need the rest of the house," I said. "We always seem to wind up here instead of inside."

"Not when it's cold or raining." Rain didn't come often in the desert, but when it did, it was a deluge. "The rest is worth it for those times alone. And for your workshop. You can't reliably carve outside."

"I wouldn't want to, even if I could. I don't like the idea of anyone watching me." The houses in the village were close together, with shared walls, and there was little privacy on the roof. We could see our neighbors on theirs and vice versa. I couldn't tolerate that when I was working. The eyes of others drained my spirit, made me self-conscious.

"Were you on the mountain all afternoon?" Kamose asked.

"Yes."

"So you will be productive tomorrow. That is good. I must go to Thebes and will be away for several days. I imagine you'll have half the ushabtis complete by the time I return."

"I won't even be through with the drawings," I said. "Why are they sending you there?"

"To meet with Pharaoh's representative and give him an update on the progress of the tomb's design. Your father is coming as well. I hope what we have to say won't be too upsetting."

"Why would it be upsetting? Construction hasn't even begun yet, has it?"

"No, but there are grave concerns about the location. We suspect it may be prone to flooding, but Pharaoh is set on the spot."

"Does he listen to expert opinion? If so, you should have no problem convincing him."

"I'm confident I could convince him, but am not so sure when it comes to his representative. Bureaucrats aren't always the most open to new ideas, particularly when they contradict Pharaoh's desires."

"I know almost nothing about Ramses. Is he stubborn? Does he surround himself with sycophants? If so, you may have trouble."

"He's a fine leader and warrior, that much is certain, but it is early in his reign, so I don't yet know the answers to your questions."

"You will by the time you return from Thebes," I said. "I shall be ready to celebrate or commiserate, whichever is called for."

Kamose laughed. "You'll be holed up in your workshop, half forgetting I've been away. Try to sleep some, will you? And eat. You're already too thin."

"Am I?" I popped the last date into my mouth. "Then perhaps you should sleep downstairs tonight. There's no point bedding down with me if I'm so unsatisfactory."

"You, unsatisfactory? Blasphemy. I shall prove to you the inanity of suggesting such a thing."

He did. And when I woke up the next morning, he was already gone.

LUXOR, 1904
11

Colin went to the telegraph office the next morning, where he collected a wire from Lord Deeley's solicitors. Aside from a handful of respectable legacies (including one to the loyal Jones), he had left his entire estate to the distant cousin who also inherited his title. "Evidently, this has come as a shock to his beneficiary, an amateur entomologist who is currently somewhere in South America searching for rare beetles. He wasn't aware he was in line for the title, let alone a fortune."

"You're quite certain?" I asked. "How could he have no idea about the title?"

"He lives in Australia and has never had contact with any of his English relations."

"So he's unlikely to be pretending to be in South America while in fact he's skulking around Luxor with his cyanide at the ready?"

"Quite."

We had finished with our breakfast and set off for Per Ma'at. When we arrived, none of the guests was in the mood for playing tourist — even Mr. Troubridge seemed gloomier today. Kat rushed to the door the moment we arrived — she must have been lingering, waiting to hear the carriage.

"Thank heavens you're here," she said, coming outside and closing the door behind her. "The atmosphere in the house is deadly."

"Not surprising after such a loss," Colin said.

"Of course, but it was made worse by some journalist — a Mr. Mallaby — poking around asking questions. Lady Wilona had words with him, and Jones had to have him bodily removed from the premises. At least that was a bit exciting. Otherwise, it's been nothing but dull. I had hoped at least one of my fellow inmates would slip and mention something that casts light on the identity of the murderer. I'm afraid it shall take direct confrontation to learn anything."

"I shouldn't recommend direct confrontation," Colin said. "It won't prove effective with this lot. You ought not be involved at all."

She looked as if she might explode. "Father, I —"

"Kat is insightful and smart," I said, remembering far too many times when I'd been told I ought not be involved in murder investigations. She had my empathy; she also had my support. I was not about to stand by and let her be cut out altogether, simply because of her age and gender, both of which could prove assets. "She's also young and beautiful and, as a result, in a position to learn rather a lot from the gentlemen in our group. They'd never suspect her of having any role in a murder investigation."

Her jaw dropped open. "Thank you, Lady Emily."

Colin crossed his arms. "I can't prevent you from engaging in conversation, but if you do anything I judge to be the least bit risky, I shall send you back to England on the next boat."

"I'm glad you won't stand in my way," she said. "It wouldn't work, you know. I made the acquaintance of three people more or less my age yesterday at the temple. One of them is the son of an English Egyptologist who's digging in the Valley of the Kings. He's quite handsome. The son, that is. Tall, dark hair —"

"Who is he?" Colin demanded.

"Oh, it doesn't matter. He's younger than

139

I am and clearly besotted with the girl who was with him, a stunning creature with an astonishing head of red-gold hair. Their friend David was sketching and is quite simply the most tremendous artist I've ever met."

"What does any of this have to do with you investigating a murder?" her father asked.

"Apparently his family is frequently embroiled in criminal inquiries. Is this common among the British?" She might be half English but considered herself Viennese, like her mother. "I told him I was all too familiar with the routine. His parents try to keep him and his friends out of it, so he's developed all kinds of clever ways to do what he wants without them catching on. Wouldn't you prefer to know what I'm up to?"

"I shudder to think of the clever ways you'd develop to hide what you're doing," Colin said. "If I find out you're not being wholly candid, or holding back any detail of your activities —"

"Yes, yes, the next boat to England."

"And you are never — ever — to go out on your own. Have someone with you at all times when you leave this house."

Her face clouded, but she agreed. I had no doubt she'd do what she pleased, but at

140

least she wasn't surrounded by loyal friends her own age ready to assist her. Colin was right to shudder at the idea of how she might hide her actions, but the truth was, he couldn't stop her.

We went into the house and asked Jones to gather the party in the sitting room. Once they were all settled, Colin informed them that Lord Deeley wanted to be buried in the European cemetery in Luxor.

"I've agreed to make the arrangements, but would welcome any suggestions for the service. I didn't know him so well as the rest of you," he said.

"Mr. Hargreaves, this is an outrageous proposition," Lady Wilona snapped, her cankeredness on full display. "What on earth could have possessed him to want such a thing? His dear wife is interred in the family tomb on the estate in Cornwall, and he belongs at her side. I am dismayed by even the suggestion that you would facilitate something so wholly inappropriate and insist that you stop at once and arrange for the body to be returned to England."

"The decision is not mine, Lady Wilona," Colin said. "Lord Deeley gave very specific instructions to his solicitors and they have asked me to assist them in carrying them out. It is not for any of us to impose our own views."

"It's dashed strange," Mr. Granard said. "Why would he want to be buried here? I suppose *you* know, don't you?" He turned to my mother-in-law as he posed the question.

"I haven't the slightest notion," she said. "He never spoke to me about it."

"I should have thought you were the one to whom he'd feel comfortable confiding such horrendously pagan ideas," Lady Wilona said.

"He's being buried in a Christian cemetery," Mrs. Hargreaves said. "There's nothing pagan about it."

This seemed the perfect opportunity to pull Lady Wilona from the group before she started an argument over burial practices. "You were kind enough the other night to offer me a tour of the garden, but dinner prevented me from accepting the invitation. Would you embark on it with me now? It's still early, so the sun won't be too hot."

"Miss Evans, fetch my hat," she commanded. The young woman scurried off.

"Kat, why don't you join us?" I asked. Between the two of us, we might be able to separate Miss Evans from her employer.

"I'm afraid I haven't the slightest interest in botany," she said, arching her eyebrows, "or any concern for floral aesthetics."

"Expanding one's horizons is always a good idea," I said, "and in this case, requires very little effort."

"I've promised Mr. Troubridge a game of chess," she said, bestowing a dazzling smile on the gentleman in question.

I had hoped she might prove an ally, particularly after I'd only just defended her to her father, but clearly she was more interested in flirting than investigation. Miss Evans returned with Lady Wilona's hat and a parasol. The three of us started for the French windows that led out of the room.

"Might I have a quick word, Miss Evans?" Colin asked.

She started to protest, but Lady Wilona interrupted. "The girl will have nothing to tell you, but if you insist on interrogating her, I shan't interfere. Don't think, however, Mr. Hargreaves, that I shan't be writing to a multitude of persons in the foreign office about your behavior. Treating your fellow citizens as nothing better than common criminals is not to be tolerated." She marched outside, the pace of her stride belying her supposed ill health. I hurried to follow, catching up to her only when she stopped so that I might open the door for her.

"Your husband thinks he's very clever," she said, as we stepped into the sun. She snapped open her parasol. "He's not. It's rather disappointing. I expected better from someone like him."

"He's tasked with a difficult job," I said. The air smelled like jasmine. "Frankly, I find it impossible to understand why Lord Deeley's close friends have so little interest in bringing his killer to justice."

"Will it help?"

"To understand?" I asked, confused.

"To find his killer. Lord Deeley is dead. Nothing can change that. So why cause further upset rather than letting us mourn?"

"A civilized society can't let murder go unpunished."

"I'm sure someone will be punished," she said and then sniffed. "This servant the Egyptian police fellow mentioned."

"We have no evidence to suggest he was responsible for the crime. The guilty party is who must be punished."

"Lady Emily, surely you are not so naïve as to believe that punishment serves any purpose beyond deterring other criminals from evil deeds? This scoundrel may not have directly killed my friend, but I've no doubt he's taken part in many shady dealings. He's bound to be guilty of something."

I felt myself starting to shake, consumed with anger at her outrageous words, but giving in to the emotion would not help my cause. I needed information about Lord Deeley. "It's all too awful to contemplate." I walked away from her, toward a hibiscus plant full of bright pink flowers. "Is this bougainvillea? The color is glorious."

"It's hibiscus. How can you not know that?" She puffed up a bit, as I expected she would. She liked knowing more than those around her.

"And those?" I pointed to a riotous mound of white and purple blooms.

"Vinca."

"Are there no roses in this garden?" I asked. "I thought an Englishman would insist on having some."

"Lord Deeley's wife grew them, but he let them go after she died. No doubt they were too painful a reminder of his loss." A butterfly landed on her arm. She brushed it away.

"Did you know her well?"

"Lady Deeley was not the sort to form casual acquaintances," she said. "Her health did not allow for it."

She hadn't answered my question, but obviously wanted me to conclude they were close. "Was she particularly interested in Egypt?"

"Heavens, no, she came for the weather. Her condition required it. She would have been better content elsewhere."

"She didn't share her husband's passion for antiquities?"

"I don't think she cared one way or another. If they made him happy, she tolerated them. She accepted his eccentricities. What else could she do? She led a lonely existence."

"Has the garden changed much since her death? Or was it just the roses?" I asked, not rising to her bait.

"I haven't been here before, so can't speak from experience but, yes, I believe it has. I remember Lord Deeley telling me he'd had everything pulled out and replaced. He had a peculiar notion about using only plants the ancients would have cultivated, but the project never went anywhere."

"Why not?"

"I suspect it's not so easy to find out what they grew. Did they even have gardens in the middle of a miserable desert?"

"The soil deposited by the annual Nile flood is some of the richest on earth," I said. "Most people would have lived near the river, not in the middle of the desert, so I imagine it's possible they had gardens."

She showed no interest in what I'd said.

"Even if they did have gardens and one could replicate them, the results might not be pleasing to the eye. I seem to recall Lord Deeley consulting your mother-in-law about it."

"I wasn't aware she had any specialized knowledge of ancient gardens."

"Nor was I, which is why I remember it. He always did like trying to impress her through flattery."

"Did you know Mr. Hargreaves, her husband?"

"They were not part of my social sphere," she said. "The both of them had decidedly odd ideas about any number of things. Of course, she had an unconventional childhood. That father of hers let her run wild. It's no wonder she turned out the way she did."

"And how, precisely, did she turn out?"

"Lady Emily, you are part of a set that holds similar beliefs, so I shan't pretend you need me to explain it to you. It's all very well to spout off about votes for women and the plight of the poor, but the fact is, there is a method by which society operates, and if we wish to live in a civilized world, that is how it will continue. There is a natural order to things. It is unwise to try to upend it."

Trying to enlighten her would be futile

and gripping her shoulders to shake her until her teeth rattled impolite. I steeled myself, again pushed my growing anger aside, and redirected the conversation. "You don't think, do you . . ." I paused and glanced over my shoulder to give the impression I feared someone would overhear our conversation. "I ought not even suggest it."

She perked up at my words. Just as I suspected, she loved gossip. "Suggest what, Lady Emily?"

"You won't repeat this to anyone, will you?"

"I am the soul of discretion."

This I doubted with every ounce of my being. "All this Egyptian nonsense . . . was Lord Deeley using it to, shall we say, *impress* Mrs. Hargreaves?"

"You've heard the stories as well, have you? I should have thought your husband would have done a better job shielding you from them." Her tone was all delight. "His mother and Lord Deeley were scandalously close before she married, you know. There was talk."

"Was there?"

"There always is, but one had to give this more credence than most. She traveled to all sorts of outrageous places. China, even.

Lord Deeley made a habit of always happening to meet her wherever she was, no matter how far-flung the location."

"They'd been friends since childhood."

"I believe you have been friends since childhood with the Duke of Bainbridge. Does he traipse around the world following you?"

The truth was, Jeremy had followed me to myriad places around the world, but I was not about to admit this to Lady Wilona. There was no need to do so; it was impossible she did not already know. At various times, Jeremy had cultivated rumors that he was in love with me. It was the easiest way to stop society matrons from trying to force their unmarried daughters on him as potential brides. Yet I also knew there was a slim bit of truth in those rumors. He had declared his love for me more than once, even after I was engaged to marry Colin. All that had happened ages ago, though, and he had long since stopped carrying his torch for me. Lord Deeley might have loved his dear friend Ann. He might even have proposed to her. Surely, however, he had not renewed his attempts at winning her affection by creating an Egyptian oasis? It was not the sort of thing likely to impress her.

"I believe Lord Deeley was in Egypt with

Mrs. Hargreaves when she met her future spouse. He would not have taken the news of her engagement well." She looked around the garden to signal that what she was about to tell me was shocking. "There may have been a scene."

"Surely you must know the details," I said, not shocked by the glee in her tone.

"Alas, no, but if you dig for information, I've no doubt you'll find it. It works for archaeologists, after all. There is much more to their story than your mother-in-law would be keen to admit."

PA DEMI, REGNAL YEAR TWO
12

I saw Sanura the second day after Kamose went to Thebes. She was with her friends — Tey's beautiful people — examining the wares offered for sale by my neighbor, a talented young potter. Like mine, her father was a painter. In a village full of artisans, it was not surprising to find talent spread among daughters as well as sons. This girl, Iset, was shy and quiet. She was past the age when most of us had married, but still lived with her parents, who encouraged her to sell her goods in the little market just beyond the village gates.

"You're wasting your time with all this, you know," Sanura was saying to Iset when I approached her stand. "Your pottery is no better than anyone else's. Frankly — and true friends ought to be honest, don't you think? — it's worse than most. Am I the only one courageous enough to tell you? You should find a husband and bear him

151

children." She was holding a beautiful vase and slammed it down on Iset's table with such force that it cracked.

"Be more careful," I said. "You've ruined the piece."

Sanura started to laugh. Her friends followed. "The two of you have so much in common, we'll leave you to discuss whatever it is people like you discuss. We've finer things to concern ourselves with." They set off in the direction of the gate that led back into the village.

"Why is she so cruel?" Iset asked. "Was she always like that, even as a child?"

"I don't remember," I said.

"She must be very sad to lash out the way she does. I don't understand it. Your brother couldn't adore her more. He treats her like a queen. Maybe she doesn't believe she deserves it."

"Of course she doesn't deserve it. She's a spouter of water." It was one of Bek's favorite insults; I rarely had cause to use it and took more pleasure than I should have at applying it to his wife.

Iset shook her head. "There is a deep trouble inside her. I can see it. She should speak to the Wise Woman or it may consume her."

"There's nothing wrong with her, not like

that. She's just mean."

"I don't believe anyone is just mean, Meryt," Iset said. "Something causes it. She reminds me of a scared child."

"A scared child?" I laughed. "No, she's nothing like that. She lashes out because she enjoys seeing hurt in other people's eyes, not because she's afraid."

"You are usually a better observer than that," Iset said. "You're letting jealousy obscure the truth."

Her words held a certain truth. Yes, I was jealous, but that had no bearing on factual observations regarding my sister-in-law's terrible personality. "This is wonderful." I picked up a bowl. She'd painted its burnished surface red and blue and formed the base as human feet that looked ready to set off on an adventure. It was a charming design.

"Take it. It will bring you luck."

"I need patience more than luck," I said.

"You and patience will never be comfortable bedfellows."

She knew me well. I thanked her for the bowl and went back to my house, thinking about a suitable gift for her from the works cluttering my studio. I never sold them; I didn't want them to bring a price. They were all too personal to me. Bek teased that

I hoarded them, but that wasn't what I meant to do. I felt life in each of them and wanted to share them with people who could recognize that as well. It was silly, but I could not change how I felt. I turned the corner onto my street and nearly ran into Sanura, who was standing in front of my door.

"Pay attention to where you walk, will you? Or were you trying to knock me over?" She pushed me away, just hard enough that I lost my balance, and then took the bowl Iset had given me, held it up above her head, and let it fall to the ground, where it shattered.

My eyes met hers. Iset was wrong. There was no fear in them, only hatred. I said nothing, only crouched down and picked up the broken pieces. Sanura laughed. I did not look up until she'd grown bored with tormenting me and drifted away, off in search of a new victim.

I put the shards of the bowl in a linen bag and tucked it into a wooden box in my workshop. I would treasure my friend's gift, even if it had lost its original form. I could still feel her spirit in it.

LUXOR, 1904
13

Lady Wilona did not accompany me back inside after our walk through the garden, explaining in excruciating detail that the exertion had exhausted her. She asked me to send Miss Evans to her and set off for her bedroom in the opposite wing of the house. When I entered Lord Deeley's sitting room, the atmosphere had changed markedly since I left. Colin and Mr. Granard were standing near the French counterpanes, arguing about politics. Mrs. Granard and Kat were playing cards. Mr. Troubridge and my mother-in-law were seated at a game table, a chess set between them. Gold ancient Egyptians faced matching silver ones on the squares of a board inlaid with lapis and ivory, the latter squares bearing lapis scarabs in their centers. Neither player had made a move. Miss Evans was nowhere to be seen. Perhaps she had anticipated her employer's needs and was already in her room.

Nothing suggested the assembled group was mourning a recently murdered friend. It was more than a little unsettling. The idea of a stiff upper lip can be carried too far. Noting that my stepdaughter looked rather dispirited and her father rather smug, I suspected there had been a tussle of some sort over who would play chess with Mr. Troubridge. Colin's face changed, however, when he heard his mother laughing and turned to see her and her opponent leaning close over the chessboard. He scowled and began attacking Mr. Granard's opposition to Irish Home Rule even more vociferously than before. So far as I was aware, Mrs. Hargreaves, although a handsome woman, had never become entangled with any gentleman since her husband's death, and she certainly was not the sort to fall prey to a seducer nearly half her age. Still, from what little I knew about Mr. Troubridge, she was more likely to be his object than Kat. If Colin had interfered with Kat's plans for chess, he was regretting it now.

I crossed to my mother-in-law. "If you've not yet started your match, might we have a word?" I asked.

"Is it entirely necessary to pull me away

right now?" she asked, her eyes turning steely as she looked at me.

"It would be best, yes," I said.

She cocked her head and smiled at the gentleman across the board. "My daughter-in-law likes interfering. Forgive me. I shall return."

Her words — and the cocked head, not to mention the smile — took me aback. I'd never seen her behave in such a way. She was almost flirting and glowered at me as she stood up. Colin's voice calmed as she followed me out of the room. I closed the door behind us and led her to Lord Deeley's study, where she sank onto one of four stools, copied from an ancient design, set perpendicularly in front of a fireplace.

"I don't appreciate being called away so unceremoniously," she said, her tone severe. "It's an inappropriate display of cheek that you should have approached me in the manner you did."

"Forgive me." I took the chair across from her. "I was speaking with Lady Wilona —"

"I am aware of that. I was in the room when you dragged her off to the garden."

"How well do you know her?" I asked.

"Enough to know better than to listen to her malicious gossip, which I presume is more than you can say for yourself. I assume that is why you've summoned me, to answer yet another set of absurd accusations from her?"

"Not at all." I slouched as much as my corset would allow, and felt slightly better. "She's a vicious old thing, isn't she? What she said isn't worth repeating. How could Lord Deeley be friends with both her and you?"

"If you intend to compliment me, don't bother. We know each other too well to play games. I'd like to know what she said."

"Nothing of note, just tried to dangle rumors of a youthful romantic attachment between you and Lord Deeley."

"She's trotting out that tired old horse again?" Mrs. Hargreaves shook her head. "I should have hoped for something more creative. Bertram adored me. The feeling was not mutual. He knew that and, as a result, never acted on it. She can believe whatever titillates her. It shan't affect me in the least."

"I must confess I don't entirely understand your friendship," I said. "He was politically . . ."

"Reprehensible, yes. It's those political positions that brought him close to Lady Wilona and her late husband. My friendship with him, however, was formed in childhood. As a result, I was always able to separate his politics from his other qualities."

"How is that possible, if you vehemently disagree on so many matters?"

"We didn't discuss it. I'd be shocked to learn that you share any of your dear friend the Duke of Bainbridge's political views."

"Jeremy doesn't have political views."

"He does what they tell him to in the House of Lords, does he not? My son would never abandon his principles in so callous a way."

"Your son has principles. Jeremy doesn't."

"You remain close to him despite this."

"Yes. As you did with Lord Deeley."

"We don't have to adore every single thing about our friends, only about our husbands," she said. "And even they, on occasion, can prove trying."

"Quite." She was correct. We all choose what things matter to us, and accept characteristics in those we care about that we would never tolerate in someone who did not have our sympathy. "I understand there was an altercation between Lord Deeley and Mr. Hargreaves years ago? Something to do with statues?"

She waved her hand dismissively. "Nicholas abhorred him. Like our son, he held fast

159

to principle. Bertram did not share that quality."

"What exactly happened?"

"Nothing of significance."

"Forgive me, but it must have been significant. It led Lord Deeley to abandon excavation and severed his connections to the academic field of Eygptology." Her face remained impassive as I spoke. "Did you enter into the dispute?"

"I was not there."

"I meant as a topic of discussion."

She shot to her feet. "I will not tolerate that sort of impertinence from you. Bertram engaged in some dubious practices. Nicholas argued with him about them. I had nothing to do with it." She crossed her arms in just the same way Colin did. "How disappointing that you can be so easily swayed by the ramblings of a foolish old woman. We will not speak of this again."

But it wasn't the foolish old woman who had told me about the argument. It was Lord Deeley's butler, who gained nothing from revealing it to me. If anything, he was the sort of man likely to hide anything that might reflect poorly on his master. Which made me more curious than ever about the altercation. Still, suggesting the gentlemen had argued about her was a mistake.

"I did not mean to impugn your character. I know you adored your husband the way I do mine. What I was trying to ask is whether it's possible that Lord Deeley's feelings for you rendered him incapable of dealing with Mr. Hargreaves in a reasonable manner. I never met him, but I suspect that Colin's temperament is quite similar to his father's. He would have to be provoked in the most outrageous fashion to throw something. Ordinarily, he grows maddeningly calm when he's angry. I, on the other hand, frequently wish I could fling things at people."

She half smiled. "You will never entirely curb your impulsiveness. It must irritate my son as much as his calm irritates you. You're correct that my Nicholas possessed the same nature. I cannot imagine what could have driven him to throw that book."

"He never told you?"

"It occurred not long before his death, and even if it hadn't, there are some things even the closest married couples do not discuss. You know that quite well."

I did, but only because my husband was an agent of the Crown and, hence, forbidden to discuss his work. His father had engaged in no such activities and had deep concerns about his son taking part in them.

"If Mr. Hargreaves was attacking his character — calling him out for unethical practices — perhaps Lord Deeley lashed out and made accusations of his own."

Her face softened; her shoulders dropped. Colin might not have inherited his calm solely from his father. "That, Emily, is impossible."

I recognized her tone. It mirrored my husband's when he voiced an opinion about which he would tolerate no further discussion. "I should let you return to your game of chess."

"Yes, you should," she said, but she didn't move. "I want to unmask Bertram's killer. Make no mistake about that. However, I know my own history with him better than anyone and can assure you that nothing in it led to his death. Whoever murdered him did so because of something far more recent."

"Do you have someone in mind?"

"I have my ideas, but they are not yet formed fully enough to share. Unfortunately, they do not focus on Lady Wilona. I should very much enjoy seeing her standing in the dock in a vain attempt to defend herself. What a pity she's not our criminal."

"She could be. We've no evidence to suggest otherwise," I said. "She's a proud woman whose station in life fell after the death of her husband. Lord Deeley has been surreptitiously helping her. She's no fool — well, at least not that sort of fool — and may not welcome the assistance."

"It would offend her sensibilities."

"Yes, but not enough that she's willing to live a quiet life of genteel poverty. What if his actions wounded her pride and forced her to admit that she's not so principled as she'd like to think?"

"Faced with her own shortcomings, she put cyanide in his tisane?" Mrs. Hargreaves did not look convinced. "It's a stretch, I'd say."

"I agree, but until we know more, we can't deny the possibility."

Now my mother-in-law smiled. "You're quite right about that. I shall see what I can wriggle out of her."

I felt relief that we were getting along better, and a sympathy for her loss filled me. "I'm very sorry you've lost your friend. I wish there was something I could do or say that would offer meaningful comfort."

"The sentiment is much appreciated." She pulled herself up straight. "As there isn't, you might direct a bit of your attention to your stepdaughter, who gives every appearance of trying to run wild. Her father is never going to take her in hand. He carries too much guilt for having had nothing to do with her for most of her life."

"That's entirely due to her mother's decisions," I said.

"Yes, but that's irrelevant to him. If she gets herself into trouble — and there are countless ways of doing so — he will never forgive himself. At the same time, he's powerless to stop her. Keep a close watch on her, for his sake."

She went back to the sitting room, but I stayed in Lord Deeley's study. She was right about Kat, but how was I any more capable of stopping her from whatever trouble might be lurking than Colin? And if I failed, would he ever be able to forgive me? Dealing with a murderer would be far simpler.

Colin and I did not dine with the others that night, retiring to the boat instead, where we ate kadashi, a mixture of rice, lentils, pasta, and a divine tomato sauce whose spices were too exotic for me to identify. As had become our habit, we went to the deck afterward. My husband passed me a glass of port, filled his with whisky, and we sat under the stars, the lights of Luxor twinkling across the river, the occasional small boat gliding by, its oars slicing into the dark water of the Nile.

"You were quite at odds with Granard today," I said.

"He's the sort who can't respect anyone who doesn't argue with him. It's no secret we're on opposite ends of the political spectrum. He used that to goad me. I reacted more strongly than perhaps I should have, but shan't apologize for taking the side of right."

"And here I thought you were out of sorts because of Kat's designs on Mr. Troubridge."

"I admit I was until it became apparent he's more interested in my mother. I hardly know what to make of it." His brow creased and he turned his glass in his hand, pretending to study the golden liquid.

"Your mother is perfectly capable of handling him."

"He's far too young for her —"

"And far too old for Kat," I said. "You don't do well with the ladies in your life having romantic interests, do you?"

"Surely you can't believe my mother is actually interested in Troubridge? Every sense revolts."

"You sound like a jealous little boy. No, I don't think she's interested. It's far more likely she correctly identified Mr. Troubridge's preference for mature, experienced ladies. Preferably married, but certainly not young and innocent." I meant Kat, of course, but upon reflection wasn't sure just how innocent she was. "Accordingly, she's allowing his attentions in an effort to send a message to your daughter that the gentleman is not, shall we say, available to her."

"It's a bloody nuisance, is what it is."

"Did you manage to speak to Miss Evans?" I asked.

"Only for a bit. Initially, she was hesitant to talk about herself, and rattled on for some time about an American girl called Mollie Fancher who claims not to have eaten for more than a dozen years. I eventually managed to get her on topic. Her mother died when she was quite small. She's the youngest of seven daughters. One of her sisters is a nun. The others are all married, but it seems she has little contact with them. She remained at home with her father. When he died last year, she was left with virtually no income and forced to seek employment. She's spent six months in the service of Lady Wilona."

"Had she known Lord Deeley before coming to Egypt?"

"Not directly, but her eldest sister is married to the gamekeeper on one of his estates.

When Lady Wilona advertised for a companion, he recommended her for the position."

"I had rather awkward conversations with both Lady Wilona and your mother." I told him what transpired between Lady Wilona and me and then hesitated. "I'm afraid I upset your mother, but I ought not spare you the details."

He listened without comment and sat silent for some time after I'd finished. "There's something decidedly odd there. Not concerning my mother and Deeley. There was never anything romantic between them, of that I'm certain, but even if there were, why should it matter? It was either before her marriage or after both of their spouses were dead. Lady Wilona enjoys gossip and riling people up. Best not give her what she wants. As for my father and Deeley and this argument . . ." His voice trailed. He tipped his head back and closed his eyes. "There's something more to that."

"Do you have any recollection of the incident?"

"I was still at Cambridge," he said. "My father had a deep fondness for Egypt. It didn't stem from academic interest or natural curiosity, but from the fact that he met my mother here. He started buying antiquities on that trip, and continued collecting thereafter."

"I don't recall seeing any at your mother's house in Normandy, nor in Anglemore Park."

"She gave all of them to the British Museum after he died."

"She kept none? Not even one from that first trip when they met?"

"They were all gone by the time I returned to Anglemore for his funeral. I asked her about it, but she wouldn't discuss it. And when she decides not to discuss something —"

"She won't so much as broach the subject. Very like her son." I laid a hand on his arm. "Do you remember anything about the pieces?"

"The ones that fascinated me the most as a child were a wooden scribe's palette and a senet game board with pieces made of blue faience. Father also had canopic jars and a large number of ushabtis, but his primary area of interest was mummy portraits from the Roman period." These vivid depictions of individuals were painted on wood and attached to the deceased's mummy. Many are strikingly realistic. "He bought every one that reminded him of my mother. She used to tease him that it was morbid, but I could see she was secretly pleased."

"Do you think that's why she got rid of them all? The memories might have been too painful."

"It's a reasonable explanation."

"Is there any chance that the decision stemmed not from your father's death but from the argument he had with Lord Deeley? The two events occurred close together."

"I very much doubt it," Colin said, "but I can't rule it out. His accident was a shock to us all. It was catastrophically sudden." His voice cracked. "I wish I could have seen him before he died." He stood up and moved to the deck's railing. I started to follow but then a voice shattered the silence around us. It was Kat.

"Father! Father! The game's up! I know who murdered Lord Deeley and have the evidence to prove it! You must come at once!"

Pa Demi, Regnal Year Two
14

I am the first to admit that I have many bad qualities. I'm quick to anger. I rush to judgment. I'm impatient. I sometimes take the best figs without first offering them to Kamose. Well, perhaps that last isn't so bad. He prefers dates. And even if he didn't, he always insists on me having the nicest things. I probably don't deserve him. I do like to think, however, that I'm a decent friend. That I'm kind more often than not. That I readily put the needs of others before my own. Except when it comes to figs.

I was in my workshop, finishing the last of the drawings of the faces I would put on my father's ushabtis. Tey was leaning against the wall, watching me. As a rule, I don't like anyone around when I'm working, but I never minded when she was there. She watched, but didn't watch, if that makes sense. She didn't make critical noises. She didn't offer suggestions. She didn't ask questions.

"I'm starting to think I've been a bit hard on you," she said. "Sanura might be as bad as you believe she is."

"What's made you come around to reason?"

"Raneb was with his friends last night. A certain amount of beer was consumed, and then a certain amount of wine, and then there was a certain amount of indiscreet conversation."

I winced. "Tell me she's not being unfaithful to Bek."

"No, I don't think she is, but it sounds as if she had a rather interesting romantic life before her marriage. You know Pentu, don't you?"

"Stonemason, the build of an ox, but not the intelligence?"

"That's the one," Tey said. "Her father took him under his wing when he first came to the village and he became close to the family. Especially to Sanura."

I shrugged. "Does it matter? She married Bek, not Pentu."

"It shouldn't, but Raneb felt there was more to the story, that there is still feeling between them."

"Not even Sanura is stupid enough to continue whatever it was they had now that

171

she's married." The penalties for adultery were severe; a woman found guilty of it would have her nose slit. Sanura was far too vain to risk that.

"No, but Pentu might try to pressure her to leave Bek," she said, "and maybe that wouldn't be a bad thing. What kind of woman marries a man when she has feelings for someone else?"

"If she wanted Pentu, I'm sure she could have had him. Why marry Bek instead?" I looked up from my drawing. "They're both well-employed, both have decent houses. It's not as if she stands to gain financially by choosing one over the other."

"Your father is one of the highest-ranking men in the village. Being associated with his family enhances her reputation."

"That's true. Look, I don't like Sanura, but this all sounds like the loosest sort of rumor. I'm trying to stay civil to her so that the rift between us doesn't hurt my relationship with Bek. You know that isn't easy for me, and you know I have a tendency to leap to conclusions when they support what I want the truth to be. I can't let myself get caught up in destructive rumors."

"I wouldn't have told you any of this if I didn't believe it was serious," she said. "I'm the one who encouraged you to not let her upset you. There's no proof, it's true, but there's something to it, Meryt, something I can't quite figure out. I had to tell you."

"Does that mean I can stop trying to get along with her?"

"No, I'm not saying that, only that it's worth paying closer attention. There's something complicated about her."

"She's a nasty piece of work, nothing complicated in that." I tried to focus on my drawing but was distracted. "What she did before she married is irrelevant. Does she still flirt with Pentu? I haven't seen it. Have you?"

"No, I can't say I have, but there's something there, Meryt. I can feel it."

I sighed. "A smoke, fire situation?"

"I'm going to watch her," Tey said. "She doesn't despise me the way she does you. I'll see what I can find out."

"She knows you're my closest friend and she isn't stupid. She won't let you see anything."

"I can be more underhanded than you think. You'll be surprised."

LUXOR, 1904
15

The sound of his daughter's shouts yanked Colin out of the melancholy that had started to envelope him as he thought about his father's death. Kat leapt across the gangplank and flew up the stairs to us on the deck. Her eyes were rimmed red, either from dust and sand in the air or crying. I couldn't tell which.

"Don't scold me. I came in the carriage so the driver is with me. I didn't leave the house alone," she said. "It's Mr. Troubridge. He killed Lord Deeley. I can hardly believe it. Nothing about him suggests he's capable of murder. It's . . . it's . . . I'm not quite sure what it is. I don't understand how he could have deceived me so."

"First, sit," Colin said, installing her in a chair. "Now, take a deep breath and tell me what happened."

"We have to go to the house at once — he could get away."

174

"He's not been taken into custody?" I asked.

"No, I came straight here from his room. No one else knows."

"You were in his room?" Colin asked, folding his arms across his chest. "Do explain."

"Oh, Father, don't be such a fossil," she said. She sniffed and rubbed her eyes with the heel of her palm. "The details aren't pertinent, but I found myself in his room."

Colin raised a hand to stop her from continuing. "The details are pertinent. Was he in the room?"

"No, no, he wasn't, and he doesn't know I was there. We ladies had been banished to the sitting room for coffee while the gentlemen remained in the dining room with their port. What a disgraceful habit, deliberately excluding us from all the interesting conversation."

"Yes, well, your stepmother shares your opinion. She caused an all-out scandal when she started drinking the port in her cellar." He met my eyes and I felt my heartbeat quicken, remembering the early days of our courtship, when he was one of the few people who did not condemn me for my love of port. "I found it endlessly endearing."

"I suppose you would," Kat said. "At any

175

rate, the whole evening was a bloody bore
—"

"Language," Colin said.

Kat rolled her eyes. "Fossil. It was deadly dull, so I decided to go up to my room and read. When I passed Mr. Troubridge's door on the way, I turned the handle to see if it was locked. It wasn't, so I went inside."

"Did you try any of the other doors in the corridor?" Colin asked.

"His is the first. I thought it an excellent opportunity to investigate and see what he'd brought with him. I knew the gentlemen would be in the dining room for some time."

"You hoped to find a convenient bottle of cyanide?" I asked.

"No, quite the contrary." She tapped her lips with the fingertips of one hand. "I hoped I'd find something that would eliminate him from the pool of suspects. It would be such a bore if the police carried him off. He's the only member of our party even slightly interesting."

I had a certain sympathy for the girl. What nearly twenty-year-old can be content taking an extended holiday with no one else her own age? I wondered if she could strike up an acquaintance with the young people she'd met at Luxor Temple. That would be preferable to cultivating a flirtation with a man closer to her father's age than her own. "You said there's evidence of his guilt," I said. "What is it?"

"I didn't find anything in his room that stood out at first. Some badly written love letters. I can't imagine why he saved them. Thoroughly disappointing. A copy of the 1884 *Laws of Cricket*. A picture of his sister and a somewhat unfortunate-looking baby. The usual sorts of things."

I raised an eyebrow but said nothing. Is it usual to travel with the *Laws of Cricket*?

"Where did you find the evidence?" Colin asked.

"In a wooden box hidden in the back of one of the armoire's drawers. I opened it, of course. It was full of apricot pits." She stopped and watched us, waiting. When neither of us replied, she threw up her hands, frustrated. "One can extract cyanide from them. Surely you're aware of that."

Colin nodded, slowly. "Yes . . . but it's not an easy thing to do. It's not a matter of simply soaking them in water. How many were there?"

"Two dozen, exactly. I counted. Which is quite a lot and you must admit that it's extremely eccentric to collect apricot pits."

We couldn't argue with that and so piled into the carriage and went to Per Ma'at. It was nearly midnight when we arrived. Mr. Granard and Dr. Rockley were still awake, smoking in the courtyard. They hailed us as we alighted and insisted on coming to Mr. Troubridge's room when Kat announced our purpose. I wished she hadn't been so blunt.

"No," Colin said. "I won't have it. The last thing we need is everyone traipsing through and making a muck of things. Emily, I want you with me. The rest of you — Kat included — stay here."

Her father was not winning points with her. She pouted but didn't argue. "I don't suppose either of you could give me a cigarette?" she asked the gentlemen. Dr. Rockley produced one. Colin pretended not to notice.

Mr. Troubridge opened the door the moment Colin knocked on it. "I say, Hargreaves, it's rather late for a social call, isn't it?" His eyes widened. "And you've brought your wife?"

"My daughter was in your room this evening, and I —"

Mr. Troubridge held up his hands, a look of horror on his face. "I know nothing about that, you must believe me. If she was here, I had no idea, and I would never dream of encouraging her. She's far too young to —"

"There's no need to continue," Colin said. "It's not that. She found a box in one of your drawers. It's filled with apricot pits."

He took a step back, nonplussed. "Apricot pits? Why on earth would I have apricot pits?"

"We were rather hoping you could enlighten us on the subject," I said.

"I do enjoy apricots. Deeley always makes a point of having them on hand for me. They're my favorite fruit, but not so dear to me that I collect their pits. What would one even do with them?"

"The trouble is that it's possible to extract cyanide from them," I said.

"Bloody hell." The color drained from his face. "I hadn't the slightest idea. Why would I? You're welcome to look for yourself. Where did you say the dashed things are?"

We entered the room. Colin crossed to the armoire and pulled open both of its drawers. There, tucked in beneath Mr. Troubridge's underthings — that Kat saw them, let alone handled them, would not delight her father — was a simple wooden box. Inside, we counted twenty-four apricot pits.

"I'm afraid we shall have to search the rest of your things," Colin said.

"Do your worst. I have nothing to hide. You won't find a vat for soaking cyanide

179

out of the pits."

He might claim to have nothing to hide, but he was clearly nervous, tapping his hands against his legs while he circled the room, watching us. Colin methodically rifled through Mr. Troubridge's clothing while I looked over everything in the small writing desk that stood in the corner of the room. Like the rest of the furniture, it was Egyptian in style, its legs gilded lions and its surface inlaid with ivory and lapis. Strangely, there were no antiquities in the room. I wondered if that was the case in the other guest bedrooms. I quickly came upon the bundle of letters Kat had read, sloppily tied together with a dark green ribbon. In the drawer beneath them I found a small leather journal. I picked it up, opened it, and flicked through the pages. A photograph fell out. It showed an attractive woman and a baby, not so unfortunate looking as Kat had led me to believe. I held it up.

"Is this your sister?" I asked.

"I don't have a sister." He grabbed it from me. "I've never seen this before in my life."

"You don't recognize the people in the picture?"

"I know the woman, but not the child. She was a friend a very long time ago."

"Does she have a name?"

"Sisley Weldon." His voice was rough.

I flipped the picture over and looked at the back. *Sis, 1896* was scrawled on the back of it, leading Kat to surmise it was Mr. Troubridge's sister. "You were close?"

Now he became irritated. "Look here, Hargreaves, is this necessary? I'm perfectly happy to help in any way possible to find Deeley's killer, but I don't see what digging into my private life has to do with that."

"Neither do we, until we know much more about it," Colin said. "Who is Sisley Weldon?"

"We were close. Extremely close, if you get my meaning, for many years. We parted ways about seven years ago. I haven't heard from her since."

"And the child?" Colin took the photograph from me and handed it to Mr. Troubridge. His hand was trembling as he took it.

"I don't know. I suppose she married and this is the result. What's it to do with me?"

"It was in your journal," I said, "in your desk."

Colin started paging through the volume more carefully. He held up another photograph, this one of a younger, bearded Mr. Troubridge and Miss Weldon standing in a garden, their arms around each other.

"It was a time when pogonotrophy — the art of cultivating a beard — was popular," Mr. Troubridge said, "and few could match my ability for it. Sisley never liked it, though. She preferred me clean shaven, even if it wasn't fashionable. I haven't seen that picture since I don't know when."

"You didn't put it in the journal?" Colin asked.

Mr. Troubridge shook his head. "Not that I recall. I keep photographs in dedicated albums, not shoved in random places."

"Do you keep any in frames?" I asked.

"Of course, but not this one."

"Why not?"

"If you must know, Lady Emily, it's a tad awkward to have pictures of one's former mistress sitting about," he said. I had the distinct impression he wanted to shock me; it did not work.

"Where does Miss Weldon live?" Colin asked.

"I've had no contact with her since we parted ways. Last I knew, she was planning to go abroad. I say, Hargreaves, you can't possibly believe I killed Deeley, especially not with apricot pits. If I had, why would I keep them on hand?"

"As tacit proof that you hadn't done it," I said. "It would be too obvious, just as you're suggesting."

Colin met Mr. Troubridge's eyes. "We're not making accusations, but you understand that we shall have to make further inquiries."

"Do your worst," he said. "As I told you, I have nothing to hide. I don't suppose you could keep this from the others, could you? I'd prefer not to have them treating me like a murderer."

"I'm afraid Miss von Lange has already revealed what she found," I said.

"I mean no offense to your daughter, Hargreaves, but this is precisely why I don't involve myself with young ladies. They're too emotional, too unreliable." He scowled. "I swear to you, I have no idea where those apricot pits came from. Someone put them in my drawer in a deliberate attempt to make me look guilty. Why would I kill the man who stood by me through all that divorce nonsense? Deeley alone treated me like more than a petty amusement. He was the only real friend I had."

"I am unwilling to draw any conclusions right now," Colin said. "I will make it clear to the others that you aren't under suspicion, but you must promise not to do anything foolish. Stay here in Luxor. Fleeing would only make your situation worse."

"It never would have occurred to me to flee," he said. "I didn't kill Deeley, and I have every intention of proving my innocence."

Lord Deeley's funeral was the next morning, the burial following in the dusty Foreigners' Cemetery on the outskirts of Luxor. The crowd gathered around his coffin — of shoddy construction and sadly cheap wood — was larger than I had expected. As Colin had predicted, Mr. Mallaby and his colleagues were publishing a steady stream of lurid stories about a pharaoh's curse. Their sensational accounts of his murder had attracted myriad gawkers.

Colin and I did not return to Per Ma'at with the others, wanting to give the deceased's friends quiet time to grieve after the service. When we arrived the next day, we were greeted by a cacophony. As usual, everyone was gathered in the sitting room, but today they were flinging the most horrible accusations at Mr. Troubridge. It was hard to imagine they'd been so sober and subdued only twenty-four hours earlier.

I clapped my hands to call them to order. "At this point, there is no evidence to connect Mr. Troubridge to the apricot pits.

Further, it is unlikely in the extreme that he — or anyone — could have extracted cyanide from them and used it to commit murder."

"What an absurd thing to say." Mr. Granard grimaced. "Obviously he did it. They were in his room, after all. Why else would he have them?"

"You know I am right here, Granard, and can hear everything you say. I don't appreciate being discussed like this."

"What would you have us do?" Mr. Granard said. "Pretend that this doesn't strongly suggest that you're guilty?"

"It's quite possible someone put them there to deliberately incriminate Mr. Troubridge," I said. "A person who has done that may do the same to the rest of you."

"You think the murderer might enter our rooms as well?" Mrs. Granard, who'd been sitting so quietly in a corner that I'd hardly noticed her, trembled. "It's too, too awful."

"I'm going to have to search each of your rooms," Colin said, "to ascertain if there's anything within them pertinent to the crime."

"That is wholly unacceptable," Lady Wilona announced in a tone — and register — more suitable to a theater stage than a sitting room. "I shall not allow it. No one is to violate my room or Miss Evans's."

"If you'd prefer, I can call the police back in," Colin said. "They will have no trouble securing whatever warrants are necessary to conduct the search."

"You're as good as blackmailing us, Mr. Hargreaves," she said. "It is not to be borne."

"I shouldn't have to make threats in order to conduct an investigation into the murder of your supposedly dear friend." Colin's voice was so low as to be only just audible, a sure sign of his growing anger and frustration.

"There's no need to be insulting," Lady Wilona said.

"You may start in my room, Mr. Hargreaves," Mrs. Granard said, sounding firmer and more confident than I'd ever heard her. "I shouldn't want to ever stand in the way of the truth."

"I knew him longer than you, so my room should be searched first." Lady Wilona's stentorian tones were starting to give me a headache.

"I do hope you're not thinking of doing this without us present," Mr. Granard said. "That would be untenable."

"What is untenable, Granard, is the lot of you standing in the way of catching Dee-

186

ley's killer," Colin said. "I've had quite enough. I'm ordering you all out of the house. Emily, perhaps you could organize an excursion to the ruins?"

"As I have no interest in frittering away more time trapped in this house, an excursion would be most welcome," Lady Wilona said.

I proposed that we set off for Karnak without delay. There was more than enough to see to keep us occupied for the entire day, leaving Colin plenty of time to search everyone's rooms. There was a brief argument when Mr. Granard refused to allow his wife to share a carriage with Mr. Troubridge, insisting she ought to be kept away from murderers.

"I'm no more a murderer than you," Mr. Troubridge snapped. "You should perhaps worry more about what Hargreaves might turn up in your room. It could be your turn to defend yourself next."

They continued to bicker as I rang for Jones and asked him to have the carriages made ready. The party dispersed briefly to prepare for the outing — parasols, hats, and smoke-colored glasses would be essential — and soon we were on our way. Because Kat and I had made our quick visit to Karnak on the day we had arrived in Luxor, we already had a sense of the scale of the place — it covered nearly two hundred acres — and were able to prioritize what we wanted to see accordingly. I doubted very much Lady Wilona would be willing to wander aimlessly.

In fact, she did not wander at all. She'd insisted on bringing her sedan chair and four of Lord Deeley's burliest servants to carry her in it while Miss Evans walked alongside. It made for an appalling scene, but one I could happily ignore in the face of such spectacular ancient monuments.

Karnak is the largest surviving ancient temple complex in the world. While it was in active use, it was the most important religious site in Egypt. The people believed that Amun controlled the seasons, the annual inundation, and nearly every critical aspect of life from here. His wife, Mut, and son, Khonsu, were worshipped at Karnak as well, a sort of ancient trinity. Physically, the complex was a reasonable distance from Luxor Temple, two miles at the most, joined by an ancient road lined with sphinxes. I longed to walk the length of it, but this was not the day to indulge myself.

Like Luxor Temple, Karnak was stolid and imposing, with towering pylons and colossal statues of the pharaohs. Sandstone was the primary material used in the structures, except for obelisks, which were each fashioned from single pieces of granite. When it was first built, every surface boasted bright paint, but the ensuing centuries had stripped away most of the color. The result was stunning, if different from what the builders intended. The hieroglyphs carved in the pale stone stood out sharply due to the shadows cast by the fiery sun, making them look even more finely chiseled than they were.

As we approached the Great Temple of Amun, Mrs. Granard pulled a fan from her reticule, flicked it open, and waved it in front of her face. She stopped walking when we reached the staircase that led to the top of the nearly 150-foot-high First Pylon.

"I know the view is spectacular," she said, turning to her husband, "but I'll stay behind if it's all the same to you. The sun . . ." Her voice trailed. "But I shouldn't want you to miss it, Inigo."

She looked awfully pale. Dr. Rockley offered to examine her, but she refused, saying it was nothing more than the heat. I volunteered to stay with her.

"I will do the same," my mother-in-law said. "That's too many stairs for me."

While the rest of the party began their

climb, we retreated to the relative cool of a shaded cloister of columns.

"I'm concerned that you're unwell," I said. "Would you like to return to the house?"

She shook her head and the color came back to her cheeks. "Sometimes I find appearing to be vaguely ill is the easiest way to avoid my husband insisting that I accompany him when I'd prefer not to. I'm perfectly capable of climbing the stairs up the pylon, but I wanted to stay behind to speak with you, Lady Emily. I'm most concerned about everything that's happened."

"Would you prefer that I leave the two of you alone?" Mrs. Hargreaves asked.

"No, please stay. We don't know each other well, but I've always had a great deal of respect for how you conduct yourself. I'm all too familiar with the responsibilities placed on the shoulders of politicians' wives and have never seen anyone navigate those difficult waters with more grace than you."

"I shouldn't share your opinion with Mr. Granard if I were you," Mrs. Hargreaves said. "He'd be horrified. He and Nicholas were bitter enemies." She turned to me. "Not in the personal sense, only in the political."

"They never agreed on anything, did they?" Mrs. Granard chuckled. She had to be at least in her mid-sixties, but her fine features were still handsome and she carried herself like a far younger woman. Her voice was clear, but quiet. I suspected she wasn't accustomed to it often being heard. "It's good that you're here, because what I have to say indirectly concerns you. That is, I believe you can bear witness to the truth of my words. I have no experience with criminals or crime or anything of the sort, but I do like a good book and am terribly fond of Mr. Conan Doyle's Sherlock Holmes. As a result, I understand the importance of motive in cases of murder. I'm sure you recall, Mrs. Hargreaves, a time many years ago now when my husband was in the running for party leadership."

"I do," she said.

"Inigo's bid failed. It was a crushing disappointment to him," Mrs. Granard said. "It all took place behind closed doors, of course. I hadn't thought about it in ages. Then, last night, when I was reading *The Hound of the Baskervilles,* I found this tucked into the pages." She pulled an envelope out of her reticule. "Read it, Lady Emily, and you will see why it's so important. It suggests that it was Lord Deeley

191

who single-handedly destroyed Inigo's political hopes. He might have been prime minister if not for his friend's interference. If that isn't motive for murder, I don't know what is."

PA DEMI, REGNAL YEAR TWO
16

Things started to become strange during the next few weeks. It was hardly noticeable at first, the odd happenings revealing themselves as such only with hindsight. Three of Miw's kittens disappeared. A loaf of bread went missing. There was a tear that I didn't remember in one of my dresses. Then I found my favorite reed brush snapped in half and laid on top of the drawings I'd made for my father's ushabtis. Two days later, our statues of Ptah and Thoth vanished from their spots in the front room of the house. That told us something was wrong. Something serious.

I've already explained that Ptah is the patron of sculptors. As such, I carried him close in my heart, especially as I'd long ago accepted that I would never receive the help of Taweret, the goddess of fertility and childbirth. Thoth, who had invented writing, was the scribe of the gods, and necessarily central to Kamose's practice of religion. Our figures of Thoth's consort, Seshat, and Meretseger, She Who Loves Silence, were lying in the center of the floor in my workshop, facedown.

Kamose stood speechless while I picked up the representations of the goddesses, but he followed me as I returned them to the platform where they belonged. "Who would do this?" I asked. "And how could they get into our house without us hearing?"

"We were sleeping on the roof," my husband said. "We are accustomed to the usual nighttime noises of the village, but not the sound of a burglar. It should have woken us."

I was unsettled. As I thought about all the other things that had happened — those I mentioned earlier — I began to see a connection. "Someone has been toying with us. She started with small things, but now has escalated to doing things that could cause us harm."

"She?" Kamose met my eyes. "You assume it is Sanura?"

"Who else would it be?"

"I can't picture her sneaking around our house to torment you. And she has no issues with me, so why would she have taken Thoth as well as Ptah?"

"I don't know." I agreed it made little sense but couldn't think of anyone else who might have it out for me. Surely Bek would notice her slipping off their couch in the middle of the night? Maybe I was being ridiculous suspecting her.

"I understand you don't like Sanura and I've come around to accepting you're right that she doesn't like you. Still, why would she attack us? What could she hope to accomplish? It's not as if she can drive us from the village. My work is here. She and Bek are married. What does she have to worry about? No matter how close you are to him, you're his sister, not his mother."

"Maybe she's afraid you'll divorce me and I'll have to move in with them."

He laughed. "That will never happen." His voice turned serious. "I can't imagine anyone stealing statues of gods. Perhaps it could be wandering demons. If we've somehow offended the goddess Sekhmet, she would have sent them. I'm going to see Bek and ask him for more red paint for the door. Then I will summon a priest. He will know the spells to stop this."

The paint would fend off demons as would spells, and I could carve new statues of Ptah and Thoth for our house, but none of that would have any effect on other threats. And it was the thought of other threats that consumed me, threats that could prove far more dangerous than demons.

Luxor, 1904

17

The envelope Mrs. Granard passed to me was heavy linen, with a stylized bee engraved on its flap. It was addressed to her husband at their London address but bore no postmark. Presumably, it had been hand-delivered. The letter inside — on the same heavy linen — was typed, not handwritten, and unsigned.

Sir:

The time has come for you to learn the truth about what transpired in the days before you lost your bid for party leadership. Lord Bertram Deeley, whom we all thought to be your closest ally and friend, worked at every turn behind the scenes to quietly undermine your campaign. He claimed doing so troubled him greatly, but that his principles would not allow him to support an individual guilty of the transgressions he shared with me and many others. Proof of these incidents is enclosed.

I have long felt unsettled at having lied to you about what happened at that time. As the evidence appeared incontrovertible, and the scandal of it becoming public would have harmed you and your family greatly, I, like my colleagues, said nothing to you. Best, I thought, to vote against you and let the matter lie buried. You asked me more than once why I did not support you. I made up an excuse about some policy detail. I now have reason to believe Deeley's evidence was manufactured and, as a result, have concluded that you ought to be afforded the opportunity to clear your name.

I apologize for my cowardice both in not coming forward sooner and in not signing my name. I'm sure you appreciate the need for discretion.

"The enclosures are not here," I said.

"No, and I've not the slightest idea what they might be," Mrs. Granard said. "I know beyond all doubt that Inigo would never have harmed Lord Deeley. Whatever this nonsense is about scandal and deception, it all happened so long ago as to be irrelevant. Inigo has enjoyed a marvelous career and has no regrets."

"He did very much want to be prime minister," Mrs. Hargreaves said, "and it would be a blow to learn that one's ambitions were thwarted by an individual one considered a dear friend."

Mrs. Granard fluttered. "Naturally, it would be a blow, but I'm not convinced there's any truth in it. I've racked my brain and cannot recall anything from those days that could have been used against Inigo or anyone in our family. There was no scandal, hence no need to clear Inigo's name. This letter, then, is a fraud, meant to cast a shadow of guilt over my husband, just as Mr. Troubridge's apricot pits cast a shadow over him."

"It's possible," I said. Mr. Granard might have been embroiled in any number of things, unbeknownst to his wife, that his political enemies could use against him. Was Lord Deeley one of those enemies? "When did you first start reading *The Hound of the Baskervilles*?"

"Last night. I'd been rereading *A Study in Scarlet* before then. The motion of boats doesn't always agree with me, so I thought while we were on the river something familiar would be a better choice than something new. In the end, I hardly read at

199

all while we were on board, hence only just finishing."

"Did you bring other books with you?" I asked.

"A Baedeker's and Amelia Edwards's memoir of her travels through Egypt. One feels obligated to have it here, doesn't one? A few other titles as well. After I found the letter, I went through them all, but none had anything hidden within."

"Are the books unpacked in your room or had you left them in your trunk?"

"They were unpacked, all of them," she said. "I had them sitting on the bedside table. I like to read to fall asleep."

Anyone who knew her habits could have inserted the letter into the book, and anyone staying in the house could have entered her room. For that matter, the servants had equal access. But where would any of them have got such a letter?

"Have you told your husband about this?" Mrs. Hargreaves asked.

"Not yet," she said. "I thought it best to consult with Lady Emily before doing so. If she were to conclude it's nothing more than a forgery or something else wholly unimportant, there would be no reason to trouble him with it."

"I do think it's important," I said. "You've

done the right thing showing it to me. With your permission, I'll share it with my husband, who can speak to Mr. Granard about it. You can count on his discretion."

"I'm most grateful, Lady Emily. I know Inigo better than anyone in the world. He is not a violent man. Why, he even kept on a footman after there were strong reasons to suspect he'd made off with a silver snuffbox. I ask you, would a gentleman capable of such forgiveness murder his dearest friend? It is inconceivable."

I made what I hoped were reassuring noises and spent the rest of the morning too distracted to give Karnak the attention it deserved. We returned to Per Ma'at in time for a late luncheon, far earlier than Colin would have liked. The others, Kat and my mother-in-law excepted, complained so vehemently about the heat that staying would have been unbearable. When we arrived, I went in search of my husband, whom I found searching Miss Evans's room. He held up a book when I entered.

"I hadn't expected Miss Evans to own a shocking collection of scandalous French poetry. Her employer would be horrified. I'd accepted that she held Lady Wilona in high esteem, but I now wonder how she can tolerate her."

"She requires the income and, as such, has little choice. I don't think there are many young women with a mad desire to serve as companions to cranky old ladies, even on the off chance that they might get a trip to Egypt out of it. How about the other rooms?"

"Nothing out of the ordinary."

"This is." I handed him the letter, which he read at once. "I didn't confront him about it. I thought that would be better coming from you."

"Quite right. I'll go to him at once."

"I'm returning to Luxor so I can send a telegram," I said. "I've had an idea as to how we might learn more about Sisley Weldon."

I could have written the text and given it to one of the servants to take to town, but I welcomed an excuse to get away from Lord Deeley's guests. I sent my message and then went to the market, thinking I might find some souvenirs to purchase for the boys. A replica pharaoh's crook and flail were perfect for Tom; I knew he saw himself in his fictional Thomasmose. For Richard, I selected three nicely made hippopotami fashioned out of blue faience. Henry was proving more of a challenge. I avoided anything with a crocodile motif, still harbor-

ing the irrational idea that he might somehow be inspired to repopulate the Nile with
the creatures. I was reaching out to pick up
an inlaid box that I thought he might like
for storing treasures when I spotted one of
Lord Deeley's Egyptian servants whom I'd
seen working in the garden. The police had
interviewed the staff, but I suspected their
efforts were perfunctory. I hailed the young
man and introduced myself.

"It is most delightful to meet you, Lady
Emily," he said, bowing. "I am Ahmed, and
I have worked for Lord Deeley for six years
now. I hope his heirs will keep me on. I love
my job."

"The garden is beautiful," I said. "I
understand it changed considerably after
Lady Deeley's death."

"Yes, madam, it did, although that was
long before my time. I only know of her
from the chatter of those who remember
her. She had many roses and many medici-
nal plants."

"She was not in good health."

"No. She hoped to find some relief for her
symptoms in the herbs she could grow here.
Alas, they did not help her in the end."

"Ahmed, may I be very direct with you?"
I asked. "Obviously, Lord Deeley's death
was a shock to us all. You and your col-

leagues have worked for him for years —"

"We none of us would have attacked him in such a way. I can promise —"

"I believe you unreservedly. Why would any of you want to harm him?" So far as I could tell, none of them would benefit from his death. More likely, they'd lose their jobs. The Australian entomologist might have no interest in a house in Egypt.

"The police have already decided Ziad is guilty of the crime. He won't ever return to Luxor. He shouldn't have run. It was a stupid mistake."

"Do you know why he left?" I asked.

"I imagine he was afraid. The police in Egypt, they will get a confession out of someone, and we all know how they do it. Their methods are brutal. Ziad's sister's husband was wrongly accused of a crime once. He confessed to stop their torture. Ziad didn't want to face the same horrors."

"What was his job in the household?"

"He maintained the building. Fixed plaster. Painted. Stopped leaks in the roof. That sort of thing."

"Was there ever any friction between him and Lord Deeley? I ask not because I suspect him, but because it is best to know everything I can to form the fullest possible picture of what happened."

"There was never any friction," he said. "Most of his tasks were completed so as not to disturb Lord Deeley, and even if they hadn't been, he kept mostly to himself. Although he did take an interest in antiquities. He found ancient burial practices fascinating. It is not right. His focus should be on Allah, but we all have our weaknesses."

"Would he have known about his employer's habit of drinking a tisane after dinner every night?"

Ahmed grinned. His teeth were very large, very straight, and very white. "Everyone knew that, madam, and everyone knew it was only for Lord Deeley. I'm surprised he did not keep it under lock and key, but then, he knew none of us would ever disobey his orders, so he must have felt there was no need."

Surely no tisane was so dear as to require a lock, but I found it compelling that Lord Deeley made such a point of it being exclusively his. It did not correspond with the generosity he displayed in every other aspect of his life.

"It came from Constantinople, is that right?"

"No, I do not believe so. It was from an apothecary here in Luxor, but I do not know which one. Jones might, or Mahmoud, the cook. I know I've seen it being delivered by a local boy."

"You're quite certain it was the tisane?"

"Well, I suppose I can't say for certain, but what else would it have been?"

"Servants see everything that happens in a house and are often the best judges of the characters of those who live there. What do you think about the current crop of guests?"

He grinned again. "You mean, who among them do I suspect of murder? It is an interesting question, Lady Emily. I am not much in the house, given my job, but I hear a great deal outside. No one has spoken directly against Lord Deeley, but they all seem less than honorable to me."

"How so?"

"They are petty in their arguments and prone to gossip. I do not know as much about Mrs. Hargreaves and Miss von Lange, as they have not been here so long. But the others? I would not want to think my friends are like them. If that is all, I must continue on my way."

When I returned to the house — after purchasing the treasure box for Henry — I sought out the ever-reliable Jones and questioned him about the tisane. He assured me it came from Constantinople, despite Ahmed's claims to the contrary. "Was it delivered by post or messenger?" I asked.

"That, madam, I could not say."

"How much did he keep on hand at a time?"

"Two tins of eight ounces each. One in use, one in reserve."

"How long did they last?"

"Each contained enough for a week."

"That suggests there were frequent deliveries. Surely you noticed?"

"I made it a point to notice nothing about Lord Deeley's tisane. That was as he wished it."

I hoped the cook would prove more useful. He was in the kitchen, stirring a pot of curry. "The loud Englishwoman will not like it," Mahmoud said. "That is why Mahmoud makes it. She is most disparaging, especially when Mahmoud tries to please her, so he abandons wanting to make her happy."

"I can't fault you for doing so," I said. "It smells delicious, just like everything your son prepares for us on the boat. I'm hoping you can help me, Mahmoud. What can you tell me about Lord Deeley's tisane?"

"It is foul. I would never let a drop of it pass my lips."

"Do you know what's in it?"

"I took one whiff and never sniffed again," he said.

"Even when you were brewing it? Or did someone else do that?"

"No, I made it. It was such an important thing to Lord Deeley, I felt I should. That did not mean, however, that I had to keep offending my senses with it."

"Where does the tisane come from?"

"Constantinople, he always said."

"How was it delivered?" I asked.

He shrugged. "I never paid attention. It was always here."

I asked him to show me where in the pantry the tisane was kept. The police had taken the partially used tin to be analyzed and found it contained the cyanide used to kill Lord Deeley. There was no other supply in the house.

"Jones told me he always had another tin in reserve," I said.

"At some point, the reserve must be opened, and at that moment, there won't be a spare."

"Until more is delivered."

"Yes."

If that was the case, a delivery should be coming imminently. "Will you let me know when more arrives?"

"Of course, Lady Emily," Mahmoud said.

"It will be Mahmoud's pleasure to assist you in any way possible."

I thanked him and sought out my mother-in-law, who was outside reading a translation of an ancient Egyptian story called "The Eloquent Peasant." Mrs. Granard, wanting to avoid the sun, remained in the sitting room working on a needlepoint project.

"She fears for her complexion." Mrs. Hargreaves was sitting on a wide rattan chair with a pot of tea on the table next to her. "She's too old to bother. It shan't make any difference, and there's plenty of shade." A covered terrace extended from the house and formed the sides of the courtyard.

"My mother would not agree with you. She's convinced there's nothing more important than preserving one's complexion. I'm quite certain she'll demand a parasol is held over her coffin when she's buried."

Mrs. Hargreaves almost smiled, but her eyes narrowed as she looked at me. "You do not follow her advice on the matter."

I bristled at the implied criticism. "I like the feeling of the sun on my face."

"You look lovely with a bit of color. I've always thought it insensible to make oneself unhappy to satisfy what are nothing more than randomly settled upon ideals of beauty."

This took me aback. Had she ever directly complimented me before? "Thank you."

She laughed. "I can see you're shocked. I've been rather hard on you over the years. Perhaps that was unfair. No one could deny you bring my son a great deal of happiness. I admit to harboring deep concerns when you first married. You were the widow of Colin's best friend. That raised a number of impertinent questions in me. Furthermore, I'd always pictured him with someone who fit my definition of an equal partner." I opened my mouth to protest, but she motioned for me to stay quiet. "We did not meet under the best of circumstances, and I judged you harshly."

To say the least. At the time, I'd recently suffered a miscarriage and was struggling to deal with the loss. She had offered me little sympathy.

"Given what you have just said about your mother, I shall admit something else. I know Lady Bromley — only very slightly — and never liked her. She embraces all the mores of society to which I object. I feared you would eventually do the same, no matter how independent and enlightened you appeared in your youth. Now, however, I see I was wrong and offer you an apology."

Tears smarted in my eyes. I blinked them away. Would we now, at last, form a meaningful friendship? The emotion of the moment took me aback. "Thank you. I know I'm not always the easiest —"

"You're impetuous, over-confident, and guided more by emotion than thought. All qualities that, on the surface, might grate. However, I am choosing to cast them in a more favorable light going forward. It is clear you adore my son. For that, I will always be grateful. It is nothing less than he deserves. When I first observed the depth of your feelings for each other, I felt a stab of jealousy. It reminded me too much of what my Nicholas and I shared and what I shall never experience again. I reacted badly. I trust there is nothing more to say on the subject and we may return to the matter at hand." She did not wait for me to reply. "What are we going to do about this murder? I shall never forgive myself if Bertram's killer goes unpunished."

I decided I would — at least for now — respect her wish to say nothing more on the prior subject and instead told her what I'd learned about the tisane. "Given there was so little left and nothing in reserve, more should be delivered at any moment," I said.

"As I'm staying in the house, I can make

a point of looking over every package that arrives before Jones does," she said. "He's efficient, but not more so than I. I don't believe he's telling you the whole truth about its source. He is the sort of man who knows everything going on, and Bertram relied on him without reserve. Given that he considered the tisane essential, there's no chance Jones wasn't ensuring it was delivered in a timely fashion, regardless of where it came from. He would never leave something so important to one of the other servants."

"Do you know how long Lord Deeley had considered it essential?" I asked.

"I'm not entirely certain when it comes to this particular blend, but it was always one of his oddities, these tisanes. This was not the first and I doubt very much would have been the last if he were still alive. He'd made a habit of drinking one after dinner for as long as I can remember, even when he was a young man. He was convinced it was good for his health. Ironic, isn't it?"

"Was he concerned with his health?"

"Not particularly," she said. "Other than the tisane, he took no measures to improve it, not that it needed improving. He was always hale and hearty. Quite fit. Had a habit of taking long walks daily."

"Did he ever talk to you about where he got his tisanes or how he chose them?"

"I believe he mentioned in passing this one was from Constantinople, but I can't say I paid much attention. It wasn't something he spoke of with any frequency."

I crinkled my brow. "It doesn't make sense. If it were coming from so far away, surely he would order it in greater quantity to ensure he always had some on hand. Yet we are to believe he kept two tins that would last two weeks? That's not enough to allow for any delay in shipping."

"It does not satisfy even the barest measures of common sense," she said. "Unless I'm wrong about how essential he considered it. Perhaps it was nothing more than affectation, and claiming it came from Constantinople lent it some exoticism."

"Are we placing more importance on it than it deserves because it provided the murderer with a simple opportunity to strike?"

"It's quite possible, but then again, it's clear there's something odd about the whole business or he wouldn't have made such a point of keeping it only for himself. Colin told me he found nothing obviously pertinent to the case in Bertram's room or study, but perhaps we should take another look.

There may be a record of the purchases somewhere, or some sort of reference to the stuff in his personal papers."

We started in his study and quickly found a ledger that recorded supplies bought for the house. There was no mention of tisane. Everything else was listed in complete detail: types of flour, specific cuts of meat ordered from the butcher, even coins given to children in response to their endless pleas for baksheesh. He ordered a slew of things from Fortnum's in London: tea, wine, spirits, biscuits, jam, and a large variety of chutneys. Everything else was acquired locally.

We turned our attention to his bedroom. Mrs. Hargreaves hesitated at the door, her face growing pale. "I don't feel quite right going in. It seems too personal a violation given how well I knew him."

"Leave it to me," I said. "There's no need for you to come."

"Then I shall return to my book." She started to walk away, then paused and turned back to me. "Thank you."

When she had disappeared from sight, I opened the door and entered the room. I've always felt that few things in a person's home are more revelatory than the contents of bedroom bookshelves. There, one finds volumes chosen not to impress, but those dear to the owner in some personal, intimate way. Lord Deeley's confirmed my view of him as someone not particularly intellectual. He had a range of the collected works of poetasters of the worst sentimental sort. Utterly unreadable, and they were the only books. Beyond that, the shelves were filled with antiquities of the highest quality, surpassing even those displayed in the public rooms of the house: fragments from tomb walls with the paint so bright it looked new, statues in near-perfect condition, smooth cosmetic containers that showed little sign of their age. He'd kept the best for himself.

The room was sparsely furnished given its size. There was no desk or table, only two chairs placed to look out the window into the courtyard, the bed, and bedside tables. I moved into the adjacent dressing room, in which stood a table with a single chair. There were no windows and the walls were lined with a variety of built-in cupboards and drawers. I went through them systematically. Most contained clothes or personal items like cuff links, cigar cutters, and a large number of dark glasses that would be useful in the desert sun. One, however, held a pen, a pot of ink, a blotter, and a leather-bound journal. I picked it up and opened it to a bookmarked page.

I know that at long last, I have won Ann's heart. It is a perilous position in which to find myself, despite how long I have wished to earn it. Should she learn those details of my past — details I dare not write even in these private pages — all would be lost. One doesn't expect the mistakes of one's youth could ever prove dangerous, but here we are. No matter what she does, I shall always forgive her.

Pa Demi, Regnal Year Two
18

After Kamose repainted our door and the priest had chanted spells to keep demons away, our life was peaceful for exactly eight days. On the morning of the ninth, I entered my workshop to find all the drawings I'd made for my father's ushabtis torn to shreds and the alabaster he'd brought me smashed to bits. I called for my husband, who was still on the roof. We'd both struggled to wake up. Together, we surveyed the destruction.

"No one could have done that to the alabaster without us hearing," Kamose said. "It would have taken loud, violent action."

"We slept too soundly last night," I said. "I could barely wake you when the sun rose. I could barely wake myself. Someone must have given us a sleeping potion."

We had dined with Bek and Sanura last evening. She was actually cordial to me. Had it all been an act? A carefully choreographed plan to drug us so that she might demolish my work? I didn't suggest it. I didn't have to. The possibility was obvious enough on its own.

Kamose ordered me to stay in the house. He went off in search of my brother and returned with him half an hour later. Bek was not working that day; he wouldn't return to the Valley of the Kings until the following day.

"Who would have done this?" he asked, surveying the damage.

I hesitated. Directly accusing his wife would create a gulf between us, one I wasn't sure we could heal. Could I be sure it was Sanura? Did she have the strength to smash the alabaster? Pentu could have done it easily enough. Maybe he was her accomplice. But why would either of them do any of this? Why would anyone? I was confused. Overwhelmed. Unsettled.

"We think someone gave us a sleeping potion," Kamose said. "Was anyone new working in your kitchen last night?"

"I'll ask Sanura, but I would hate to think a member of our household would do such a thing. She will be horrified. She was only just telling me how she hopes that the two of you can find your way to being friends."

Guilt surged in me. His tone softened so

much when he said her name. He adored her, of that I had no doubt. "We drank water when we returned home," I said. "Someone could have tainted it while the house was empty." We didn't have any servants who lived with us, only day help, so no one should have been in the house.

The three of us went to the kitchen. There was only one jug with water left in it from the night before; I hadn't yet collected more that morning. It smelled and looked like ordinary water. I lifted it and drank. We waited, but I did not grow tired. We all walked to Bek's house.

Sanura looked skeptical when her husband told her what had happened. "There was no one new in the kitchen," she said, "and even if there were, we all ate the same dishes and drank the same wine. Bek and I were not overtaken with fatigue. Maybe something else exhausted you. Maybe you're both ill." She shrugged. "I don't see why sleeping soundly is such a bad thing. Whoever came into the house and moved your statues probably thought it was a good joke."

"Stealing statues of the gods is not a joke," I said.

"No, I guess not." She frowned.

"Neither is smashing alabaster," Kamose said.

"Maybe someone objects to your work, Meryt," Sanura said. "We live in a village of artisans. Your father having you make some of his grave goods takes the work from someone else. Someone who needs the money."

"Everyone here is well paid," I said. "Such a small commission would hardly make much of a difference to any household."

"Some people are incapable of living within their means," she said. "Some people have vile habits. I'm sure you'll find your culprit among them."

It wasn't the worst idea, but it didn't explain how we'd been drugged. Sanura was staring at me, her eyes narrow, her lips curved into a sinister smile. I didn't trust her, yet I wasn't ready to accuse her. Maybe that was her genius. She could torment me without leaving enough evidence to turn Bek against her. But why? Why would she hate me that much? There was something I wasn't seeing. Something that would explain it all. And I hadn't the slightest idea of how to go about figuring out what it was.

LUXOR, 1904
19

I have won Ann's heart? I read the words over and over but did not know what to make of them. The entry was dated 18 August 1903, months before Lord Deeley had set off for Egypt. Why would he have left a bookmark there, instead of at the spot he would start writing his next entry? That's what I always did with my diary. I took the journal back into the bedroom and sat on one of the chairs by the window. I flipped to the front of the volume and skimmed, looking for references to my mother-in-law. None came before 18 August, and nothing in that entry illuminated why Lord Deeley believed he had won her heart.

A quick but thorough examination of the rest of the journal revealed nothing about Lord Deeley's tisanes. I decided to take the book with me, wanting to read it more carefully when I returned to the boat. I made another circuit of the bedroom to ensure I hadn't missed anything and noticed a crack in the glass of a picture frame on one of the bedside tables. The frame displayed a fragment of papyrus. I picked it up and saw that the backing was damaged. I pulled it out and found a photograph behind the papyrus: one that showed a young Ann Hargreaves and Lord Deeley mounted on camels in front of the Great Pyramid. This, I could believe he would keep, particularly if he harbored a long-standing affection for his friend. But why was it covered up if he had come to believe that he had at last won her heart?

I couldn't accept his conclusion. Mrs. Hargreaves might not choose to emulate our late queen and dress in mourning forever, but it was clear she still grieved her late husband. I had heard the pain in her voice when she referred to him as *my Nicholas* when we were talking in the garden. In all the years I'd known her, she'd never shown the slightest interest in forming another romantic attachment.

Although she had flirted with Mr. Troubridge. Or at least let him flirt with her. But surely that contradicted the notion of her having fallen for Lord Deeley? I wondered if she knew he had her photograph next to his bed. Given that she was making an effort at being more friendly to me, I was not about to hide it from her. I took it out to the garden, where she was reading.

"Where on earth did you find this?" she asked as I handed it to her.

"It was in a frame on Lord Deeley's bedside table, hidden behind a papyrus."

"How did he come to have it? I thought I possessed the only copy." She frowned. "In fact, I know I did. Before I married, I spent much of my time traveling, preferring far-flung parts of the world. I studied the art of photography long before cameras were as easy to use and as portable as that Brownie Kat carries with her everywhere. When I returned home, I would develop the plates and place the pictures in albums, one for each trip. Bertram made a habit of meeting up with me on these youthful adventures, and on this particular voyage" — she held up the photograph — "we spent a lovely fortnight exploring the sites around Cairo before I met Nicholas. This shot is from that day, taken not more than half an hour before my fateful climb up the pyramid. It's very strange . . . . I had every intention of bringing my album from that year with me here, but I couldn't find it. It wasn't with the others. I thought perhaps I'd given it to Colin years ago, and that he had it at Anglemore. It contained the first pictures of me with his father and the only photograph taken on our wedding day."

"I've never seen it," I said.

"He was always quite sentimental about his father. It wounded him deeply that he wasn't able to get home before we lost him, although it wouldn't have made much difference. Nicholas only regained consciousness briefly after his accident. Those days are still foggy to me. It all happened quite suddenly."

"I'm so sorry."

"It was ages ago and is best left in the past. May I keep the picture or is it required as evidence?"

"Even if it is, I see no reason that you shouldn't be the one to hold on to it."

She was still staring at it. "We were so very young." She gave herself a little shake. "Did you find anything else?"

I hated even to mention it. "There was one passage in his journal that confused me. He was writing about you in a rather personal fashion. I apologize for reading it, but —"

"Show me," she said. I opened the diary to the page in question, handed it to her, and watched as she read. She squinted and raised her eyebrows, the rest of her perfectly still. She then pursed her lips, slammed the journal shut, and flung it across the garden. It landed in a bed of vinca. "What an outrageous suggestion. First, Bertram never had my heart and never would, no matter how long he lived. He knew that better than anyone. Second, I would never prove a danger to him, regardless of whatever these absurd details of his past might be." She was angry.

"You need not convince me. I find it all insensible, but I thought I should tell you nonetheless."

"I do appreciate that, Emily," she said. "If we are to be friends, we must always be honest with each other. There is nothing more important. I admit that Bertram long carried a torch for me. Our families were close and we spent much time together as children. His father would have been delighted had we married."

"And yours?"

"He would never have allowed me to make such a foolish mistake. He wanted me to lead an extraordinary life. That's how he always phrased it. *An extraordinary life.* He encouraged me to travel. My brothers, of course, had all done their Grand Tours, but I remained at home with him after my mother died. He didn't require any care, but appreciated the company and the sacrifice, although I never considered it a burden. What else was I going to do? I had as little interest in getting married as he had in seeing me leave home."

"Did he travel with you?" I asked.

"Quite often, but not always. He wasn't in Egypt when I met Nicholas. Our marriage took him entirely by surprise, but he thoroughly approved of my choice, something he wouldn't have done if I'd come home Bertram's wife."

"Why is that? Your families were so close, one would half expect a marriage between you to have been arranged when you were children."

"It wasn't that he didn't like Bertram. He enjoyed spending time with him and certainly encouraged our friendship. However, he knew me well and rightly concluded that Bertram and I would not be a good match. He would have proved too traditional a husband. Too old-fashioned. A fossil, as Kat might say."

I nodded. "Have you any idea why Lord Deeley might have believed that he'd won your heart?"

She looked down at the closed book in her lap and considered the question. "He wrote that in August . . . it was about that time that I told him I would come to Egypt."

"Did you accept the invitation in writing or in person?"

"In person. He came to my house in France to proffer it. We neither of us was getting younger, and I thought it prudent to go before I'm too old to travel."

"You are nowhere close to those days," I said.

"I don't require idle flattery, Emily. When I lost Nicholas, I learned that one cannot rely on one's health, no matter how good it may seem to be. It may be taken from one in an instant."

She was right, of course. The poet Horace tells us *carpe diem, quam minimum credula postero:* pluck the day, put no trust in the future. "He doesn't specifically mention coming to Normandy in the journal, although it's clear he was with you."

"He stayed only two days," she said. "He was on his way to Paris. We discussed nothing that could be construed as romantic."

"How long had it been since you'd seen him?"

"A few years at least. As you know, I spend almost no time in England. He popped in to see me at home whenever he happened to be in France, which was not often."

"Do you correspond?" I asked.

227

"A few times a year, rather erratically. Old friendships like ours don't require frequent nurturing. When we did see each other, it was as if no time had passed, but we were no longer involved in each other's daily lives. If you'd like to search my room, go right ahead. I didn't bring any of his letters with me, but you ought not take me at my word in the midst of a murder investigation."

"I don't need to search your room." Colin had already done so and I did not feel comfortable violating her privacy in so dramatic a fashion, particularly as we were finally beginning to get along.

"As you wish," she said. "I do hope you won't come to regret it." Her tone was all jovial joking, but the words sat a bit uneasy with me. I wouldn't have given anyone else the same courtesy; I would have insisted on combing through their possessions. Instead, I returned to Lord Deeley's study to take a closer look at his correspondence, hoping he might have kept her letters to him. It was there Colin came to tell me what had transpired during his conversation with Mr. Granard.

"He is adamant that he's never before seen the letter his wife found in her Sherlock Holmes," he said. "He reacted quite badly, which isn't altogether surprising, but he managed to more or less keep his composure. Insists he has no idea what Deeley accused him of doing. I stopped at the telegraph office on my way back and found this waiting for you." He pulled an envelope out of his pocket and handed it to me.

I tore it open and read. It was a response to the message I had sent to a friend at Scotland Yard, Inspector Fenimore Cooper Pickering. He'd assisted me on a case some years ago and we had been close ever since. He was more sensible than most of his colleagues and was always willing to offer help when he could.

"Sisley Weldon died by suicide in 1896 — that's the year on the back of the photograph," I said. "It was shortly after she'd given birth to and given up a little girl. She's survived by a sister who lives in Durham. He's included her address. I'll write to her at once. A family in Dover took in the child and Lord Bertram Deeley sent them monthly funds to pay for her keep."

"Deeley?" Colin asked. "That's unexpected."

"Perhaps it was his child," I said.

"I'm not sure Troubridge would be keen to learn his friend was involved with his mistress."

"Motive for murder?"

"Certainly, if Troubridge knew."

"He claims never to have seen the photograph," I said. "Just as Mr. Granard claims never to have seen the letter."

"Convenient, isn't it?" Colin asked, his forehead creased. "I'm beginning to question whether any of Lord Deeley's guests didn't have a reason to want him dead."

We summoned Mr. Troubridge to dine with us on the boat that evening, knowing it would be the best way to confront him without alerting the others. He might not have appreciated the hawawshi our cook prepared — a simple dish of crisp pastry stuffed with mince and spices — but he did not object to the privacy the setting provided. The *Daily Yell* had published a story that morning that mentioned both the apricot pits and an incriminating letter found in Per Ma'at; someone in the house was leaking information to Mr. Mallaby. I had no interest in reading about our conversation in tomorrow's paper.

Mr. Troubridge reacted violently to the suggestion that Lord Deeley might be the father of Miss Weldon's child, primarily because he did not believe his friend would engage in such shocking behavior.

230

"He wouldn't do that to me, not Deeley. It's an affront even to consider such an accusation. A bloody outrage."

"So he knew about your affair?" Colin asked.

"I had no reason to hide it from him," Mr. Troubridge said. "It's not as if Sisley or I was married."

"It would have been more discreet to keep her identity secret," I said. "I'm thinking in terms of her reputation."

"I understand your point, Lady Emily, but I assure you I was quite discreet. Deeley wasn't the sort to gossip, not ever. I'd faced a number of daunting challenges. He could see that I was happy for the first time in ages and wanted to know why, so I told him."

"If you were so happy, why didn't you marry her?" I asked. "You admit that you were both unattached."

He shifted nervously in his seat. "I'm not the marrying sort."

"I don't believe that, Mr. Troubridge," I said. "Everyone is the marrying sort when they meet the right person. Are you saying Miss Weldon wasn't the right person?"

"You've already mentioned her reputation," he said. "Think of the shambles that is mine. I'm a cad at best. Having a husband named as co-respondent in a divorce case would hardly improve her standing in society."

"Did she care about such things?" I asked.

"Don't all women?"

"To a degree, perhaps. However, I would argue that a woman willing to become a mistress is not desperately concerned about her reputation."

"You may be correct, Lady Emily, but I never looked at it that way. At any rate, she threw me over, so there's no reason to think marriage to me was something that appealed to her."

"Why did she leave you?" I asked.

"Here now, Hargreaves, you can't expect me to discuss this sort of thing with your wife. It's bloody uncomfortable."

"No more so than discussing it with me," Colin said. "Why did she leave?"

"If you must know, she didn't really explain beyond saying that she no longer felt a passion for me. I didn't press for details."

"Did you ever introduce her to Lord Deeley?" I asked.

He balked. "Heavens, no. He was a dear friend and accepted my shortcomings, but he wasn't the type of man who would keep a mistress or want to meet someone else's.

He would have considered it undignified. Old-fashioned values and all that."

"How, then, did he come to pay to support Miss Weldon's child?" I asked. "You can understand, I'm sure, why one might suspect him of being the father."

"Of course, of course," he said and sighed. "I can't answer your question. Sisley knew we were friends. Perhaps she wrote to him and begged for his assistance."

"Is that the sort of thing she'd be likely to do?" I asked.

He dropped his head back against his chair. "No, but I can't think of any other explanation. I know they were not acquainted, let alone involved."

"Why didn't she contact you if she needed help with the child?" Colin asked.

Mr. Troubridge looked chastened. "I suppose the truth is I always believed I was fonder of her than she was of me. I didn't behave as well as I ought to have when she left me. I'm rather ashamed of that. After the things I said, she wouldn't have dared ask for my help."

"Is it possible you are the father of the child?" Colin asked.

The question tempered Mr. Troubridge's mood. "I suppose I could be. We parted ways five or six months before the baby must have been born. I had no idea — you must believe me — no idea that she . . ." He dropped his head into his hands. "If I'd known . . . I wanted a child, very much. Always did. I would have married her, and given her condition, she might have agreed if I'd asked. I loved her. Never understood why she left. So far as I knew, it came out of nowhere."

"Was she aware of your feelings?" I asked.

"It wasn't something we ever discussed. One doesn't, does one, in those circumstances?" He frowned and his features lost all of the charm they normally had. "Do you have any information about the child?"

"She's called Marian," I said. "Beyond that, I know nothing."

"My mother's name." His voice was a whisper. "Where do I find her?"

"You don't," Colin said, "not now, at any rate. You're staying in Luxor until we find out who killed Deeley."

"Come now, Hargreaves, be reasonable. I have to go to her."

"We don't know that she's yours," Colin said, "and even if we did, we're in the midst of a murder investigation."

"This proves I had nothing to do with it," Mr. Troubridge said. "Deeley was taking care of my child. I shall never be able to repay him for that. He would have been waiting to tell me until she was old enough to understand what had happened between her mother and me. When she was, he would have brought us together. Of that, I'm certain."

"It would have made a great deal more sense to involve her father when her mother died," I said.

All the color drained from his face and his hands started to tremble. I could not doubt the news was a shock to him. "Sisley's dead? Are you sure."

"She took her own life shortly after giving up her child," Colin said.

"Took her own life?" He looked stricken. "Did Deeley know that?"

"I don't know," Colin said.

"No." His eyes were misty. "He couldn't have. He would have told me. He knew how I felt about her, how devastated I was to lose her."

"Both of which argue against him telling you," I said. "Why cause further pain?"

He buried his head in his hands. "What a disaster. If only I'd known. If only —" He lifted up his head and looked Colin in the eyes. "I must have these questions answered. Is the child mine? Did Deeley know? How did this all come to happen? If anyone stood in the way of me discovering the truth . . ." His voice had grown louder and louder as he spoke. He no longer looked stricken; he looked furious.

"If someone did stand in your way, what would you have done?" Colin asked.

"I would have killed him, plain and simple, without the slightest hesitation. Sisley was everything to me."

Pa Demi, Regnal Year Two
20

My mother came to see me the day after the destruction in my workshop. We had always been close — just as she and Bek were — but she rarely interfered in my life. That probably went a long way in explaining our closeness. I should have taken her as a model and not meddled in my brother's life. The wisdom of that choice would become obvious only when looking back, when it was too late to change anything. But those days were still far away, and I had no idea as to the gravity of the situation.

"I don't like it," Mut said, shaking her head. "I don't like any of it. Kamose is correct — this is not the work of a disgruntled villager. It comes from the gods. You must appease them, Meryt, and restore the proper balance of Ma'at."

"The priest has already been here," I said. "We've done everything he told us to."

"I recognize the tone in your voice. You

blame a person, not the gods, for this. Sanura, I presume?"

"Who else?"

She sighed. "Meryt, you pose no threat to her. You see her hand in this because of the trouble dwelling in your own heart, not hers."

I didn't want to hear someone else chiding me for allowing jealousy to cloud my judgment. I'd let her think I agreed with her. "I'm sure you're right. She raised an interesting suggestion — that someone is angry that Eetee is having me make his ushabtis instead of hiring a sculptor he'd have to pay."

"It might have been nothing more than a drunken prank that got out of control. Not everything is a plot. More often, chaos is to blame. If you've done what you must to make things right with the gods, there's no sense in giving this any more thought. Focus on your work and your husband and let yourself return to normal life."

I didn't argue. What good would come from upsetting her? She wanted the problem tucked neatly away, even if her explanations were woefully inadequate. Kamose and I had been drugged. Chaos didn't do that, and neither did the gods. I made vaguely reassuring noises to her, but after she'd left,

I went straight to Tey's house.

Her three sons were playing outside in the street, shrieking with laughter. Her daughters were inside, one still a baby, the other two years old, clinging to her mother's skirt. Tey's pet monkey, spoiled more than her children, was eating plump grapes handed to him by one of the servants. Tey had two, one of whom lived with her and helped with the children. She needed all the assistance she could get, especially until the boys were old enough to begin their studies.

"They are a joy, but an exhausting one," she said, as if she could read my thoughts. "Let's go for a long walk so we can have some peace." She handed the baby to the nurse and kissed the toddler's chubby cheeks.

We headed for the river. It was the place I always craved when I needed sanctuary and peace, so different from my desert home. The sun was hot, but it could have been worse, and I felt relief as we passed through the village gates, as if I had escaped an enemy. Tey knew this without me having to say a word. She put a slim hand on my shoulder.

"I saw your mother this morning, so I know you're supposed to be working and not thinking about anything else. Personally, I think what you need is distraction that will free your mind from ruminating."

"I can't sit back and do nothing when someone has violated my home."

"I agree, but right now, we don't know what it is you should do. Your heart will figure it out, if you let it alone to work. Sometimes thinking too much makes it impossible to find a solution."

"You're wise beyond your years," I said.

"Let's not think about the years. They're passing at an alarming rate and we'll be old and shriveled before we know it."

The walk to the river was pleasant, despite the heat. We were used to it, after all. We reached the edge of the flood plain quickly and soon were sitting on the bank, our feet dangling in the water. The spot we chose was across from the towering columns of the temple complex, with a view of the god Amun's barque docked on the river. This boat, called *Userhetamon* — Mighty of Brow Is Amun — mirrored the one Ra journeyed in daily, moving the sun across the sky. Ra, god of the sun, and Amun merged, sometimes. Or at least Amun took on his characteristics and became Amun-Ra. Amun, who once was a god local to Thebes, eventually became the king of the pantheon. Religion is confusing; it's not for me to understand or explain, only to accept, even when it contradicts itself. Anyway, the barque was a spectacular conveyance, built from Lebanon cedar and covered with gold leaf, and was the center of the annual festival of Opet, when Pharaoh himself would come to Luxor to be reborn in the confines of the sanctuary, his right to rule renewed. The statue of the god Amun would then board his barque and glide along the river. Preferring feasting to ritual, I was always more interested in the celebrations that followed the divine procession. For the moment, though, I was content to study the reflection of the barque's gold covering as it shimmered in the water, my worries seeming to magically recede. Perhaps it was the intervention of Amun, perhaps something else, but for those few hours, I didn't think about Sanura once.

Tey and I discussed her children, our husbands, the problems with unreliable servants. I described for her the progress I'd made on my father's ushabtis and the challenges presented by one of them, whose face I had not yet managed to paint to my satisfaction. We proposed and objected to potential husbands for our friend Iset, the potter.

"She should marry," Tey said. "It would

bring her happiness."

"It would bring her parents happiness," I said. "I'm not sure about her." We listed every single man we could think of in the village but could come to no agreement as to who would be best. It was a delightful distraction, particularly when we laughed so hard we almost choked as we came to the most unsuitable candidates.

"Anyone would be better than Pentu," I said. The mention of his name stopped our laughter the way an unwelcome cloud blocks the sun. Except that we lived in a desert and welcomed clouds. I understood, in theory, however, that a cloud might be undesirable. Things are always more complicated than they seem, aren't they?

"It's high time Pentu found a wife," Tey said, stacking a small pile of pebbles she'd collected. "We know Iset won't marry him. Will anyone?"

I laughed, glad to feel the sound burbling. "Not everyone puts the same value on intelligence we do. Some women might prefer a husband who's stupid."

She tossed one of her pebbles into the water. "He's not exactly stupid, is he? It's more that he's crass and coarse. Which is unusual for the men of the village. Artists

242

and craftsmen tend to have a finer sense of things."

"True," I said. "He couldn't be inconceivably stupid and still do his job, but I'd argue he's more cunning than smart."

"Cunning people scare me," Tey said. "You can't trust them. They manipulate. They're always out for something."

And then, as if our conversation had conjured him, Pentu appeared, a hundred yards or so down the river from us. He didn't notice us; he was engrossed in conversation with a woman who had wrapped a fine linen cloak around her shoulders and over her head so that it was hiding her face. I would recognize her figure anywhere. It was Sanura. On that, I would bet my life.

LUXOR, 1904
21

Mr. Troubridge's admission that he would have killed anyone who stood in the way of his learning he was little Marian's father did not convince me he was responsible for Lord Deeley's death. First, he seemed genuinely shocked at the news that Miss Weldon had killed herself. I did not believe he already knew anything about her death. Second, we could not be sure he was the child's father. Perhaps what mattered more was whether Mr. Troubridge believed he was. He claimed not to have known about her existence and insisted he had never seen the picture of her with Miss Weldon, but he could be lying. Finally, even a barely competent murderer would refrain from making death threats in his current circumstances. Unless he'd done so deliberately to throw us off track. He'd balked at the idea that he'd kept the apricot pits in his room, stating emphatically that it would have made no sense if he was the killer. This gave me pause. Had he deliberately adopted a strategy of setting up evidence in just such a way that it would appear someone else was trying to frame him?

After Mr. Troubridge left the boat and I'd written a letter to Miss Weldon's sister, Colin and I took our usual positions on the deck with the awning rolled back to reveal stars pricking through the velvety blue sky. I hadn't yet told him about what I'd learned concerning his mother and Lord Deeley and it was time he knew. He blanched a bit when I showed him the pertinent passage in the dead man's journal but accepted his mother's position that there was no romantic connection between them.

"Deeley must have imagined it," he said. "Mother has never shown any interest in having that sort of relationship again. It had to be a flight of fancy on his part."

"I agree, but it's rather odd, isn't it? He doesn't strike me as having been a particularly romantic man. I believe that he long carried a torch for her and can accept that he might have become more sentimental as he aged, but nothing rings true in his claim to have at last won her heart."

"There's no truth in it and we have no way of discovering what led him to write such a thing. I'm not convinced it matters in the least. It couldn't have anything to do with his death," he said. "I didn't remove the papyrus from the frame to see if there was anything behind it. It was sloppy of me."

I did not suspect — not in the slightest — that Mrs. Hargreaves had poisoned her childhood friend. Still, I could not entirely dismiss the possibility that Lord Deeley's claims, even if untruthful, were relevant. Why had someone covered up the photograph of the two of them? Had Lord Deeley done it, and if so, why? Was he harboring affection for someone else? Someone who might be angered by the picture? Who, other than his servants, would have been in his bedroom to see it?

I was saved from having to pose any of these questions to Colin by the arrival of Kat, who once again made a late-night appearance on our gangplank. She hadn't come in the carriage this time, but on horseback, and was wearing a pair of jodhpurs, copied from the style of garment worn by the members of the Jodhpur Polo team who visited England in 1897 for Queen Victoria's Diamond Jubilee. They made it possible for her to ride astride and were surprisingly flattering. I'd always considered myself a dedicated horsewoman, but rode sidesaddle, as society expected. Perhaps it was time to broaden my horizons. A pair of jodhpurs with a tailored jacket in gentian blue would suit me nicely. They'd also be useful for exploring ruins. Trailing skirts were always a hindcrancc.

"Don't scold," Kat said. "No one is going to attack me when I'm riding. I'm too fast. It would have been cruel to force the poor coachman out at this hour and keep him waiting around for who knows how long while I'm here."

"You promised you would not leave the house unescorted —" Colin started. Kat ignored him and turned to me.

"Did you tell Mr. Troubridge to stop speaking to me?" she asked. "He's behaving very strangely."

"How so?" I asked.

"Did you forbid him to speak to me?"

"I did nothing of the sort." I sighed. I'd hoped we were moving to a more cordial relationship. "What makes you think otherwise?"

"He hardly talked at all after he returned from dining with you, so what else am I to surmise?" she asked. "We were having coffee in the courtyard when he arrived. He poured himself a whisky and sulked. Lady Wilona, the old bat, called him out for not doing his social duties. Accused him of letting us all down."

"That suggests he wasn't singling you out and hence makes it unreasonable for you to assume I am behind it," I said. "Perhaps he was not in an affable mood."

"If he wasn't, it's because of something you said to him while he was here." She glared at me. "You're not my mother, you know. It's not your place to decide whether a suitor is worthy."

"She may not be your mother, but I *am* your father and it *is* my place," Colin said. "Mr. Troubridge isn't an acceptable suitor. He was out of sorts not because we forbade him from courting you, but because he learned that he may have a hitherto unknown daughter. Such revelations tend to take a gentleman by surprise."

Her eyes widened. "How old is she?"

"Quite young," Colin said. He told her what we knew.

"This is most interesting," she said. A sadness flickered in her eyes. I wondered if she was thinking about her own childhood. "I obviously know something about how these things work. My mother had a valid reason to hide my existence from you. Did Miss Weldon fear something awful might happen if Mr. Troubridge knew he was the baby's father?"

"I can't imagine what," Colin said.

"Why did she abandon the child?" Kat asked. "Mother sent me to school, but that's hardly the same thing."

"Miss Weldon must have felt she could not raise a child on her own," I said. "It's all but impossible to overcome the stigma of having a child out of wedlock."

"She could have moved abroad and told everyone she was a widow," Kat said. "It still might have been difficult, but not impossible. She'd have had loads of sympathy from all corners."

"It's unlikely she had the financial resources to support the child," Colin said. "She had the baby placed with a family who could care for her and then killed herself, which suggests an untenable level of despair."

"If she'd told Caspian the truth, he would have taken care of her," Kat said. "He's a bit of a rogue, but a gentleman underneath it all."

"Mr. Troubridge, not Caspian," Colin said.

Kat looked up at the sky and muttered something unintelligible about old-fashioned gentlemen. "If he loved her he wouldn't have let her leave him, even if he didn't know about the baby."

"Love is not always enough to prevent someone from leaving," Colin said, and I knew he was thinking about his relationship with Kat's mother. He'd proposed to her; she had refused him. "We know very little about their relationship, but if Mr. Troubridge took it at all seriously, he would not have skulked about having an inappropriate affair. There was no reason he couldn't have courted her openly."

"Perhaps he didn't know how much he adored her until it was too late," Kat said.

"It is never too late to behave appropriately," Colin said. "Neither of them was married. He could have proposed."

"Could he?" I asked. "I've written to her sister, but until I receive a reply, we shan't know much about Miss Weldon. Was there something in her background that made legitimizing the relationship impossible?"

"Even if there was, he was quite clear about his feelings for her and stated unequivocally that he would have married her if he knew about the child," Colin said.

"Or so he claims." I was not entirely convinced.

"There's no need to disparage him. He's not nearly so bad as you think," Kat said.

She pulled an envelope from her jacket pocket and handed it to her father. "I didn't come here only to admonish you about him. I was poking around the house after everyone else went to bed and found this under the chessboard. It's a rather argumentative letter from Mr. McLeod to Lord Deeley. Apparently the latter was refusing to fund his archaeological endeavors despite having earlier promised to."

Rather argumentative was not a strong enough description. Mr. McLeod's tone was decidedly rude. "I was thinking we could go see him at Deir el Medina tomorrow," Kat said. "Descend upon him when he's unaware and coax him into revealing something he shouldn't."

"It's not a bad idea," Colin said. "I'll go first thing in the morning."

"I'm coming with you," Kat said.

"It would be better if I spoke to him, gentleman to gentleman."

"I don't agree," I said. "I've a keen interest in archaeology. I'll speak to him, civilian to professional. And Kat will accompany me. You've said all along direct confrontation is not the best approach for this murder inquiry. Two ladies curious about daily life in the New Kingdom will appear wholly unthreatening. We'll bring a picnic."

Colin and I met Kat at Per Ma'at early the next morning. We left him behind as we mounted donkeys from Lord Deeley's stable and set off with a guide who would lead us to Mr. McLeod's dig. Perched atop the animal, I came to the conclusion that riding such a beast sidesaddle was even more ridiculous than doing so on a horse. Kat's jodhpurs had set me on a path. I pulled alongside her as we made our way through the desert and asked for the details of the dressmaker who had made them.

"You can't be thinking of riding astride," she said. "Father would go apoplectic. He's such a fossil."

"He's far more enlightened than you give him credit for."

"Enlightened for a fossil, not a modern man."

"Are you bound and determined to always have a nemesis?" I asked. "It must be exhausting."

"You're not very nice to me."

"I could lob the same accusation at you. Wouldn't it be simpler to accept that we're not going to like everything about each other and focus on what we do have in common? I'm quite taken with your sense of fashion and your talent for photography."

"I don't despise the fact that you study ancient Greek."

"Well that's something," I said.

"I confess that I took up Latin to annoy you," she said, crinkling her nose. "It didn't work, did it?"

"Not a bit."

"I don't like being told what to do. I suppose that's the long and short of it. The nuns at school never had any meaningful control over me. They were deliciously easy to manipulate, but even so, I was still there, in the convent. Trapped. Now, I have freedom and I want to take full advantage of it."

"I wholeheartedly encourage that you do."

"So long as I don't flirt with Mr. Troubridge."

"In theory, I'd prefer that you keep away from anyone suspected of murder, but then, when I was first falling for your father, I thought he might have killed his best friend."

"Your first husband," she said.

"Yes. I was wildly off the mark, but the point is that we love who we love, even if we suspect them of the worst."

"You didn't really think Father murdered

253

the Viscount Ashton?"

"For a brief period of time, it seemed quite possible."

She gave me a sideways look, as if she was considering me in a new light. "Was it quite exciting, thinking he might be guilty?"

"Ever so slightly titillating, but only because I knew how it would torment my mother."

Kat's eyes went wide and her jaw dropped open. "I may have underestimated you, Lady Emily. You could have great potential as a modern woman."

"Kat, darling, the desire to torment one's mother — or any parent, for that matter — is hardly a modern invention. I'm quite certain Alexander — before he was Great — caused Philip much grief."

"Even more impressive to rile up one's father if he's a king," she said.

We rode on in silence. As the sun rose higher in the clear, azure sky, so did the temperature. The dry air caught in my lungs, and every bit of my person was coated in a fine layer of sand. It was marvelous. I felt more like a real explorer than I ever had in my life. There was a wildness to Egypt I'd never before experienced. I scanned the horizon, half hoping to find a band of Bedouins approaching. Instead, I had to be satisfied with a caravan of camels off in the distance. They were exotic enough to suit me.

At last we approached Mr. McLeod's dig. The area was small, with a towering mountain and a large hill separating it from the rest of the desert. There were as yet no large monuments or obvious buildings excavated, only bits of walls peeking out of the sand. It felt to me like a land of endless possibility. Anything could be buried here. I'd always been drawn to Greece, with its golden ratio and epic poetry, but there was something magical about Egypt, a civilization already ancient when Pericles ruled Athens.

I called out to Mr. McLeod when I saw him. He startled, then collected himself and came over, removing his pith helmet when he approached.

"I say, Lady Emily, this is a surprise. If you'd told me you were coming, I could have arranged that things weren't quite so . . . so . . . ." He looked around, helpless.

"Sandy?" I asked, laughing. "I assure you, sir, I have no lofty expectations when it comes to archaeological sites. They ought not be sanitized."

"And visitors mustn't keep you from your work," Kat said. I could not help but notice Mr. McLeod subtly appraise — and approve of — her unconventional appearance. "It's too important."

He raised his eyebrows. "If you're trying to get into my good graces, you're succeeding, Miss von Lange. Are you a student of ancient Egypt?"

"No." She surveyed the site around her. "But perhaps I ought to reconsider. There's something about this place. I hope you don't mind that I plan to take a perfectly disgraceful number of photographs. I've never been anywhere so romantic." There was none of the usual cynicism in her voice.

Mr. McLeod laughed. "You've got a decidedly strange definition of romantic. Come, we've a canopy set up where you can have some water. You must be parched after the ride here."

"I could do without the donkeys," she said, looping her arm through his. "A nice Arabian horse would be preferable, but I couldn't persuade Lord Deeley's groom to let us take them. He said donkeys are best for tourists, but I know it's only because I took one of the horses last night without asking. He was furious about that. Still, I'll manage. I always do. It's one of my finest qualities." Her silvery laughter bounced off the hills surrounding the ruins of the village. Despite his sunburned face, I could see Mr. McLeod blush.

"We've brought you an enormous picnic," I said. "It's the least we can do to make up for interrupting your work."

"Unnecessary, I assure you. Although, you've come just when we were ready for a little break and I'm sure whatever is in that marvelous hamper is superior to our luke-warm water and hard-boiled eggs."

Mahmoud had prepared a feast for us: a vast selection of sandwiches, heaps of grapes, pomegranate seeds, figs, and a tin of anise biscuits, all to be washed down with cold tea. I'd asked him to include a dish an Egyptian might eat. He shook his head and said that the English only like what the English eat. I reminded him that I loved the traditional dishes his son served on the boat, but he didn't back down all the way until I pointed out that it would irritate Lady Wilona if he gave me Egyptian food. Eventually he relented and prepared a small container of chickpea puree seasoned with sesame paste and lemon and soft, puffed bread to go with it.

I covered the rough table I found under the canopy with a cotton blanket, spread our bounty on it, and insisted that Mr. McLeod invite all of his workers to join us. Many of them looked at Kat and me with skeptical eyes, but they gave every sign of enjoying the food. I envied them their flowing linen robes, far better suited to the climate than European garb.

Kat must have been thinking along similar lines. "They don't suffer from the heat like we do in our stiff jackets and ridiculous boots. At least the men don't. The poor women are always swathed in black. I shouldn't like that."

"No, neither should I," I said. "We shall have to dress like men if we want to be comfortable."

"Don't so much as consider it. Hargreaves will never forgive me for corrupting you," Mr. McLeod said.

"He knows better than anyone how futile it is to curb my enthusiasm when I set my mind to something," I said. The food was nearly gone and his men were returning to work. I longed to follow them, to sift through the sand in search of artifacts. When I said something to this effect out loud, Mr. McLeod laughed.

"It's not nearly so glamorous as you imagine. Lots of dust. Lots of sand. Lots of sunburn."

"And all worth it the instant you find a potsherd," I said.

"For me, yes."

"It would be for me as well." I drew in a deep breath, inhaling the baking smell of the desert. "I don't require spectacular finds. It's more satisfying to hold something ordinary, something used daily by the people who lived here. Touching objects the ancients did, thousands of years ago, forges a connection between us. At least to my mind. Someone would have made the pot, perhaps someone else painted it. I like to imagine their lives."

"It's easy to do so in a place like this, a village for craftsmen," Mr. McLeod said. "Perhaps I ought to hire you on."

"I should like that very much."

"I'd like it more," Kat said. "Shall I report for duty in the morning?"

"Before you start hiring more staff, there's something we need to discuss." I removed the letter Kat had found from my jacket pocket but didn't give it to him. "I apologize for acting as if our visit was for pleasure alone. It's come to my attention that you and Lord Deeley had argued — vehemently — about his decision to revoke funding he had promised you. It confused me because you were adamant you'd never discussed anything of the sort with him."

"You're rather good at ferreting out dark secrets, aren't you?" He winced. The slightest trace of a Scottish accent crept into his words. "It was foolish of me. I admit it. I hadn't asked him for anything. Not a penny. One evening at the end of the excavation season last year, I was dining with him and he offered to fund my work. It came completely out of the blue. I wasn't in a position to refuse him and honestly never considered that it might affect our friendship. Also foolish, of course. I never could figure out what changed his mind, but I behaved badly — abominably, in fact — when he pulled the funding. I should never have sent that letter. I expected we'd never speak again, but when he returned to Egypt this year, everything had changed, in ways that I could never have imagined. He didn't reject me, instead he pulled me closer. It was almost as if he'd become a different person."

Pa Demi, Regnal Year Two

22

Tey and I shouldn't have gone after them. It was foolish. Reckless. Impetuous. In other words, very like me. Just the sort of thing my friends would expect me to do and that my mother would warn me against. I couldn't help it. I wanted to confirm my suspicions. I wanted to catch Sanura with Pentu. Tey tried to stop me, but I pulled away from her.

"It's not as if I'm doing anything dangerous," I said. "Pentu is an acquaintance. If he spots me, I'll pretend I was coming over to say hello."

"It won't seem so innocuous if Sanura is there. She could turn it around on you and tell Kamose you're the one flirting."

"That is beyond ridiculous. Kamose would never believe it."

And so we skulked along the bank of the river, weaving our way through the palms and acacia shrubs until we were close enough to hear their voices. Of course, that meant we were also close enough for them to see us, but the shelter provided by a group of trees hid us.

"That's not enough," Pentu was saying. "You know that."

"You always demand more." I recognized Sanura's voice. "That's why you like me." He laughed. She said nothing. "So when, *when* will it be?"

"I'll figure that out as soon as I can."

"Leave a message in the usual way," he said. "Don't make me wait too long."

"I would never do that." Her voice was soft, melodious. I hated the sound of it. "I would touch you if I could, but it's too public here."

"You're a good girl." Pentu stepped closer to her. "I like that. I like that very much."

"I know what you like." She started to turn away from him but hesitated. "Not before Bek goes back to the Valley."

Pentu shrugged. "You'd better hope you recognize when the time is right. Everything depends upon it."

She walked away, the cloak still covering all of her face but the eyes. Pentu did not follow. I wanted to run out and slap him, but Tey had me firmly by the arm. We waited for him to leave, but he didn't. It

262

was almost as if he knew we were watching and wanted us to confront him. So I did.

"Pentu!" I shouted as I walked toward him. "What brings you to the river? And why was your lovely companion obscuring her face?"

"I never bother to ask why women do anything," he said, his eyes narrow and probing. "Maybe she doesn't like the sun. Have you come here to beg the priests to intercede with the gods for you? I hear stories that you have angered them." He was grinning but with malevolence. For a second, anyway. Then his face changed. His eyes warmed. His smile softened. "I shouldn't tease you. It's serious what happened at your house. It is not good when Ma'at is disturbed. Kamose must better protect you."

I spoke without thinking, wanting to defend my husband. "We were drugged. No sound would have woken either of us. There was nothing he could have done."

"You're certain?"

"I am."

"You are not the first household this has happened to, you know," he said, looking not at me, but at a skiff slicing through the river. "It was years ago, when I was not yet living in the village."

"So, what you mean is, you don't actually know anything about it firsthand," Tey said. She was glaring at him. All the softening in the world wouldn't make her like him.

"No, but when I first came to work at Pa Demi, Sanura's father, Dedi, trained me. I have no other family here, and it is much harder to find one's place in the village without that. Dedi taught me how to improve my skills, but also welcomed me into his family. In addition, he shared with me the tales of what came to pass years ago in the house of a scribe and his wife. First there was destruction of property. Then one of their children disappeared. Soon thereafter, the wife died for reasons no one was ever able to explain. For months afterward, the entire village lived in fear."

"And you are suggesting Meryt and Kamose are being attacked by this same person?" Tey asked, her irritation at him evident.

He made a gesture — half shrugging, half shaking his head — that gave every appearance of humility. "I can't claim to know that, but what was done so long ago scares me, and I am a man who doesn't get scared."

"Did they ever find out who was responsible?" I asked. I didn't believe him, not entirely, because I'd never before heard mention of any of it. And if it had been so alarming that it left the whole village terrified, I would have heard stories. We all would have.

"I can't answer that question with any confidence," he said, "but I have my ideas. Someone important must have been involved because the incident was covered up and never spoken of. Everyone knew better than to mention it."

"Everyone except Dedi, apparently," I said. "What moved him to tell you?"

"One morning, some tools were missing from my house. The next day, three pots in my kitchen were broken. I heard nothing, saw nothing. It was strange, so I told him. It reminded him of those events in the past, so he shared with me what he knew, hoping the knowledge would help me protect myself from further attacks. I kept vigilant, and nothing else ever happened. I am only telling you because you and Kamose need to know so that you, too, can escape anything more serious."

Tey looked as skeptical as I felt. "So why was Sanura here with you?"

"I asked her to meet me and didn't want anyone else to see us. She's married to your brother, so obviously she knows what's going on. I wanted to get all the details from her. She doesn't like you much. Girls are very, very petty, aren't they? Still, she told me everything."

"Why meet so far from Pa Demi?" I asked.

"Someone inside our village walls, someone who walks among us, has returned to his evil deeds. I don't know you well, but I have a great deal of respect for both your father and your husband. They are men of honor and great intelligence. I will not stand by, idle, when their family is threatened. And when the threat comes from within a place that should be safe, a wise man does not discuss it where he can be overheard. The deeds of this man were hidden before, which tells me he is powerful. Revealing that I am trying to stop him would put me in danger. Much as I want to help you, I have little interest in endangering myself, especially when it's not necessary."

I was not sure what to make of any of this. It felt odd. Unbalanced. Unbelievable. Yet, someone had attacked our household. There was no denying that. If there might be a connection to a past event, I would be foolish not to explore the possibility. So I thanked Pentu. Told him he could come see Kamose. And then Tey and I walked back to the village, silent as we left the green of the floodplain and felt the hot desert sand on our feet.

"It seems fantastical, but if it's true, it would explain a lot," she said, once we'd passed through the gates and were back on familiar streets. "I'll ask Raneb if he's heard any of these stories. It's likely, though, that your father would know more."

"Can we trust Pentu?" I asked.

"I've never particularly liked him. He's crude and crass, but I've never thought of him as dishonest. In the end, does it matter? It's true or it's not, and he isn't the person who can prove it either way. If he's deliberately sending us on a meaningless chase, it won't actually hurt us. And if he isn't . . ."

"If he isn't, Kamose and I may be facing a situation more dangerous than I ever imagined."

It didn't feel real. Things like that never do. We easily embrace our fictions and our fantasies, but when does an actual threat stop feeling surreal?

"Lord Deeley seemed like a different person?" I asked. The workers at the dig had started to sing, their voices bouncing off the cliff walls that surrounded Deir el Medina. "How?"

Mr. McLeod pushed his hands together and cracked his knuckles. "I may be overstating things. As I said, I half expected he'd never speak to me again after I'd sent that letter. He certainly didn't reply to it. He arrived in Egypt months later than I did, which wasn't unusual. I'm here to work and don't mind the heat that often lingers into the early autumn. Ordinarily, I'd call on him when I got word he was here, but for obvious reasons I doubted I'd be welcome. So you can imagine, given everything, how shocking it was to receive a letter sent from Alexandria, asking me to meet him at the dock when his boat arrived in Luxor." He was still rolling his *R*s, sounding more Scottish than usual. Evidently whisky wasn't the only thing that brought out his accent.

"I suppose you expected he was summoning you to read the riot act after what you'd written to him," Kat said.

"Precisely." He drew his eyebrows together. "I prepared myself for a very public dressing-down. Instead, however, he greeted me like a long-lost son, introduced me to his guests, and pulled me firmly back into the fold. It was as if nothing uncomfortable had ever passed between us."

"Did he ever mention your letter?" I asked.

"I brought it up that evening — he had insisted that I dine with him. I pulled him aside so that we could speak discreetly, but he stopped my apology before I'd had much of a chance even to start it. He told me to never mention it again."

"Are you known for having a bad temper, Mr. McLeod? I mean no offense by the question," I said.

"No offense taken. I'm not proud of it, but I am quick to anger."

"And Lord Deeley was aware of this?" I asked.

"He was. Often poked fun at me about it. My emotions cool as quickly as they heat up."

"Lord Deeley left you in a lurch. I would have been furious," Kat said. "It's unconscionable to dangle assistance and then pull it away. You claim he offered no explanation for changing his mind?"

"Claim?" He flashed a wry smile. "I do hope I haven't lost your goodwill and trust, Miss von Lange. It was the night before he was going back to England. All he said was that circumstances had changed and that he didn't believe he owed me an explanation. It was his smugness of manner when delivering the news that infuriated me. We argued. I lost my temper and was not polite. When I returned to my rooms, I wrote the letter in your possession. I behaved badly and, frankly, had no justification for being so rude. He had the right to spend his money in whatever way he chose. I ought to have better managed my disappointment."

"No one would take such news well." Kat furrowed her brow and the color in her cheeks rose. "It's demented, really, to expect otherwise. Furthermore, it is my belief that he did owe you an explanation."

"He knew I had enough to fund this year's excavations. It was the following that would prove problematic, and, given that, he left me plenty of time to seek other sources. Had he waited until the end of this season, it would be an entirely different matter. Could he have softened the blow? Perhaps, but I would have been angry regardless. Cozying up to potential donors isn't my strong suit."

Kat was watching him with keen interest. It wouldn't surprise me if she offered to fund his work. She certainly had the money to do it. "Aside from his so thoroughly forgiving you, how was Lord Deeley behaving like a different person?" I asked.

"I'm afraid I've led you somewhat astray. Forgiveness wasn't out of character for him. He wasn't the sort to hold a grudge, but he did hold one accountable for one's actions, and that can make one rather uncomfortable after having behaved badly. I expected he'd require a discussion and an apology. He deserved no less. When I first saw him on the dock in Luxor, he looked different. More relaxed. I suppose his not taking me to task was a result of whatever caused this newfound contentment."

"What was he like in other years?" Kat asked.

"He had a great deal of nervous energy. Not a bad thing, mind you, but it could be rather exhausting. He was always embroiled in some scheme or another. One year it was harassing the donkey boys to take better care of their animals. Another, it was a campaign to prevent holidaymakers from being besieged by children begging for money. The constant pleas for baksheesh can be overwhelming to Europeans. No reasonable way to stop it, though, not unless someone can find a way to pull their families out of poverty."

"I didn't realize he was so concerned with the plight of the poor," I said. Frankly, it surprised me, given his politics.

"I don't know that I'd describe it quite that way." He pulled off his smoke-colored spectacles and blew the dust from them. "His projects did immensely benefit those less fortunate than himself, but he was, perhaps, more taken with how they improved his reputation and standing in the community. There was always a hint of insecurity behind his bluster. His good works helped assuage this. Please don't think I say this to minimize his contributions in the slightest. It's merely what is no doubt a flawed observation on my part."

From my brief interactions with Lord Deeley, I doubted very much Mr. Mc-Leod's observations were flawed. Lord Deeley had always struck me as a man keen on impressing those around him. He wasn't wholly cynical, but taking on charitable causes to bring glory to himself sounded perfectly in character.

"May I ask, Miss von Lange, how you came to possess this appalling letter of mine?"

"It was under the chessboard in the sitting room at Per Ma'at," Kat said.

"That's dashed strange," Mr. McLeod said. "When I started my attempt at an apology, he pulled what I thought was the letter out of his pocket and tore it to shreds. I suppose it must have been something else."

I unfolded the document and held it out to him. "You're quite certain this is your original letter?"

"There can be no doubt."

"Lord Deeley must have used some other letter he had in his pocket to reassure you that the matter was closed," Kat said.

"I imagine so. I shouldn't have thought he'd have carried it all the way back to Egypt with him."

"You sent it to him in England?" I asked.

"Yes. As I said, he was starting his journey home the next morning. I figured it could be there, waiting for him, when he arrived. Also, I suppose I knew deep down I wasn't behaving honorably, which is why I didn't have it delivered to him at Per Ma'at before he left. I didn't want him to be able to easily confront me."

"Yet he did bring the letter back to Egypt with him," I said. "Why, I wonder, if he had no intention of discussing it with you?"

"It's quite strange," Kat said, furrowing her brow. "Surely he anticipated your attempt at apology, but the action of tearing up whatever paper it was he pulled out must have been spontaneous. I suppose it doesn't matter, does it?"

"I imagine not," Mr. McLeod said. "Still, it's odd."

Odd, indeed. And I was not convinced that it didn't matter. Not in the least.

Our ride back from Deir el Medina was uneventful. Despite the dust, I was utterly captivated by Egypt. I adored the desert: its open expanses, its narrow, twisting wadis that would flood when rain came. It was an environment of contrast and extremes so unlike the richness of the Nile and its surrounding floodplain. Each was alluring; it was as if they were competing for a suitor's attention. When Kat and I reached Per Ma'at, the household was in disarray. That much was evident from the shouts echoing across the courtyard. Jones did not open the door for us; Mahmoud the cook did instead.

"It is madness, Lady Emily, all madness," he said. "I would not come inside if I were you. The nasty English lady has been poisoned."

"Lady Wilona? Poisoned?" I asked.

"She has collapsed in a heap on the sitting room floor. Miss Evans is hysterical. Mrs. Hargreaves slapped her. The Englishmen are about to come to blows."

"Where is Jones?"

"He has invaded Mahmoud's kitchen. He thinks to find the poison there, which is absurd, so Mahmoud has invaded his territory in turn. But I do not like the task of opening and closing the door. It requires no art."

Kat brushed past me and ran down the antiquities-filled corridor toward the sitting room. I urged Mahmoud to return to the kitchen and followed my stepdaughter. The shouts had quieted by the time we reached the room, where, much to my surprise, Lady Wilona was sitting on the settee, upright and very much alive. Colin, who gave every sign of having reached the limit of his ordinarily endless patience, was standing in front of her.

"I assure you, Lady Wilona, it is not possible to spontaneously recover from cyanide poisoning," he said. He was holding a teacup in his hand. "Neither Dr. Rockley nor I have found the slightest indication that there was anything wrong with your tea."

"I will not tolerate this impertinence, Mr. Hargreaves. A gentleman ought never question the word of a lady. I was poisoned — that should be evident to anyone with even the substandard intelligence you are currently demonstrating. Truly, I fear for the Empire if men like you are charged with preserving it. As for Dr. Rockley, he's barely qualified. I demand that another physician be fetched from Luxor without delay."

"Dr. Rockley is perfectly well qualified," Colin said, "and if you mean to intimidate me with insults, you'd best brace yourself for disappointment."

"Given the behavior of your mother — slapping dear Pandora, what an outrage! — I ought to expect nothing better from you. I shan't be distracted by your antics. It's clear what's going on here. Your party arrived the very night Lord Deeley was murdered."

"What are you suggesting?" Colin asked.

"Isn't it obvious? No one tried to kill Lord Deeley until you got here. Someone in your little family circle must have committed the crime, and now you're trying to cover it up, silencing me in the process. Well, sir, you have failed on that count. Your cyanide did not beat me!"

"Your irrationality is not to be tolerated." Mrs. Hargreaves, who had been standing next to Miss Evans, her hand clamped around the girl's arm, released her grip, crossed the room, and motioned to her son. He stepped away and she took his place in front of Lady Wilona. "I will not stand by silent when my son is being slandered. You have, perhaps, heard stories of the lengths mothers will go to protect their children. Do not draw my ire."

Colin drew in a long, deep breath. Lady Wilona laughed. "Mummy has to come protect him, has she?" I wanted to reprimand her, but the last thing Colin needed was another lady coming to his defense. I met his eyes. His expression, cold and calm, hid the rage I knew must be simmering inside.

"I shall not allow this to descend into further madness," he said. "Dr. Rockley, will you take this tea into Luxor and have it tested for cyanide? On your way back, please bring one of your colleagues to examine Lady Wilona so that we may be reassured about her condition, miraculous or otherwise. Granard, I shall ask you to stand guard and let no one harm her in the meantime. Emily, come with me." He turned on his heel and stalked out of the room, holding the door for me and then closing it — softly, ever so softly — behind us. He took my hand and pulled me along the corridor into Lord Deeley's tomb-like study. Once that door was closed, he covered his face with his hands and started to laugh.

"Forgive me, I ought not" — he could hardly speak for laughing — "it's only that I've never witnessed such a ridiculous scene."

"You find this amusing? I was certain you were enraged."

"No one that absurd has the power to enrage me." He dropped his hands to his sides and kissed me, hard, on the lips. "Thank you. I feel much better composed now. The day was largely unremarkable. I had worthwhile conversations with Rockley and Miss Evans. I pulled her into the courtyard to speak with her when Lady Wilona had stepped out of the room. When she returned, she came to the French windows and saw us. She then poured a cup of tea, added a dash of milk and two lumps of sugar, took a single sip, and made a great show of collapsing on the floor, but not

278

before she carefully placed her teacup on a table. She feigned unconsciousness for approximately eleven minutes before springing back to life, so to speak. My mother timed it with her watch."

"Lady Wilona poured the tea herself?" I asked.

"Yes. Mrs. Granard and Mother both saw her do it."

"Did anyone else drink from the pot?"

"Troubridge and Mrs. Granard."

"Lady Wilona didn't want you to speak to Miss Evans," I said. "So she caused a distraction."

"That's quite likely, but it was badly done. She made a point of preserving the remaining tea in the cup. If she'd let it crash to the floor with her, it would be more difficult to prove it's not poisoned."

"She succeeded in stopping your conversation."

"Not quite soon enough. Miss Evans is very guarded in her speech, careful never to say anything that might implicate her employer in any wrongdoing," Colin said. "However, I was not asking her about her employer. I was making broad inquiries into her childhood. In the course of learning more than I'd like to know about preserving fruit — apparently one of her sisters has a passion for it — she mentioned that she visited Deeley's estate in Cornwall regularly. That's where her sister, who is married to Deeley's gamekeeper, lives. I gave no indication of finding this in the least interesting, which, naturally, led her to explain that she had, in fact, met Deeley more than once before obtaining her position with Lady Wilona. She hadn't wanted to admit this, as she feared it might make us suspect her of having killed him."

"That gives her no stronger motive than anyone else in the house," I said.

"Indeed. More interesting is that she was at the estate once when Troubridge was visiting. They didn't meet, of course, but she came upon him in the grounds, not far from the gamekeeper's cottage. He was arguing with Deeley. She ducked behind a convenient hedge and listened to them row. She couldn't make out all that they were saying, only that it was something about a baby."

"Marian?"

"Quite possibly. It's all a bit too commodious for my taste. Everyone in this house is gossiping, fueled by the articles that wretched Mallaby keeps writing, so there's no doubt she's heard about Troubridge and the child. I suspect she's conjured up this story to protect her employer."

"Surely she can't think Lady Wilona is guilty? The woman may be despicable, but she's not the sort to put herself in danger of facing prison, let alone the hangman. Lord Deeley's death stands to hurt, not benefit, her. He's no longer there to discreetly help her out financially."

"I agree," Colin said, "but we don't know how Miss Evans sees all this. She may know very little about Lady Wilona's financial situation and is instead focused on nothing but her own. If her employer is arrested, her income will disappear."

"Did she give you any specific details concerning the incident she overheard? The date, for example?"

"She believes it was vaguely sometime in the autumn of 1896, but isn't certain as to specifics."

"The year written on the back of the picture. Autumn, when one would assume a gentleman would be in the country, shooting birds."

"Quite."

"I wonder . . . what if she did meet Mr. Troubridge? He was frequently in Cornwall, and he has an eye for the ladies. Might he have trifled with a gamekeeper's sister-in-law and left her bereft?"

"And desperate for revenge?"

"When she finds herself in Egypt with the man who destroyed all her hopes, she is furious. Hurt. Desperate."

"She wouldn't kill Deeley as a result," Colin said.

"No, but when someone did, she might have decided to frame her nemesis for the crime." I frowned. "It doesn't quite work, though. Mr. Troubridge isn't the sort to involve himself with someone like her. He prefers married women."

"Sisley Weldon wasn't married. We know very little about her background. She, too, might have been someone's sister-in-law. Still, it stretches credulity. Miss Evans happens to be on the trip where Deeley is murdered, happens to be in a position to frame Troubridge?"

"It doesn't quite hold water," I said.

"No, but it does raise interesting questions. Do you think we could induce Kat to befriend the girl? They can't be all that far apart in age, and Miss Evans has no one here to confide in. She might tell Kat something she wouldn't reveal to either of us."

"That's an excellent idea, and it won't take much to convince Kat," I said. "It's just the sort of thing she likes to do. Does

Lady Wilona give Miss Evans any time of her own?"

"She has a morning once a week."

I cringed at the thought of anyone being forced to spend so much time with Lady Wilona. "She'll be all the more thrilled to do something with Kat. In the meantime, I want to have a little tête-à-tête with Lady Wilona."

Pa Demi, Regnal Year Two
24

I decided to talk to my father before I went home to Kamose. Neither would return to the Valley for another two days. Even on his days off, Eetee worked. Not for Pharaoh, but for anyone willing to pay him. He was a brilliant painter, but also loved making furniture, smoothing the wood — sycamore, fig and tamarisk, acacia and willow — oiling and decorating it. His pieces commanded high prices from the nobles in Thebes. I expected to find him in his workshop, but it was empty, which meant he must be at his tomb.

I walked out of the village and across the hot sand to the western necropolis, the hills and the Peak looming above me. Tombs and monuments littered the hillside. Many of the older ones were relatively simple, at least on the outside. The newer ones were topped with pyramidions and had courtyards that led inside to chapels and contained multiple burial chambers. All boasted intricate decorations. A few generations earlier, tombs were intended for individuals, but we now preferred to bury families together. My parents would be interred there, and Eetee was making sure there would be space for my brother and me — and our spouses — as well. I can't say I thrilled at the idea of spending eternity in proximity to Sanura, but it wasn't my place to decide.

The necropolis was quiet. My father was one of the only people working there that day. I climbed the brick stairs and passed through the door leading into the courtyard of his tomb, which was surrounded by a wall constructed — like the rest of the structure — from stones and mud bricks. Only the pyramidion on top was formed from limestone. Columns marked the entrance to the tiny chapel, where I found my father. Smooth plaster covered the walls and the vaulted ceiling. My brother had marked squares on it to ensure the figures he drew with red ochre were perfectly placed. Today, Eetee had black charcoal in hand to mark and correct Bek's few mistakes. I always felt strange in this place, knowing that someday I would bring offerings to my parents here. I shivered a little despite the heat.

"This is a pleasant surprise," my father

said, embracing me. "What brings you to the cemetery? I hope nothing bad has happened." Worry crossed his face.

"Nothing new, no," I said. "Tey and I saw Pentu in Thebes. He told us a story about a time, years ago, when a scribe and his wife suffered attacks similar to what Kamose and I have experienced."

Eetee shook his head. "That was a different matter altogether."

"So it's true?"

"Meryt, some people are not formed right. They disturb Ma'at, they care not about decency, they are incapable of telling the difference between right and wrong. They offend the gods. The man responsible for what happened to that family . . . he was this sort of man."

"Who was he?"

"I cannot tell you that."

"Because you don't know, or because it's forbidden?"

"The latter."

I wouldn't ask again. There was no point. When the village officials forbade something, few people dared question them. My father certainly never would. Partly because it was not in his character and partly because, as the leader of the Right Gang — one of the two groups of the village's workers — he was an official. But that didn't mean I couldn't ask other questions. "Is this man still in Pa Demi?"

"He is not."

"You're certain?"

"I am."

"Is he still alive?"

"Yes."

"That doesn't bring me much comfort. Had he left the village by the time Pentu came here?"

"He had. Pentu is a skilled worker, diligent and capable, but he angers quickly and likes to believe he knows more than those around him. Sometimes, a man like him needs to be tricked into behaving in the manner expected when adapting to a new way of life. When he came to the village, he was not always easy to manage. Someone decided to scare him into assimilating. Given what Dedi told him, I'd say he was in on it. Whatever they did was harmless and it worked."

"Do you know for a fact that this happened?" I asked.

My father shrugged. "I heard murmurs of plans and the result tells me they carried them out. Pentu gives no one trouble anymore. He's a fine stonecutter, much to be admired. He's a bit gruff, but is the kind of man you come to like the more you get to know him."

I wondered if he'd still believe that if I told him I'd seen Sanura with him by the river, but said nothing to tar her. Regardless, I didn't like Pentu. Getting to know him better wouldn't change that. "So where does that leave Kamose and me? No one is trying to get us to adapt to a new way of life."

He put his arm around me and pulled me close to him. "I wish I knew, Meryt, but I don't. The entire village is aware of what has happened at your house. They know of my displeasure. If it was some sort of prank that went too far, whoever is responsible won't do it again."

"And if it's something else?"

"You've had the priest in. You've repainted the door. Those things will protect you."

"Unless the responsible party is some other person not formed right who doesn't care if he disturbs Ma'at."

"I cannot envision a scenario in which either you or Kamose would have caught the attention of someone like that. You keep to yourselves. You contribute to village life. You have no children."

"And therefore, nothing to envy," I said.

"Not exactly, but someone unhinged who

has no heir might try to interfere with the domestic tranquility of those who do. Now, if Tey and Raneb started getting meddled with, I'd tell them to keep their sons close to them."

"Tey might be willing to barter one of them for guaranteed domestic tranquility — a thing she insists is impossible with too many children underfoot."

He smiled. "I am glad you have a friend like her."

"Me, too." I touched the cool, smooth-plastered wall next to me. Bek had outlined a figure of my father, showing him with his hands raised in prayer. On either side of him were spells that would guide his journey to the afterlife and images of protective symbols. The room would be stunning when the decorations were complete. Stonemasons had dug out the burial chambers beneath the chapel, accessible from a shaft in the courtyard. It was strange to think of them ever being filled.

"Try not to focus too much on this trouble, my child. You are prone to worry. Your mother is, too. Remember that it doesn't help."

He was right, of course. But I'd feel better if there was something that would.

LUXOR, 1904
25

I waited to speak to Lady Wilona until the doctor from Luxor had finished examining her. Not surprisingly, he found nothing wrong, but the manner in which he handled his patient was nothing short of masterful. He explained that her attack, while not brought on by cyanide, was almost certainly catalyzed by the keen sensitivity she felt for her murdered friend.

"You're wholly incorrect," she said, protesting. "I vividly smelled bitter almonds just as I took that fateful sip of tea. The poison acted at once, which is why I collapsed. Obviously the miscreant who put it in the cup didn't use enough."

"An active mind — as yours clearly is — can simulate any number of vivid sensations." The doctor was packing up his bag. He was an older man, grizzled and gray, serious and measured, with an air of confidence and reliability. "I suggest that you smelled what your mind thought you should. If I may be so bold, may I inquire whether you've ever experienced something that could only be explained by supernatural means?"

"Good heavens, no."

"We humans like to think we're evolved and enlightened, but there is much we do not understand," he said. "Some among us — a very rare group of extraordinary individuals — possess the ability to see truth that remains hidden from the ordinary world. You smelled bitter almonds because your brain was trying to tell you something about Lord Deeley's murder, something most people lack the skills to interpret."

"Surely you're not suggesting I have psychic abilities?"

He placed a hand on her shoulder and spoke in the gravest of tones. "That is precisely what I am suggesting, madam. There are many charlatans who claim such powers; most are frauds. As a man of science, I have no difficulty in recognizing the difference. Why, just last week, I met with a duchess who has had experiences very similar to yours. I have a colleague in Luxor whom I trust implicitly. She is an expert in these arts. Might I send you to her? She could offer guidance in how to hone your skills."

"A duchess?" Lady Wilona was sitting up straighter. "I shall give the matter serious thought."

I followed the doctor out of the room as he went to leave the house, curious about his methods. A wide grin split his face when I questioned him.

"Some would condemn me for it," he said, "but I find it remarkably useful. I see countless patients who share Lady Wilona's affliction. They are bored, forgotten, and generally have seen a loss in status. They mistake malaise for a medical condition. I make them feel special. The woman in Luxor I mentioned — she's actually a trained nurse — gives them something else to focus on. No doubt they occasionally irritate their friends by insisting on demonstrating their psychic powers, but it's harmless. Within a few weeks, their imagined physical symptoms stop plaguing them."

"How very clever of you," I said.

"You may not think so if your friend insists on hosting regular séances, but I suspect that once she feels she has something unique to offer, she'll become less of a pest."

Back in the sitting room, I ordered Colin

— adopting a fair copy of Lady Wilona's stentorian tone — to help her to her bedroom. "I shall sit with you this afternoon," I said. "Don't try to dissuade me. I shan't brook any argument. Miss von Lange, I am certain Miss Evans could use some fresh air. Would you be so good as to take her for a walk? I can only imagine how desperately upset she is by all that has happened." Colin had already told her we hoped she could befriend the girl. As we expected, she was delighted to take action.

Once Lady Wilona was tucked into her bed, a mountain of pillows propped up behind her, Colin left us alone.

"Would you like me to read aloud?" I asked, giving a cursory glance at the two books — the Bible and William Le Queux's *The Great War in England in 1897* — on the desk across the room. She was just the sort to get stirred up by fictional thoughts of England falling to her enemies.

"I don't require you to sit in attendance on me."

"So no reading, then? Good. I confess I'd hoped we could chat. The doctor's words didn't surprise me. From the moment I met you, I felt you were a person of special talents. Insights. You observe things others never notice. I didn't understand it at first, which is probably why you don't much like me, but now, I can only imagine the onerous burden you carry."

She puffed herself up. "I've known for ages that I have the gift, but I've never tried to use it. I don't like prying into other people's business."

"Of course not. Still, it could be helpful rather than hurtful, if deployed correctly. Like this afternoon, for instance. You smelled cyanide because somewhere, hidden in your mind, is a detail about Lord Deeley that will point us to the identity of his murderer. The scent was your subconscious calling out to you to recognize what you already know. I wonder . . . what if we go back further than the night he died. Your husband was a close compatriot of Lord Deeley's. Did they ever have a falling-out? An argument over principle? Perhaps he had to intervene to prevent his friend from making a grievous political error? I did not know him, but I have paid attention to your character and am confident that you would never have married a gentleman who did not possess the highest moral standards."

"That is an observation, Lady Emily, that even a simpleton could make. Sir John always stood on the shoulders of giants, yet he was no dwarf. He had a sharp intelligence, but never got bogged down in too much book learning, if you take my meaning. He frequently guided Lord Deeley through difficult decisions."

"No doubt" — I paused, then spoke with more force. "No doubt, you are aware of the contents of the letter Mrs. Granard found in her book."

"It pains me to have heard any of it. I abhor gossip, but one cannot avoid all conversation. Naturally, I insisted on reading the letter. I don't like to draw conclusions from the unreliable reporting of others."

"As the wife of a powerful political player, you must not have been entirely surprised by what you read. Surely Sir John relied on your insight and your discretion and, hence, shared with you many things of a confidential nature."

"Indeed he did. He joined with Lord Deeley and the others in blocking Mr. Granard's bid for party leadership. I agreed with his decision. I can't say I know specifically what scandal the anonymous letter refers to, but there was at least one incident in the past that made me hesitate to think Mr. Granard should be prime minister."

"Is that so?" I raised an eyebrow. "Would it be too much to ask that you share your knowledge?"

"For me, it was nothing lofty or political. No disagreement with policy. It was something far more personal. It happened long ago, back when they were all at Oxford. Sir John was always much more serious than his peers, but he was living in college when it happened, and was close enough friends with Lord Deeley to hear the story. Mr. Granard and Lord Deeley got embroiled in some sort of elaborate prank. I can't recall the details — it was something to do with climbing on a roof — but the specifics don't matter. What does is that their actions resulted in serious injury to the son of a local shopkeeper. The boy never walked again. It was an accident, of course, but tragic all the same. Fortunately for the young gentlemen, their fathers were able to hush it all up. I'm sure the shopkeeper was given some sort of remuneration and everyone came out of it well enough."

I doubted very much that the boy's father would agree, let alone the boy himself. "So the conclusion you drew from this was that neither Mr. Granard nor Lord Deeley possessed the character necessary to lead the nation?"

"It was never clear which of them was responsible for what happened. Yet it seems to me that Mr. Granard was likely the instigator."

"Is there a particular reason for your belief?"

She looked like an extremely satisfied cat. "Only my talent for observation. Lord Deeley had the nobler spirit. Sir John never was as close with Mr. Granard."

I wondered if she had always referred to her husband by his title. "Did this incident become common knowledge later?"

"No, not at all. Sir John shared the story with me not long after our marriage, one evening when we had dined with the Granards. He did not wish me to become overly familiar with them."

He sounded like a controlling lout. "But you suspect this accident in Oxford was what prompted the failure of Mr. Granard's bid for leadership?"

"No, no, I don't. It is simply the explanation of why I find him unfit." She blinked several times and then closed her eyes. "For the rest, it doesn't feel right. That, in my opinion, had to do with a scandal more politically-centric. It would make more sense. You know, I'm feeling much better now, but I don't want to have to face the others. I could use a decent cup of tea. I think I'll run over to the Luxor Hotel and have some there. Leave me, please, so I can prepare."

Her shift in mood was so sudden it took me aback, but I was happy to do as she asked. I left the room, which was at the end of the corridor, where large French casements opened into the courtyard. I could see Mr. Granard through them, smoking outside next to a tinkling fountain surrounded by jasmine, and decided to confront him about what Lady Wilona had told me.

"What a lovely space," I said, walking toward him. "I've never smelled flowers more fragrant. Who would have expected to find such an Eden in the desert?"

"It's merely a variation on the oasis, I suppose," he said, and offered me a cigarette. I refused but was surprised he made the gesture. He didn't seem the sort to approve of ladies smoking.

"I apologize for what I need to ask you. I've learned about something tragic that happened when you were at Oxford and am wondering if that is the scandal that prevented you from becoming prime minister."

"Very bad form for Hargreaves to allow you to traipse about like this asking impertinent questions. Shocking, truth be told. You can't really like it, can you? What can he be thinking? He ought to let you live the life of a lady and deal with this sort of distasteful work himself."

I ignored his own impertinent questions. "Oxford. A roof. An injured boy. I'm sure you remember."

He stiffened and took a deep drag from his cigarette. "It was a hideous mess. I'm ashamed of the part I played in it. But how did you come to hear about it? It happened more than thirty years ago. Lady Wilona, I imagine. The old bat never did know when to keep her mouth shut. I give you my word as a gentleman that what happened that night had nothing to do with my losing the bid for party leadership. As a result, it wouldn't give me motive for wanting to see Deeley dead and is not worth discussing."

"I can't agree, Mr. Granard," I said. "If the story became common knowledge, it absolutely could have hindered your political goals."

"I give you my word that it didn't."

"Your word is not enough. I require a full explanation."

He dropped his half-smoked cigarette onto a paving stone and crushed it with the toe of his boot. "The story did come out, though not in any widespread way, years before I had any sort of reasonable shot at

299

leadership. I confided in one discreet colleague. He spoke of it to no one else. Of that I am certain."

"You'd have me believe you sabotaged your own career?"

"It wasn't mine that suffered," he said. "It was Deeley's. It all started when we heard about the antics of a student at Christ Church in the seventeenth century. He was described as a *person of notorious and incorrigible debauchery* and was caught *debauching with a gentleman commoner.* It didn't sound to us as if he'd done anything worthy of such notoriety, although among his offenses, he stole and killed a local woman's pig, which made for a most unpleasant mess. We thought it high time we earned similar accolades. We gathered up a number of bicycles and determined to get them onto the roof of Tom Tower, but reconnaissance told us that would be too difficult, so we settled upon the Hall instead. Deeley asked a local lad — the shopkeeper's son — to join in, figuring that was close enough to debauching with a gentleman commoner. He was our age, but wasn't all that eager to take part. Deeley could be rather persuasive, you know. He did everything he could to convince the fellow. Twice I told him to back off, that it might prove dangerous, but he wouldn't listen. Eventually, calling the poor bloke a coward changed the boy's mind."

"And he fell off the roof and was left paralyzed."

"Yes. I'm not proud of what we did. It was reckless and foolish."

"Did you blame Deeley for the result?"

"Not entirely. I could have tried harder to stop him. It wasn't precisely necessary to involve a commoner."

As if that was what made the incident so outrageous. "You, Mr. Granard, are a gentleman commoner," I said. "A shopkeeper's son isn't. Lord Deeley pressured him for no reason at all."

"We were young and had consumed a great deal of alcohol. I regret it wholeheartedly."

"All the regret in the world will do very little for the injured boy."

"Quite." He opened his silver cigarette case and snapped it shut, three times in rapid succession. "About a decade later, when Deeley and I were both firmly ensconced in our political careers, we each were considered candidates for ministerial positions. I was still young enough to be rather embarrassingly idealistic and felt that we weren't worthy, specifically because of that incident at Oxford. I confessed as much to the prime minister. He wasn't as horrified as I expected — boys will be boys, that sort of thing — and, in fact, was impressed that I had the courage to tell the truth. As a result, he named me a minister, but not Deeley. The PM felt that by continuing to hide what happened, Deeley revealed a weakness of character."

"Was Lord Deeley aware of any of this?" I asked.

"Not so far as I know, but I couldn't swear to it," he said. "It's conceivable that, eventually, the prime minister mentioned it to him, but even if that were the case, it wouldn't give me motive for killing Deeley. Quite the reverse. Deeley wanted to be prime minister. He'd have known that this scandal, if it came out, would absolutely preclude the possibility."

I thought about what Mr. McLeod had said about Lord Deeley and forgiveness, that he could be magnanimous but ordinarily required a discussion about the transgression and an apology. I had no doubt that if he had learned what Mr. Granard had done, there would have been a great deal of discussion. Mr. Granard would gain nothing by lying to me about it. Even supposing that it was he, not his friend, who goaded the local boy into participating in the prank, that would give Lord Deeley cause for anger, not Mr. Granard. It did not appear to shed any light on his murder.

All the same, it did shed light on Mr. Granard's character. He was willing to betray a friend when he thought his moral code required it. He was fortunate not to lose his chance at becoming a member of the prime minister's cabinet as a result. Was his explanation honest? Was it true he had been rewarded for being brave enough to speak honestly? Or was he lying, then and now? He could have said anything to the prime minister, including denying his involvement altogether. I could accept that the PM might never have revealed what he knew to Lord Deeley. Why bother? If he had, it would have caused upset and scandal, neither of which politicians like to court.

"Are we quite finished here?" Mr. Granard asked. "It's beastly uncomfortable discussing any of this with you. Should the need to interrogate me rise again, I'd ask that you have the decency to send your husband to do his own work. This is not a job for ladies."

I stared at him, unblinking, and said nothing. A person like him, whom I could never respect, had no ability to insult me. I had no interest in his views about women. Far

more fascinating were the broader implica-
tions of the story he'd told me. Lord Deeley had a motive for wishing him harm. I
might not yet know how, directly, this
impacted our investigation, but I was certain
it did.

PA DEMI, REGNAL YEAR TWO
26

After I spoke to my father in his tomb, life returned to normal for long enough that I almost forgot to worry about the destruction in our house. Almost. Dread never disappears altogether, does it? It wakes you in the middle of the night, with a burning sensation in your belly. Or it tweaks you from behind when you're enjoying a quiet moment with your husband or your friends and makes you incapable of continuing to relax with them. In either case — or by any of the thousands of other ways it disrupts your contentment — it gnaws at you, never letting go. Not all the way.

So most of the time I was all right. I worked on my father's ushabtis. I flirted with my husband. I gossiped with my friends. Pentu started making friendly overtures to Kamose and socializing with my father. I still didn't like Pentu, so that irritated me, but otherwise, things were all very ordinary. Until Sanura came to see me. And then it wasn't all right.

"I know what you're doing," she said.

I'd invited her inside and offered her a cup of beer. I was trying to be cordial. I had no ulterior motive. "What I'm doing is giving you a drink and a place to sit. Neither is generally considered controversial."

"Stay away from Pentu. He doesn't need a friend like you."

"I don't need a friend like him. You're the one who seems attached to the man."

"I'm not." Her voice was uncharacteristically forceful. "Not any more than the rest of my family. We've been close to him for as long as I can remember. It's not easy to wriggle out of that sort of thing. You'll find it the same now that he's insinuating himself into your own family."

Did she want to wriggle out? This interested me. "I'm sure it won't break Bek's heart if you let Pentu drift away."

"That's not what I meant," she said.

"I've never been much good at reading people's minds."

"I'm not sure I believe that. I know you dabble in magic."

"I don't dabble in anything."

"If you didn't, your sculptures wouldn't breathe."

"My sculptures don't breathe. No sculptures do."

"I disagree," she said. "They aren't like those made by others, even by artists far more talented than you. Their technique may be perfect, but you put something in yours that makes them come alive."

"I promise you, I've never seen any of my sculptures hop off the shelf and start walking around."

"That's not what I mean. They look at you. They seem to know what you're thinking. They pass judgment. In ways, they appear more human than any of us. It scares me."

I debated how to reply. Should I point out the inanity of her claim or ask her the more compelling question? I chose the latter. "Why does it scare you?"

"We all have secrets. Even you. Even your father. Your sculptures know. I can tell. Even those cats you gave Bek and me. I can feel their eyes following me. They know everything I do."

Now I went from being mildly bemused to getting a pit in my stomach. Sanura was not well. Maybe a demon had possessed her. Maybe she was going mad. Either way, I didn't want any part of it. But I knew I couldn't walk away. We were in my house, after all. And even if we weren't, I wasn't that kind of cruel.

"I promise you, I never use magic when I'm working, or at any other time, for that matter," I said. "You've been subject to a lot of upheaval — you left your parents' house, you married, you're running your own home now. It's not an easy adjustment for any of us, no matter how madly in love with our husbands we may be. They're a lot of work, men, and most of it is duller than dull."

"You misunderstand. I couldn't be more content with my life." She drained her beer and put her cup on the small table between our chairs. "Dismiss my warning if you want, but you will come to regret doing so. Destroy your sculptures and stop working. They will see if you don't."

"Who will see?" I asked.

"The gods." A strange look crossed her face and then, an instant later, she became herself again: pretty, scheming, and mean. "Leave Pentu alone. Haven't you got enough friends already? Well, no, I guess it's only Tey who can tolerate you, and only barely at that. Pentu doesn't need the kind of trouble you bring."

She rose from her seat, picked up the empty cup, and dropped it on the floor,

laughing as it shattered. "On top of everything else, you're a terrible hostess." She
laughed again, the sound following her out
of the house.

For a while, I stayed there, sitting, im-
mobile, not sure what to make of any of this.
Had Sanura been playing me the whole
time, pretending to be unhinged before flipping back to her normal self? But why?
What purpose could that serve? She'd
lobbed vague charges of using magic at me
before. They were toothless and unfounded.
Today, however, she'd stuck this old com-
plaint in the middle of trying — commanding, really — that I stay away from Pentu. I
doubted this was because she was jealous of
sharing a friend. She was afraid I'd find out
what was really going on between them. I
could slur her in any number of ways, but I
couldn't claim that she was stupid. She
knew that if I found out she was having an
affair, I would tell Bek. And she wouldn't
like the consequences of that.

So was she playing crazy to convince me
that it was best to keep away from both her
and Pentu? Hoping that I'd conclude I
didn't need the aggravation? None of this
made much sense. And things that didn't
make sense troubled me, because I knew if
I understood them fully, they would make

sense, and I was afraid of what that might reveal.

310

LUXOR, 1904
27

Colin and I were in dire need of respite from the other members of the party, whose bickering and pettiness was relentless, all the more so with the daily barrage of accusations published in the *Daily Yell*. This morning came a sordid report of Lady Wilona's supposed poisoning and a mention of Lord Deeley's romantic feelings for Mrs. Hargreaves. Tired of the gossip, Colin and I invited Kat and Mrs. Hargreaves to join us for a peaceful dinner on the *Timsah* that evening. Cramped quarters and the sounds of the city were preferable to the tension in the Per Ma'at. Somehow, Kat had managed to win over Lord Deeley's groom, and they rode the fine Arabian horses over instead of taking the carriage. I envied them the journey on those magnificent beasts, across the desert under clear, dark skies, the path lit by the moon. The night was chilly, so we stayed below deck, even for our after-dinner drinks, retiring to the divans built in beneath the saloon's windows.

"It's not nearly so romantic here as I expected," Kat said. "I envied you the boat, and I still do to some extent, but only because you're not trapped at the house with all those dreadful bores. Docked here, though, with Luxor right across the river isn't dreamy and private. That's what I would require if I was staying on a dahabiya with the man I adored."

Colin frowned, no doubt wondering if she had identified someone as the man in question. I thought this entirely unlikely. Mrs. Hargreaves, untroubled by the possibility of an impending romance, commended her granddaughter's opinion.

"Nicholas and I felt the same," she said. "We traveled up the river every winter, always on the same dahabiya, and never docked near civilization if we could avoid it. I can't say the crew much appreciated our eccentricities, but the young rarely care about such things."

"You weren't young, though," Kat said. "You were nearly forty when you married!"

"Positively ancient, yes," Mrs. Hargreaves said. "You should be careful not to give your heart to any man in the near future. Falling in love has much to recommend it, but it does tie one down. You've barely traveled, hardly seen the world, and ought to resist settling down until absolutely necessary."

"I'm hoping it shall never be necessary."

Colin rose from his seat and started to pace, a sure sign of distress. I couldn't decide which appeared to trouble him more: the idea of Kat in love, or of Kat deliberately remaining unattached for the rest of her life.

"That, my child, is a vain hope," Mrs. Hargreaves said. "Eventually, we all find the person we belong with, and when we do, there's nothing to be gained by trying to deny it."

"I should so like to have a story as inspiring as yours." Kat sighed. "Falling in love halfway up the Great Pyramid, engaged by the time you were at the bottom."

"They were both fortunate it was a good match," Colin said. "Grand passions don't always turn out so well."

"Do you speak from experience?" Kat asked.

Knowing his relationship with the countess had stemmed from just that sort of passion, I intervened before he could answer. "Tell me, Kat, how are you getting on with Miss Evans?"

She drew in a deep breath, pressed her lips together, and paused before letting the air rush out of her lungs. "I suppose you'd prefer to avoid awkward conversations. I shan't challenge you on the point. Pandora is something of an enigma. She's smarter than she lets on, but in a manner that is frightfully tedious. She remembers all kinds of random facts — although I wonder about the validity of some of them — but she pulls them out at the strangest times. I can't tell if it's affectation or a failing. She despises her position, which is no surprise, but not for the reasons you'd think. Lady Wilona doesn't bother her in the least, particularly since she started making a habit of taking tea at the Luxor Hotel. It gives Pandora a welcome break."

"I'm surprised she doesn't take Miss Evans with her," I said.

Kat shrugged. "I am as well, but it didn't give Pandora any pause. Apparently she's used to the whims of overbearing battle-axes. Makes me wonder what her sisters are like."

"So what does she dislike about her work?" I asked.

"Her inability to have control over her life," Kat said. "While she's pleased to have the opportunity to see Egypt, she would have preferred India. And she would have rather traveled next winter, not this, for reasons she was unable to articulate."

"Did she say anything about Dr. Rockley?" Mrs. Hargreaves asked. Naturally observant, she, too, had noticed the doctor's attachment to the girl.

"She's rather stupid when it comes to men. Hasn't the slightest inkling that the doctor has fallen for whatever it is he views as her charms. I wouldn't want her to be my only confidante after a particularly interesting ball. She'd be worse than useless when it comes to parsing what gentlemen say."

"Were you able to get her to speak about Mr. Troubridge?" I asked.

"There's something funny there, that much is certain," Kat said. "I made up a little story, telling her that he'd mentioned that he'd been at Deeley's estate in Cornwall at the same she was staying in her sister's cottage. She showed no inkling that this was, at best, a tenuous claim, and at worst an outright lie. Why on earth would he have been aware that the relative of a random servant was there? And why would he know her name? He would have had no occasion to meet her. She ought to have been skeptical at the very least."

"She wasn't?" Colin asked.

"No. Only said that she doesn't think he's

the gentleman he presents himself to be. I pressed her as to why, but she gave the worst sort of flimsy answers. His eyes don't seem honest. A gentleman his age ought to be married. That type of inanity. Nothing concrete."

"And no mention of Miss Weldon or the baby?" I asked.

"No, and I don't think that is due to her trying to hide anything from me. She made no secret of being relieved to have found a friend in me. Instead, I would say she was making it all up when she talked to you, Father, in an attempt to protect the hideous Lady Wilona. It's insensible, really. She should run from the woman. No income is worth what she's forced to tolerate."

"Yet you admit that Lady Wilona doesn't bother her," I said.

"I do, but I don't like it. Not a bit. It's absurd. Knowing what she'd told Father, I tried to approach the subject every way I could, all with the goal of uncovering *why* she would shield such an odious woman. It must be because of the income, but that's a most unsatisfactory answer."

"This case is full of unsatisfactory answers," I said. I shared with them what I'd learned from both Lady Wilona and Mr. Granard.

"It's dashed odd," Colin said. He was sitting again — growing more relaxed the further we moved from discussing his daughter's hypothetical romantic life — and ran a hand through his tousled curls. "Like you, Emily, I feel as if this is more significant than it seems at first glance. Not the details of the story, but the fact that Deeley might have borne a grudge against Granard."

"Bertram never held a grudge in his life," Mrs. Hargreaves said. "He wouldn't, even when he should have. His ability to relegate the wrongs he suffered to a metaphorical box, locked up, never to be opened again, was astonishing."

"I'm always dubious when people claim they can forget the past altogether," I said. "We all carry the hurts we've suffered."

"I assure you, he succeeded in putting it all aside," she said. "I witnessed it too often not to give credence to it. It worried me sometimes, but never seemed to have an ill effect on him."

"Is there anything in your own past that might have hurt him?" I asked.

"My past? Heavens, no. I told you he admired me, but he always knew there was no possibility of anything beyond friendship between us. If that had wounded him, we wouldn't have remained close for so many

317

decades."

"I imagine he was more affected by your marriage than he let on," Colin said. "He'd followed you to Egypt, after all, only to watch you fall in love and forsake him."

Mrs. Hargreaves laughed. "You do paint a picture, don't you? First of all, he wasn't on the Great Pyramid with Nicholas and me, so he did not watch me fall in love. That took only a few moments and was done and dusted by the time we came back down and met him by the camels."

"I must interrupt to express my disappointment at not having had the opportunity to ride a camel on this trip," Kat said. "I feel robbed of the experience."

"It's far more uncomfortable than you can imagine," Mrs. Hargreaves said. "That is why I have not included it on our itinerary. Even a donkey is preferable."

"We're getting off track," I said. "I'm asking these questions not to pry, but to determine what similarities — if any — can be found in the relationships Lord Deeley had with each of those whom he invited on this trip."

"Given what we've already discovered, I'd say the common ground is that you all had reason to be upset with him." Kat stretched her legs out in front of her and crossed her

318

ankles, just the way Colin had a habit of doing. She was wearing another pair of her flattering jodhpurs. I wondered, not for the first time, if I could get away with such daring attire. The mere fact that I was questioning whether I might made me feel crushingly ancient. I hadn't been all that much older than Kat when I fell in love with Colin, yet it felt like a thousand years ago.

"I have no reason to be upset with him," Mrs. Hargreaves said.

"Is that really true, Grandmama? He argued with Grandpapa, didn't he? Made him so angry that he threw a book and broke something, behavior that, so far as I can tell, is the sort abhorrent to the Hargreaves clan. Fortunately, I get my emotional side from my mother, who had no such restrictions on how one ought to act."

"Arguments are not unusual," Mrs. Hargreaves said, "and each of us has the potential to lose our tempers during them and act in ways we would normally find reprehensible."

"Grandpapa died only a few days later, did he not? I apologize if I'm not supposed to speak openly about such things. You must remember I'm Viennese, not English. I talk about uncomfortable subjects instead of burying them."

"I'm not sure what that has to do with being Viennese," Colin said, half under his breath.

"The thing is, there are so many subjects the lot of you consider verboten that I've had to take matters into my own hands to learn things I have a right to know. I always thought it was strange that I know no details about Grandpapa's death, only that it happened entirely out of the blue. Did he have some hereditary condition I ought to be concerned about? Not only for myself, but for my own father?"

"Katharina, this is not something —"

She interrupted Colin. "No, of course, not something to be discussed. I know all too well how you feel about it, but I don't share your point of view. I do want to know. So I confronted the doctor who treated him. He didn't want to speak with me, but felt that he ought to, as I was so concerned. Grandpapa fell into a coma, not out of the blue, but because he received a grievous injury to his head."

"He was struck by a carriage," Colin said. "The injuries he suffered caused him to slip into a coma. He was unable to describe what happened, but we have no reason to doubt it was anything but an accident."

"Surely you had it investigated?" Kat asked.

Mrs. Hargreaves looked like a wounded animal. "Knowing who caused the injury wouldn't have brought him back. There was no point suffering through the indignities of an investigation."

She was sounding too much like Lady Wilona. "This occurred at Anglemore Park?" I asked. I'd heard nothing about it until now. All I knew was that Colin's father had died suddenly and unexpectedly.

"In Dunsford Vale, one of the villages on the estate."

"No one saw anything," Colin said. "I interrogated every single person who might have witnessed the accident. It was late on a winter evening, already dark and no moon in the sky. Father had only just returned from London."

"Where he'd argued with Lord Deeley," Kat said. She placed an envelope on the settee in the space between her and Mrs. Hargreaves. "I decided to search everyone's rooms again today and found this in yours, tucked in a set of nightclothes in the armoire. Inside, there is a sheet of paper with a coat of arms drawn on it and a single typewritten sentence: *Painted on the side of the carriage that ran down Nicholas*

321

"It's Lord Deeley's coat of arms," I said, examining the page. "It's the same stationery — heavy linen, with an engraved bee — used for the letter Mrs. Granard found."

"Someone is toying with us," Colin said. "Deeley would never have attacked Father. And at any rate, he was in London."

"Can you prove that?" Kat crossed her arms and pulled a belligerent face.

"This goes too far," Mrs. Hargreaves said. "What happened was a dreadful accident, not a deliberate attack. Bertram was angry, but would never have physically injured someone. Furthermore, how would he have known Nicholas would happen to be in the village that night? He only went because one of his tenants was ill and asking for him."

"Who was it?" I asked.

"John Thomas. He had some sort of fever and his wife was desperately worried that if he died she'd have nowhere to live. Nicholas reassured her that he would always look after her and the children."

Colin frowned. "Thomas married a girl from Cornwall, didn't he?"

"Yes, Judith. She worked in the kitchen. I can't recall her maiden name," Mrs. Hargreaves said. "Her mother was a parlor maid for Bertram —" She stopped. We all sat, silent.

"Is this the first you've heard of any of this?" Colin asked his mother.

"I never before made the connection."

"That doesn't answer my question."

"Bertram's housekeeper recommended the girl, which does not mean she was some sort of spy in the house. She wasn't even working for us anymore after she married Thomas."

"She could have been in contact with Lord Deeley," Kat said, "and agreed to summon Grandpapa to her house at a set time on the pretense of her husband being ill."

"This is absurd," Mrs. Hargreaves said. "Bertram would never have involved himself in such a scheme. He wasn't that sort of man. Nicholas's death was a tragic accident, nothing more."

"But whoever hit him didn't stop to see if he was all right," Kat said. "Why not?"

"Most likely because he was afraid of the consequences," Colin said. "It's unfortunate, but not altogether unusual."

Mrs. Hargreaves's face was bright crimson and tears pooled in her eyes. "I won't have this all dragged up again. It's pointless. Bertram was in London, not Derbyshire."

"I didn't only receive the coat of arms," Kat said. She pulled another sheet of paper out of the envelope and unfolded it. "There was this, as well."

Colin, who had started pacing again, took it from her. "It appears to be a page ripped from Deeley's journal, dated this past October." He read aloud. *"It was cowardly, but for so long I could not bring myself to confess my Great Sin to Ann. I'm so ashamed of what I did, but I posted the letter, and she has at last replied — five weeks later; imagine the anxiety plaguing me, waiting to hear what she would say! She doesn't despise me. It's hard to fathom. And she will still come to Egypt. Perhaps she will unleash her wrath on me in person; I shan't blame her if she does. But at least — at last — there shall be no more secrets between us. I know there will be consequences. I shall live with them, fully aware that what I've done is well and truly unforgivable."* He lowered the paper and looked at his mother.

"This is an outrage," she said. "I never received any letter from him that included a confession of any sort. If we are meant to assume he is admitting to having" — she gulped — "having injured Nicholas —"

"That's precisely what we're meant to assume," Colin said. "And from that, we are

324

meant to draw another conclusion: that you sought revenge for your husband's death and took it in the form of poisoning Lord Deeley."

Pa Demi, Regnal Year Two
28

Kamose, usually the more level-headed one in our relationship, reacted even more strongly to Sanura's strange visit than I had. He was preparing to leave for the Valley the next morning, pulling out clothes from the chests in our living room. He would be gone for the usual eight days.

"I don't like this at all," he said, packing a bundle of personal items he'd take with him: clothing, kohl, his razor, and whatever else he deemed necessary. "She is not well. She may be possessed. I don't want you to see her while I am away and you're unprotected."

"I'm not completely useless, you know. I'm certainly capable of defending myself against loopy females."

"This isn't the time to joke. I'm worried about you being in the house alone."

"I can ask my mother to come if it would put your mind at ease, but I don't think it's necessary."

"I'd feel better if she was with you."

So she came to stay, arriving shortly after the Right Gang had left for the Valley. Like me, she thought the men were overreacting. Father had sided with Kamose. In his view, it was better to take precautions, even if they proved unnecessary, than to have something bad happen. A reasonable enough point of view, I suppose. Mut kept out of my way while I was working, taking over the kitchen from our servant, who wasn't a gifted cook. I had almost forgotten how much better I'd eaten when I still lived with my parents.

Two days passed without event. On the third, shortly before we planned to sit down to eat, Pentu appeared at my door. He explained that he wasn't in the Valley with the other men because he'd been ill.

"It's passed now, though. Only a sore throat, more of a nuisance than anything. I will go back to work tomorrow. I came to see how you are doing."

My mother, standing behind me, urged him to come inside. "It's nice to have a visitor," she said. She brought out beer for all of us, along with some nuts and dried fruit.

"I couldn't have walked past the house without stopping, not only because I wanted to say hello, but because of the delicious aromas coming from within. I have heard stories about your meals. Ahmose is constantly bragging that his wife is the most skilled cook in the village."

I was annoyed that he was flattering my mother. She, however, was amused. "Oh, Pentu, I know how it is with you single men. You eat very badly. You will join us for dinner — that will give you good food and me the opportunity to pressure you to take a wife. You're too old to still be living on your own."

"I know you're right, but I've never thought married life is for me." His tone was serious, his posture humble. Very unlike him. "I'm interested in nothing but my work and wouldn't give a wife the attention she deserves. It would be a failure."

"Not if you found the right woman," my mother said. She was endlessly optimistic. "You're not all that unusual, Pentu. All the men in the village are devoted to their work. It is an honor to hold such a worthy position, to be trusted with working on Pharaoh's tomb. It does not, however, mean that you should shun having a family." She shot him a severe look that made him squirm, but he laughed.

"Not everyone is as lucky as your son when it comes to finding a wife."

"Sanura is a beautiful girl," my mother said. "If only she had an unmarried sister for you." Neither of us mentioned her bizarre behavior, my mother, because she was polite, me, because I had no interest in stirring up drama with Pentu.

"I'm content on my own and am aware of the many bad habits I have that would drive any wife to a constant state of fury. Not all men are meant to be husbands."

My mother shook her head, but I knew she hadn't given up. She called for our servant to bring us plates laden with hot, fresh bread and perfectly cooked duck seasoned with cinnamon. There was wine of the highest quality, as well as pomegranates and figs, and honey cakes to come as well.

The food was heaven, but I would have enjoyed it more without Pentu. His manners were atrocious. He stuffed his mouth too full, chewed loudly, and grunted every time he swallowed. I can only assume these were a few of the bad habits he had referred to, and I agreed that no woman should have to suffer through living with him. It also made me suspect he snored. Not that I had any reason to connect his eating habits to snoring, but doesn't it seem reasonable to expect a person possessing one set of appalling behaviors to also possess another?

Maybe that's not fair; snoring can't be controlled. But Pentu was the kind of man who wouldn't control it even if it were possible.

The conversation as we ate wasn't too aggravating. Some might even describe it as pleasant. I would have, if I trusted Pentu. As it was, I wasn't thrilled by the way he was ingratiating himself with my mother. What was he after?

That was a question that would have to wait for another day, because just as I took my first bite out of a honey cake, we heard someone pounding on the door.

Luxor, 1904
29

I took the page from Lord Deeley's journal out of Colin's hand and scrutinized it. The handwriting looked authentic, and the paper was jagged on one edge. The leather-bound volume from which, presumably, someone had torn it was still in my possession. I retreated to the small cabin we used as a study and pulled out the diary, flipping to the entry nearest by date to the one Kat had found. When I bent back the spine, I could see — only just — the tiny remaining bits of the ripped-out page.

I sat at the desk for a few moments, considering how to best proceed without unnecessarily upsetting my mother-in-law. Could Lord Deeley have followed Nicholas Hargreaves back to Derbyshire after their argument and run him down with his carriage? Of course it was possible, but it wasn't reasonable, not in the least. Furthermore, if he had done so, why on earth would he have been moved to confess his actions to the woman he claimed to love, all these years later?

A question — bizarre and unsettling — started to percolate in the back of my head. I returned to the saloon. "The page does appear to have been ripped out of Lord Deeley's journal and is written in his hand. What any of this means, however, is less clear."

"I did not poison Bertram," Mrs. Hargreaves said.

"I believe you," I said. "Someone — our murderer — has done a rather smashing job of providing strong motives for Mr. McLeod, Mr. Troubridge, Mr. Granard, and you, Mrs. Hargreaves, to want Lord Deeley dead. The letters we have found were all written with the same typewriter. I'm going to telegraph the housekeeper at Lord Deeley's estate in Cornwall to see if there is a machine there. If so, she can send us a sample of the type. It's possible that whoever is responsible is a disgruntled member of the staff — or former member of the staff."

"That would be something," Mrs. Hargreaves said, "but I'm not convinced it would bring us any closer to identifying the murderer. I haven't been to Cornwall in ages, but both Mr. Troubridge and Mr. Granard were frequent guests. Either of them might have used the typewriter deliberately, to throw the police off course."

"Every bit of evidence helps us gain a fuller picture of what happened," Colin said. "Motive isn't the only thing required to prove guilt, compelling evidence is also necessary."

"What about Lady Wilona?" Kat asked. "And Pandora, for that matter?"

"Lady Wilona could have discovered that Deeley was propping her up financially," Colin said. "That would wound her pride, but hardly be reason to poison him. Miss Evans seems entirely peripheral to the case. Her claim about overhearing Mr. Troubridge is nothing more than an amateur attempt at protecting her employer and, hence, her own position and income."

"Let's not forget there is also the missing servant, Ziad, who fled Per Ma'at after the murder, afraid he would be wrongly arrested," I said.

"I'm not sure we should assume arresting him would be wrong," Kat said.

"We can't prove his innocence," I said, "but neither can we offer any explanation of why he would have committed the crime."

"He — like all of the servants — had opportunity," Colin said. "They have access to the butler's pantry."

"And any of them could have acquired cyanide," Kat said. "It's not extraordinarily difficult. Chemists stock it. But surely one must sign a poison register of some sort when buying it?"

"It certainly could be acquired in Luxor," Colin said, "but I have canvassed the chemists there and found no record of anyone known to us buying cyanide."

"A smart person would have used a false name and even a disguise," Kat said.

"Regardless, we know that whoever poisoned the tisane managed to get cyanide, whether in Luxor or elsewhere. If in Luxor, he — or she — did not leave a trail," Colin said.

"Poison often points to a female killer," I said.

"If I ever decide to murder someone, I'll choose a much more hands-on method," Kat said. Her eyes sparkled alarmingly. "I don't take to standing back and watching something happen. A shot to the head or a well-placed stab to the neck is more my style. Active, rather than passive."

"I'd prefer if you stayed away from the business of murder altogether," Colin said.

"Don't be so old-fashioned, Father. I

wasn't suggesting that I'm actually planning to kill someone. There's no need to over-react."

"There is something interesting in what Kat says." I considered the matter. "Women do tend to use poison. It's more difficult for them to physically overpower their victims, particularly if they are men. If I were a man bent on murdering Lord Deeley, and I wanted to implicate Mrs. Hargreaves, I would choose to poison him."

"And then hide evidence giving her a motive," Kat said.

"I'd do that first," I said. "One can't be certain what will happen in the immediate aftermath of a murder, so the only sensible course of action would be to plant the fraudulent evidence before committing the crime — just not too soon, lest someone discover it early. I'd also include something that would cast suspicion on myself. Otherwise, it would be glaringly obvious who was behind it all. Our murderer appears to have done just that. We must figure out which motive catalyzed the actual poisoning. I propose that we look again at everything that happened on the last day of Lord Deeley's life, focusing on the movements of his guests and his servants as well as his own."

"I can remind you what I did," Mrs.

Hargreaves said. "After we docked in Luxor, I remained on the *Timsah*. I took a nap, bathed, and read some of a most disappointing novel by Dickens. Sometimes, the man is simply too much. The only time I left the boat was to post a letter, but I couldn't have been gone more than a quarter of an hour."

When initially describing her actions the morning after Lord Deeley's death, Mrs. Hargreaves had said she'd never left the boat. Which version of her alibi was the truth? Why would she have posted a letter herself? There was a silver tray in the saloon upon which we'd all placed our outgoing mail throughout our trip. If she'd wanted something to be sent urgently, she could have given it to Selim, our indispensable crew member.

"I needn't have gone out at all, of course," she continued, "but I wanted to be certain the letter went out, and you never can entirely trust servants. And a little walk after so many days cooped up on a boat never hurts."

Now, she didn't even sound like herself. I would have expected that sort of explanation from Lady Wilona or some other stereotypically hopeless English holidaymaker. Mrs. Hargreaves was nothing of the sort.

She didn't disparage servants — especially not those she had chosen herself. This behavior was strange and out of character. "What about you, Kat?" I asked.

"I was on the boat and then with you, Lady Emily. We took a quick excursion to Luxor Temple."

"And you?" I asked Colin.

"We've all given our alibis before," he said. "I don't see the use of doing it again. More helpful would be reconstructing Deeley's actions and those of his guests and servants on the day of the murder."

"They've given their alibis before, too," Kat said.

"I trust them far less than I do us."

Conversation was rather stilted for the rest of the evening. Kat and Mrs. Hargreaves discussed their mutual interest in photography but did not stay much longer, and Colin was uncharacteristically quiet when we retired to our cabin. I didn't query him about his reticence. I knew he, too, recognized the change in his mother's story. I saw no reason to doubt the authenticity of the page ripped from Lord Deeley's journal. What he had written appeared incriminating, but there was no specific mention of what he'd confessed, nor of Nicholas Hargreaves. Admittedly, Lord Deeley's words made it sound as if he had committed some grievous offense, but without details, we could only speculate as to what he had done.

Mrs. Hargreaves insisted that Lord Deeley had made to her no confession of any sort. Was she telling the truth? Much as I wanted to believe her, I could not be sure. She'd changed the details of her alibi. What other lies might she be telling?

The next morning at Per Ma'at, we followed the strategy upon which we'd agreed after dinner. Colin would glean what he could from Lord Deeley's guests about the day of the murder, with Kat and Mrs. Hargreaves following up any interesting bits in the guise of making casual conversation. I would focus on the servants.

Querying the gardener and the footmen provided me with no new insight. They all swore they hadn't veered from their normal duties and insisted there was nothing unusual in any of their interactions with their master on the day of his death. The groom mentioned that Lord Deeley set off on a donkey rather than one of his horses when he left for his ride, but explained that this was not unusual. For most Europeans, donkeys were the preferred method of transport when going into the desert.

One of the maids saw her employer going into Mr. Troubridge's room with a dish of apricots, but she was certain it was the fresh fruit, not pits. She said he knew they were his friend's favorite. I then went to the kitchen to see Mahmoud, who had started to seem like an old friend. He liked that I enjoyed his food and that I shared his dismay about Lady Wilona. He was able to give me details of everything Lord Deeley ingested on his last day. He'd started with a cup of tea (no milk, no sugar) in bed at sunrise, followed by kedgeree and coffee for breakfast in the dining room about ninety minutes later. He skipped luncheon in favor of a ride but returned to the house in time for afternoon tea, when he had smoked salmon and dill sandwiches, three scones with clotted cream and strawberry jam, and a frosted tea cake. Finally, of course, came the dinner he had shared with all of his guests, and then, the fatal tisane.

"Did he often forsake luncheon for a ride?" I asked.

"No, it was most unusual. He had a magnificent appetite. I imagine he wanted to save me from preparing something for him to eat. The others were lunching in Luxor, you understand. I was busy with dinner. He had given very specific directions for what he wanted, and you know what a feast it was."

"Was it usual for him to plan elaborate menus?"

"No, he left it to Jones to manage them for the most part and generally ate lighter food when he was here. That is better for the climate in Egypt. These heavy meals . . ." Mahmoud shrugged. "I do not understand why the English want such things."

"Did he tell you why he himself planned the menu for that night?"

Mahmoud grinned. "It was all to impress Mrs. Hargreaves. He carried a flame for her. Is that how you say it? He did not confess this to me, of course, but Mahmoud could see it."

"Did he tell you specifically it was to impress her?"

"Yes, yes he did. He said he wanted her to feel like the queen of Windsor Castle."

"Did you speak to Lord Deeley the day he died?" I asked.

"No, Lady Emily, I did not. Mahmoud, he stays in his kitchen. He does not like going elsewhere in the house."

"When was the last time you saw him?"

"I could not say. I did not realize I should have noted the occasion. It was a grave error, and one I will regret. Mahmoud took for granted his master would always be here."

The next person in line for me to question was Jones, whom I found in his pantry, well-placed to overhear my conversation with the cook. He made no attempt to hide that he'd been eavesdropping.

"I expect you want me to go over my and Lord Deeley's movements on that last day," he said. "The only uncharacteristic thing he did was take that ride. Everything else was perfectly normal." He proceeded to tell me, in excruciating detail, everything that occurred that day and then explained himself. "I only know it so well because I've gone over it countless times in my head, thinking there must have been something amiss, that if I had noticed would have enabled me to stop this awful tragedy."

I was rather horrified at how much Jones recalled. But then, he did seem particularly attached to his employer. I shouldn't have liked it if Davis kept such close watch over me. There is a difference between attentive service and intrusion. That said, the details weren't particularly interesting, let alone enlightening. Lord Deeley left the house early, breakfasting before his guests, to meet us at the dock, and returned soon after the others had gone into town. He retired to his room and remained there until he announced to Jones that he would not take luncheon in favor of a ride.

"How long was he gone?"

"Several hours, I believe, but I can't say I kept track exactly. When he returned he bathed, put on fresh clothes, drank a very fine single malt scotch, and joined his guests in the sitting room. They played charades until the gong rang and it was time to dress for dinner."

"Was it usual for him to drink scotch in the middle of the afternoon?"

"No, madam, it wasn't. I can offer no explanation for why he chose to do it that day."

Perhaps something had happened during his ride that upset him. I wished I knew if he had arranged to meet someone while he was out, or whether he had run into a friend or acquaintance. Otherwise, it was hard to imagine what might have, as it were, driven him to drink. Then again, it was entirely possible he simply liked the sound of a splash of scotch. These might sound like meaningless musings, but nothing in a murder investigation is trivial.

"Were you aware that Lord Deeley felt an attachment to Mrs. Hargreaves?" I asked.

"Heavens, no, madam." Jones looked well and truly horrified. "Lord Deeley would never speak of such things to me."

"Perhaps not, but you are an observant man," I said. "You might have noticed something."

"They were always close, from the time they were children. If there had been an attachment, they would have married. They didn't, so, as far as I am concerned, there is nothing more to be said."

"Lord Deeley is dead, murdered, quite possibly by someone close to him. The more I know about the details of his life, the more likely we are to bring his killer to justice." Beads of sweat appeared on Jones's forehead. He was struggling. It was not easy for a man like him to act in ways he considered undignified. It was unfortunate that I needed him to do so. "I know how loyal you are, and how much Lord Deeley appreciated that quality in you. Nonetheless, speaking freely now wouldn't be a betrayal. It would be a help."

"I'm not sure Lord Deeley would agree. He was an extremely private man when it came to certain parts of his life. It is, I fear, a betrayal to say more, but in the circumstances, I don't know what else I am to do. My own observations told me that he did carry a torch for Mrs. Hargreaves, but he never spoke of it or acted in any way that was less than honorable. So far as I could see, she was never more than a friend to him. I believe this wounded him, but, nonetheless, he carried on admirably, accepting that she could not offer anything beyond friendship. He certainly never pressed her on the subject."

"No, he wouldn't have, would he?" Truth be told, I didn't know whether he would or wouldn't, but I wanted to soothe Jones, just a bit. I could see he was aching to tug at his collar and wipe the sweat from his brow, but he would do neither in my presence. "Mahmoud said that Lord Deeley gave very specific direction for dinner the night we arrived in Luxor."

"Yes, he wanted it to be a particularly festive occasion."

"To impress Mrs. Hargreaves?"

"That was the conclusion I drew."

"Why?"

"He mentioned in passing that she was fond of consommé à la Monaco and that raspberry soufflés glacés had long been a favorite of hers, but made no comments about the food preferences of his other guests."

I nodded. "What do you know of Ziad,

the servant who ran off after the murder?"

"While I'd very much prefer him to be guilty than a friend of Lord Deeley's, I cannot imagine any reason for him to have murdered the man who made it possible for him to support his family. Lord Deeley pays wages far superior to most Europeans here. Ziad won't find any other position that offers similar recompense. If I may speak candidly, the Egyptian police are notorious for torturing suspects. I imagine it was fear of such treatment that prompted him to flee."

"Have you any idea where he might have gone?"

"He comes from a village called Gurneh. I believe all of his family is still there, including both of his wives. His brothers all work for the archaeologists excavating in the region. If I remember correctly, one of them is employed by Mr. McLeod."

Jones didn't know the man's name, but it was enough, for now, to learn that he worked for Mr. McLeod. Knowing that the groom had balked when Kat asked to take horses to Deir el Medina, I asked Jones to arrange for Colin and me to take them, so that we could reach Mr. McLeod's dig as quickly as possible. As I was not dressed for riding, I then sought out Kat, who was close enough to me in size that I could borrow something from her instead of having to return to the boat to change.

"I'm not likely to have anything you'd consider appropriate," she said, a wicked grin on her face. "My boots will be too big, but not dreadfully so. You're welcome to whatever you want, so long as you promise that Father doesn't come down too harshly on me for your appearance."

She meant me to wear her jodhpurs.

PA DEMI, REGNAL YEAR TWO
30

The pounding was so loud, I shot out of my chair, knocking it over. Pentu, on his feet in an instant, grabbed my arm hard enough to leave a bruise.

"Don't answer it," he said. "Let me."

I didn't argue with him, but I didn't obey either. It was my house; I was perfectly capable of answering the door, no matter how loud the knock. I padded into the front room and pulled open the door, Pentu and my mother close behind. No one was there. No human, at least. Sitting on our stoop, pristine and undamaged, were the statues of Ptah and Thoth that had disappeared the last time my tormenter visited the house. I bent over and picked them up. Pentu examined the door. The paint was badly scratched.

"They must have banged on it with a cudgel," he said.

"I don't like this, Meryt," my mother said.

347

"Perhaps you should come to my house. It's not safe here."

I didn't want to leave my house. Maybe that sounds irrational. Irresponsible. Stupid. It probably was all of those things. But I wasn't about to leave my workshop unguarded. I'd already had alabaster destroyed. My father's ushabtis and all the rest of my pieces would be vulnerable if I abandoned them. My mother anticipated that.

"You can bring your work with you. Pentu can help us pack it all into a cart."

"I won't be driven out of my own home," I said.

"How will you be able to sleep, wondering if this person is going to come back?" my mother asked. "When Kamose returns from the Valley, you can go home, Meryt. Until then, you're staying with me."

"I can keep her safe if you will let me," Pentu said. "It's not difficult at all. I can easily reinforce the door so that no one can enter from the front, and I will sleep on the roof, so no one can come in through there. I understand wanting to stay in your own home after such an event. I know you don't like me, Meryt, but you can trust me. You know I experienced something similar, soon after I arrived in Pa Demi. I stopped it before, I can stop it again."

I was feeling more irritated with him than I had any right to be, and it made me feel a twinge of guilt. I didn't like him; he was correct about that. He was ignorant and oafish and coarse. All of that was bad enough, but it was his friendship with Sanura that gave me pause. How could I trust someone who was close to her?

I sighed, ready to accept the least aggravating of the options before me. "Fine. Stay here, protect me. Will that satisfy you, Mut?"

She agreed that it would. "Pentu is a strong man. He will keep you safe."

"I will, of course, not come down into the house at any time unless you call for me, Meryt. I would not disturb you."

"Promise me you'll be careful," my mother said. "I know I can trust you to look after Meryt, but you must not take any unnecessary risks. We want you safe, too."

"I give you my word."

We went back into my living room, where our food was still on the table, but I no longer felt like eating. Pentu was much less disturbed. He finished his meal, then asked to have the rest of mine, saying it was too good to let go to waste. My mother was flattered. I was annoyed. All I wanted was for Kamose to return from the Valley.

Luxor, 1904
31

Kat's clothing fit me better than I had expected. The freedom of movement allowed by the pair of khaki jodhpurs she loaned me was nothing short of astonishing. The expression on Colin's face when he saw me suggested I cut a fine figure in them. I felt rather satisfied. It must be noted he appeared in equal measures impressed and horrified, but he voiced no objection.

Lord Deeley's Arabians, a pair of matched grays, with their chiseled heads, elegant necks, and lithe bodies, were some of the finest horses I had ever seen. They moved like poetry, rhythmic and endlessly graceful, a joy to ride. Because I remembered the way to Mr. McLeod's excavations at Deir el Medina, we did not need a guide. Colin and I were alone, leaving me free to admire his fine seat. Had he possessed golden curls and blue eyes rather than being all dark, he would have been the picture of Alexander the Great astride Bucephalus. Regardless, even Alexander would have envied him if he stood watching that day. We flew across the desert atop the magnificent steeds, the cliffs that ringed Deir el Medina rising before us all too soon. I should have liked another hour's ride at least, but one cannot indulge one's whims during a murder investigation.

There was no sign of Mr. McLeod when we first dismounted. I saw his foreman, a tall man called Hasan, standing in front of the tomb the crew was excavating. The archaeologist, he explained, was inside. The door to the structure was clearly visible in the hillside, leading to a space carved into the rock, but the passage beyond it was dark and close, strewn with rubble. Hasan called to Mr. McLeod, who emerged from the opening covered with dust, a grin on his face.

"Capital to see you both," he said. "I'd love to offer you a tour, but there's not much to see yet. Clearing out this debris is more time consuming than you might think."

Every bit of my body ached to dive inside. Or, rather, crawl. The doorway was tall enough to walk through, but the corridor lowered quickly. How tantalizing to explore such a place, to walk on stones not trod upon by other humans for thousands of years! Despite Baedeker's warning that *a visit to the interior of the Great Pyramid is comparatively uninteresting to the ordinary tourist,* I had enjoyed every hot, dusty, cramped moment of my explorations there. It would have been far more pleasant with fewer ordinary tourists (who were, indeed, unimpressed) and if the guides hadn't been set on rushing us through as quickly as possible. Mr. McLeod's tomb would have neither of these inconveniences.

"It's tempting, McLeod, most tempting," Colin said, "but unfortunately we're here on business. One of your workers is the brother of Ziad, the servant of Deeley's who fled after the murder. We'd like to speak to him."

"Right. I've not the slightest idea who it is, but Hasan should be able to help us figure it out. If, that is, the fellow is willing to be found. Given that the police are interested in locating Ziad, his brother might prefer to remain anonymous."

Fortunately, this was not the case. Hasan himself was Ziad's brother. We sat down with him under the canopy where Kat and I had picnicked with the archaeologists. Hasan seemed a serious, intelligent man, who spoke in measured tones, carefully considering the words he chose.

"I am not happy that Ziad has run off. It is cowardly, even if it is understandable," he said. "If you hope to find him, I'm afraid I will be of no help. He could be anywhere."

"Presumably, he is not being hidden by your family," Colin said.

"No," Hasan said. "That would only serve to put them in a considerable amount of danger. The police in Egypt are not gentle in their methods."

"So I understand," Colin said. "What about Ziad's wives? Have they fled as well?"

"No, no, they are in their home, the house next to my parents' in Gurneh. It is a small village near the mortuary temple of Seti I. Ziad would not have taken his wives with him, not only because it might subject them to the scrutiny of the police should they be found, but also because their presence could prove cumbersome. They do not get along particularly well."

I couldn't imagine they would. Two wives sharing the same husband sounded to me like a perfect recipe for disharmony.

"He would not have gone back to Gurneh, nor would he have tried to disappear in Luxor," Hasan continued. "The town is too small for that. He never liked Cairo and doesn't know it well enough to hide there.

My belief is that he has gone into the desert. There are caves that could offer protection, that are too far away from civilization for the police to find. They do not like the hardships endured without notice by those of us used to the desert."

"Is there any way to trace him?" Colin asked.

Hasan considered the question. "Not after so many days. The sand will have blown and covered any tracks he might have left. I understand you want to find him, but I ask this: Why? I know beyond all doubt that he did not kill his master. A wise man does not bite the hand that feeds him. Is that not an expression of the British? Ziad has two wives and seven children who need to be fed. He would do nothing to risk their well-being. He ran to keep them safe."

"I can't argue with your position," Colin said, "and accept that he had valid reasons to flee. I don't suspect him of murder, but I do believe he may be able to provide crucial details about what happened the day Lord Deeley died."

"You need him to bear witness." Hasan nodded slowly. "This I understand. It is a noble thing to do, and something Ziad would agree to gladly, if his safety could be guaranteed."

"I would never ask you to contact him unless I could be absolutely certain you would not be followed," Colin said.

"Such promises are not often kept," Hasan said. He did not deny the possibility of delivering a message.

"Indeed they are not." Colin held the other man's gaze. "When I give my word, when I offer protection, I consider it sacred. I would never knowingly betray my oath."

"You acknowledge that sometimes things go awry, even among those with the best intentions?" Hasan asked.

"It would be dishonest not to. I'm skilled in my work. I know how to cover my tracks, how to avoid being followed. I'm always discreet. Still, I am only a man, and therefore, fallible. Should you choose to carry my message to your brother, I will do everything in my power — a power that is not inconsiderable — to protect both you and him. Of that, I give you my word."

"McLeod admires you," Hasan said. "He speaks highly of you and has told me that you are a man of honor."

"Am I a man you can trust?" Colin asked.

"I believe you are," Hasan said.

"I need more than to have you simply deliver a message," Colin said. "This situation is too complicated for such things. I must sit with your brother, drink tea with him, and converse. Can that be arranged?"

"The police know you are looking into the matter of the murder," Hasan said. "They do not like it because it undermines them. They have closed the case and already decided Ziad should be condemned. Your meddling is not welcome. I am certain they are keeping a close eye on you. It would not be safe for him to meet you."

"Are they keeping a close eye on me?" I asked.

"On you, Lady Emily? No, I shouldn't think so. A woman doesn't intervene in the affairs of the police."

"So if you were to take me into the desert, to show me something of archaeological significance, for example, they would not take notice, would they?"

"Lady Emily, I would never agree to such an expedition. It would be irresponsible of me —"

"I am an excellent rider and a keen enthusiast when it comes to all things ancient. No one would think twice about me going off into the desert in search of antiquities."

"It would not be appropriate for him to meet with you alone."

I considered my options. Kat was the obvious choice, but I doubted she would satisfy

Hasan's desire for a chaperone. Mrs. Hargreaves's age brought with it more propriety. She was a decent rider and had an adventurous streak. This expedition was just the sort of thing she would have done in her youth, when she traveled the world. "My mother-in-law is a woman of great dignity. Her presence would preserve your reputation, and including my stepdaughter will ensure it looks like an ordinary tourist outing."

Hasan nodded, slowly. "That would be satisfactory. Again, however, I can make no promises. I will alert you when I have further information."

"The quicker all this can happen, the better," Colin said. "If we can prove who killed Lord Deeley, your brother will no longer have to hide."

"That would be good," Hasan said. "Very good."

Shouts came from the direction of the tomb and echoed off the sides of the hills surrounding the site. Hasan leapt to his feet and ran, Colin and I following close behind. We scrambled up the rocky way to the entrance, where Mr. McLeod stood, an enormous grin on his face.

"Don't get too excited," he warned. "We've reached the tomb's chapel, but there's good and bad news. The bad is that, unfortunately, it appears someone was here before us, which may bode poorly for the burial chamber — or chambers, if we're truly fortunate — when we find them. The good, however, is that I can't think when I've seen something so beautiful. You must come inside, if you don't mind crawling and getting rather filthy."

"I don't mind at all," I said. I stepped forward, Colin behind me, and we went with Mr. McLeod into the passage and beyond the door, which he explained would have led into a courtyard.

"Entrance to the burial chambers will be via a shaft either in the courtyard or in the chapel." The passage grew low ten feet or so from the doorway; we had to crouch. We crept along for another hundred feet or so — it was difficult to tell, as the only light came from the lanterns we each held — and then he cautioned us to stop. "We're nearly there now. You'll need to wriggle through the opening, but once you're past it, you'll be able to stand upright."

He went first and guided me as I followed. Kat's jodhpurs made everything easier. Never had I known such easy movement, particularly in such a tight space. Without petticoats to hinder me, I had no trouble crawling into the chapel. Mr. McLeod grabbed my hand and helped me to my feet. I gasped as I looked around.

The chapel was not large, but every inch of it was covered with colors so bright, they might have been painted yesterday. The vaulted ceiling hung over us, an inky sky replete with glittering gold stars. Rows upon rows of hieroglyphs filled the walls, interspersed with scenes depicting gods and a man who, presumably, occupied the tomb.

Colin let out a low whistle after he shimmied through the narrow opening into the room. "Extraordinary. The condition —" He stopped, not finding words adequate to describe what we were seeing.

"It's remarkable," Mr. McLeod said. "There's dashed little damage."

"You said someone was here before you," I said. "Is that why there are no burial goods?"

"A chapel wouldn't necessarily have much in it. The dead man's family would have used it, visiting to honor the deceased, whose name was Ahmose." He held up his lantern, illuminating the hieroglyphs on the wall. "You can see it here. The reason I know that we're not the first to breach the room is because of what's inside. Come."

We followed him to the far corner of the

chapel, where the remains of a wooden box sat on the floor. Mr. McLeod squatted and, with great care, picked up a piece of wood to reveal an alabaster statue, approximately ten inches tall.

"A ushabti?" Colin asked.

"Precisely." Mr. McLeod rose to his feet and held it out to us. "It's alabaster, exceedingly fine quality. Look at the detail on the face. I'm fairly certain this tomb is from the Nineteenth Dynasty. Think Seti I and Ramses the Great. Now, in this period, ushabtis didn't always depict the deceased. Instead, they were shown as servants, which, of course, is what they were intended to be. Here we have a man — you can tell by the style of his wig — with an extraordinarily expressive face. He looks sad, doesn't he? As if he's in mourning for a beloved master, although that might be pushing my fiction too far."

"Is the fact that there is only one what tells you someone else was here?" Colin asked.

"There shouldn't be any ushabtis in the chapel," Mr. McLeod said. "They belong in the burial chamber, where they can serve the tomb's owner as necessary. Finding one here leads me to believe that the tomb was robbed."

I knelt down and looked at the remains of the box. "Perhaps the thief was caught, or at least startled, and dropped what he was carrying. The container broke, but the statues survived. He gathered them up and ran off, never noticing he'd left one behind."

"Your flair for fiction is nearly as fantastical as mine." Mr. McLeod smiled. "It certainly could have happened that way, particularly if the shaft to the burial chamber can be accessed from here. If it's in the courtyard, however, I'm not quite sure how the ushabti wound up here."

"Perhaps the ushabti belongs to a different tomb," Colin said, "and was left here by whoever robbed it."

"That's also possible," Mr. McLeod said.

"Are the chapels always attached to their tombs?" I asked. "I'm thinking of what I've read about the pharaohs' burials. A wholly different matter, of course, but I seem to recall that their mortuary temples aren't always next to their tombs."

"That's correct when it comes to royal tombs," the archaeologist said. "It allowed offerings to be made without anyone knowing the location of the actual burial. A measure of protection against tomb robbers, who were quite active throughout Egypt's history."

"Which suggests the pharaohs' subjects weren't quite so obsessed with religion and ritual as one might think," Colin said. "A man willing to steal from a royal tomb isn't overly concerned about the weight of his heart against that of the feather of Ma'at."

"I suspect it was someone unlikely to have any fear of his heart being devoured by a demon." Mr. McLeod knelt down and picked something up from the floor, something decidedly modern: a Bryant & May's matchbox with a picture of a tiger on it. "I can't hold out much hope for the burial chamber now, but even if there's nothing else to be found here, the painting in the chapel and this charming little fellow make it all worthwhile."

I stood close to him to better see the ushabti. Its face truly was astonishing. It was stylized, like all Egyptian art, but there was such life in his eyes! His lips looked on the verge of a sad smile. No one could doubt he was eager to serve his master in the afterlife, even as he mourned. "What do the hieroglyphs say?" I asked.

"It's a standard text that essentially is the ushabti saying *I am here,* here to work, that is, ready to do whatever is required of him." He carefully moved the little sculpture, turning it over to see the back, and then again to look at the bottom. Something he saw there made him grunt. He sat on the floor, cross-legged, and brought his lantern closer to the sculpture. "This is most unexpected. Egyptian artists didn't sign their work. Yet here, on the bottom, we have a phrase. It's hard to read, the hieroglyphs are so small. Let me see . . . *my way is good.* Not a signature as such, then, but still interesting. I've never seen anything like it."

Colin crouched down. "May I?" Mr. McLeod let him take the statue. Colin squinted at the signs on the bottom of the figure's feet. "This is familiar to me somehow. But surely that's not possible."

"I shouldn't think so," Mr. McLeod said. "Do you read hieroglyphs?"

"No, no, I don't mean to suggest the Egyptian is familiar, but rather your English translation. My father was a collector. I could swear he had a piece with the same phrase written on it."

"What sort of piece?" Mr. McLeod asked.

Colin frowned, then shook his head. "I can't recall. My mother might."

"Maybe it is a signature of sorts," I said, "left by an artist who didn't want his — or her — identity known."

"It's a romantic notion, to be sure," Mr. McLeod said, "but unlikely in the extreme.

Egyptian artists weren't known by name. That is, people did not talk about them as we might banter about Monet or Renoir or that Klimt fellow. They weren't famous in that sort of way."

I couldn't help but relish his examples, as all three were among those I considered friends. "Presumably, someone knew their names, though, at least in the village where they lived."

"Naturally," he said. "Your idea that our artist could have been a woman is unlikely, but not impossible. Sculptor was not a profession normally held by women. They were more likely to be potters or basket weavers. Some worked with textiles, and of course there were the singers in temples. In a village like this one, however, where every family contained craftsmen of the highest skills, it wouldn't be surprising to find talent among the children, girls included."

Colin had gone quiet. He was still holding the ushabti, staring at it, his lips pressed together in a hard line. Something was troubling him, that much was obvious.

"Mr. McLeod, is it possible there was an earlier, legitimate excavation of this tomb?" I asked.

"Absolutely not. There have been concessions granting the right to dig at Deir el

Medina, but there is no record of this tomb in particular."

"So whoever left the matchbox was digging illegally?"

"Yes, there's no question of that. Had it been an authorized excavation, the find would have been reported and recorded. It smacks of someone looking to gather up plunder to sell on the black market. We're fortunate he didn't hack up the walls of the chapel to sell in bits."

"We need to return to Per Ma'at," Colin said, handing the ushabti back to Mr. McLeod. "I must ask my mother what she remembers about my father's collection. Something is not right."

Pa Demi, Regnal Year Two
32

I'll never quite understand how he managed it, but Pentu convinced my mother that she should go home and leave him to protect me. This came as a relief. I wanted to stay in my house, but I didn't want my mother next to me all night. I wanted privacy. The sight of the missing sculptures on my doorstep shattered me. I was desperate for Kamose to come home. That night, I slept on the couch Pentu moved from the roof to our living room; I found no peace there. I was used to watching the stars in the sky above me until I fell asleep. I would wake when the dark blue gave way to streaks of pink and gold, and the sun god Ra, the Horus of the Horizon, was reborn to begin his journey across the sky in his solar barque. That night, inside the house, it felt as if the walls were closing in on me.

When morning finally came, I pulled on the sheath I'd worn the day before but didn't bother to wash my face or apply kohl around my eyes. I called up to Pentu that I was going to see my mother, then slipped out the front door before he could offer to come with me. When I reached her house, I pulled the door open and stepped inside. Neither Bek nor I ever knocked; she didn't like us to. I was about to shout a greeting when I heard Sanura's voice. I crept along the wall of the front room until I reached the doorway that led to the living room. I stayed still and listened.

"It's very, very concerning," she was saying. "Bek would be beside himself if he knew, but I haven't breathed a word to him. He already has enough to worry about. And as for Kamose, it is not my place to warn him about his wife's behavior. That is why I've come to you. She's your daughter. She can be fierce with me and call me a liar, but she won't do that to you."

"I cannot believe any of this, Sanura," my mother said. "Meryt would never betray Kamose. It is not in her to do so."

"I wouldn't have thought so either, but would you have me ignore what my own eyes have seen? She's orchestrated everything to make it possible to have Pentu sleeping in her house!"

"Meryt has no interest in Pentu."

367

"Meryt is skilled in the art of deception."

My mother laughed. "Sanura, Sanura, it is kind of you to be so concerned. You are a good sister. In this case, though, your worry is misplaced. There is nothing between Meryt and Pentu. She does not even consider him a friend, although that may change after what he's doing to try to help her. If it does, such a friendship is wholly appropriate. Pentu is not going to be living in her house. He will only be there until Kamose returns. He got permission to stay away from the Valley so that he could help us. I have decided to consult the Wise Woman for advice. She will know how to best protect Meryt and Kamose from whoever is tormenting them."

"They are in need of no protection. It's all a deliberate invention by Meryt, meant to make it easy for the lovers to meet."

I should have stayed silent, but outrage overwhelmed me. I stormed into the room, grabbed Sanura's arms, and jerked her out of the chair she'd been sitting in. I stopped myself before I slapped her, but only just barely. "You are a liar of the highest order," I said, pushing her away and releasing her arms. She fell back on the floor. "If anyone's husband should be worried about infidelity, it's yours. Bek wouldn't be too happy to hear about your secret rendezvous with Pentu in Thebes."

"You don't know what you're talking about," Sanura said, standing up and straightening her sheath. "Pentu is like a brother to me. I agreed to meet him in Thebes because he told me you were in danger. I thought I was obligated to as you're family. Now it's clear that all of this is nothing more than an attempt to hide your affair. Adultery comes with stiff penalties, Meryt. You should be careful. Stop now, before it's too late."

"Mut, you can't believe her." I was shouting. My mother took me firmly by the shoulders and marched me out of the room and up to the roof, where she ordered me to stay while she dealt with my sister-in-law. She returned a quarter of an hour later. I was pacing and still furious.

"Before you say a word, Meryt, drink this." She gave me a cup of beer. "Slowly. And sit down."

I did as she ordered. It calmed me, a little, which I resented. I had every right to my anger and would get more satisfaction from relishing in it than letting it dissipate. I waited for her to speak.

"Sanura should not have lobbed accusations at you," she finally said, after I'd finished the beer, "but you must remember that her intention coming here was not to incense you. She wanted to talk to me, to appeal for my help, my intervention."

"If she believes I'm involved with that lout Pentu, she's crazier than I thought." I recounted to my mother what had happened when Sanura came to see me, warning me to keep away from Pentu, how she had raved like a mad woman. "If anything, it all makes me think she's the one hiding an affair."

"No, Meryt, there is nothing but friendship between her and Pentu. You know that in your heart, if you will let yourself listen to it."

"You can't know that any more than I can," I said.

"It is true I can't know her feelings, but Pentu's were written on his face last night. He has a deep affection for you. He is a simple man, but I believe an honorable one, and would never act on those feelings. Given how close he and Sanura are, she has no doubt noticed the same thing."

"I agree with nothing that you're saying, but suppose it is true. If they're such great friends, wouldn't she also believe him to be honorable? If that's the case, she wouldn't be flinging accusations at me."

"She does believe Pentu is a man of honor. She thinks you are corrupting him."

I jumped out of my chair. "That's even more outrageous. I am the seducer?"

"Don't let yourself get carried away," Mut said. "No one who knows you well would give credit to such a notion. Sanura does have some strange ideas, ideas that, if aired publicly, could have a bad effect on your reputation, even though they're false. Can you not find it in your heart to better get along with her? She's . . . well." She sighed. "She's not the most intelligent girl in the village. She's a new bride. She feels insecure and threatened by you because she knows how close you and Bek have always been. She's lashing out."

"And that's my fault?" My anger — no, my rage — was making every inch of me tremble.

"Of course it's not. But you're older. You're more mature. You have more experience. You're the one in a position to stop her nonsense. Make friends with her, Meryt, and all of this will go away."

I felt tears spring to my eyes, which infuriated me all the more. "I have tried. Tey has tried. Even she's all but given up. And why is that? Not because she finds Sanura mind-numbingly dull, but because she started to see what Bek's wife is really like. Bek is the one who should be worried, not Kamose."

Somehow, I would have to find a way to prove my position. Otherwise, this torment would never stop.

LUXOR, 1904
33

Colin and I did not go directly to Per Ma'at after we left Deir el Medina; instead, we stopped at the boat. We were both filthy and desperate to bathe. I went first, expecting that Colin would, as was his usual practice, follow me into the bathroom so we could discuss all that had occurred and read the latest outrages in the *Daily Yell,* but he didn't. When I emerged from the tub and went into our cabin to dress, I found that Selim had worked a miracle on Kat's jodhpurs, brushing away all signs of the dust that had coated them. Colin and I planned to ride the horses to the house, so I pulled the trousers back on, along with a crisp cotton blouse and a tailored riding jacket, piled my unruly damp hair on top of my head, and went in search of my husband, whom I found on the deck, a ledger in his hand.

"I hadn't noticed my mother brought

this," he said. "I hadn't even realized it existed, though of course it did. One does keep records of one's collections. My father was a meticulous man. He logged everything."

"This is a list of his Egyptian antiquities?" I asked.

Colin nodded and read aloud. "Three animal sculptures. Baboon, falcon, and cat. Nineteenth Dynasty. Private tomb. Deir el Medina. Hieroglyphs reading *my way is good* on the bottom of the feet."

I sat next to him and looked at the page. The hieroglyphs drawn in the description matched those we'd seen on the ushabti at Mr. McLeod's dig.

"So your father purchased items found in the village," I said. "That's neither shocking nor noteworthy. Mr. McLeod said that no one has officially dug at the specific tomb where he's currently working, but that doesn't mean the sculptor of the ushabti he discovered today didn't make sculptures for other tombs as well."

"No, it doesn't, but given the signature — if we may call it that — is unknown to those in the discipline, how did my father come to have objects bearing it? I assumed, and I presume you did as well, that the argument between him and Deeley about statues was

374

catalyzed by Father learning that Deeley had acquired them illegally. What if it was the other way around?"

"I doubt your father would have bought something illegally," I said, "unless he wasn't aware he was doing so. Perhaps Lord Deeley sold these objects to him, and when your father found out he'd been deceived as to their origin, he was angry, angry enough to throw a book. I imagine he wasn't someone who tolerated his honor being put into question."

"He wasn't," Colin said. "Suppose your theory is correct. We know their argument led to the Egyptologists in Luxor freezing Deeley out. If my father was the one who pressed the issue and made it public, perhaps Deeley was angry enough to follow him to Derbyshire and run him down with a carriage."

"That was only a few days after their altercation, not long enough for Lord Deeley to have any idea that his reputation in Egypt would be irrevocably harmed."

"I don't agree with that," Colin said. "My father could have made it perfectly clear in the course of the argument. He might already have contacted the archaeologists Deeley longed to consider colleagues."

I shook my head. "No, I don't believe it. I

375

didn't know your father, but I know you, and everything your mother tells me suggests you both subscribed to the same principles. Your father — like you — would have privately given Lord Deeley the opportunity to make things right. He wouldn't smear the man's reputation first."

"Granted, but even so, Deeley could have refused. He might have insisted he'd done nothing wrong. Furthermore, it's conceivable that my father was wrong about Deeley's involvement in the situation and accused him unjustly, which would have incensed him."

"We need to speak to your mother," I said. "We're getting carried away with rampant speculation. She is surely in possession of more facts than we are."

He looked more unsettled than I could ever remember seeing him. On our cruise up the Nile, I'd combed through every book we'd brought on the *Timsah* and had never seen the volume detailing his father's antiquities. Mrs. Hargreaves must have brought it with her and kept it in her cabin until she went to Per Ma'at. An understandable choice, given that she had met her husband in Egypt. She might have been feeling nostalgic about the things they'd bought on subsequent trips. Yet, she'd given the entire collection to the British Museum; I was surprised that she'd kept back his records. Surely the keepers would have wanted — insisted, even — they remain with the objects.

Colin returned, wearing a fresh set of tweeds. We set off without delay. The Arabians would have loved to gallop all the way to Per Ma'at, but he kept to a slow, measured pace. I did not blame him for being less than eager to confront his mother. When we arrived at the house, we rode to the stables and handed the horses to the groom. I was sad to leave them. The experience of flying across the desert to Deir el Medina was incomparable; I longed to do it again.

Inside, Lord Deeley's guests were dispersed in their usual fashion. Mrs. Granard was in the sitting room working on her needlepoint while her husband read the *International Herald Tribune.* Even that paper was reporting on the troubles in Luxor, sparing the reputations of no one staying at Per Ma'at. Dr. Rockley was on the settee with Miss Evans, looking through a book of watercolors depicting ancient Egyptian ruins. Lady Wilona was nowhere to be seen; Miss Evans explained she had gone to meet an acquaintance in Luxor for tea. Kat was at the chessboard but had no opponent. She had inherited from her father a love of solving chess problems; a volume devoted to them was next to her. Even so, she jumped up when she saw us and came along to find her grandmother.

Mrs. Hargreaves was in the courtyard with Mr. Troubridge, who went inside as soon as Colin asked to speak to his mother privately. He showed her the ledger. "Why didn't you tell me you still had this?" he asked. "Or that you'd brought it to Egypt?"

"Because neither is true," she said. "All the records pertaining to your father's collection went to the British Museum. I haven't seen them since."

"This was on a bookcase aboard the *Timsah*," Colin said.

"I can offer you no explanation as to how it arrived there."

"We can consider that question later," I said. "There's something more important at the moment." I told her about the animal statues and the hieroglyphic signature.

"Do you remember where he bought them?" Colin asked.

"What you're really asking is whether Lord Deeley and your father argued about them, isn't it? And if so, did that inspire Bertram to run down my husband with his carriage?"

"It's rather fantastical," Kat said.

She sighed. "I'm afraid your speculation has some truth to it. It was the provenance of those statues that spurred the argument, and yes, Nicholas acquired them through Bertram. I wasn't privy to the details. Beyond that, I can tell you nothing except that I have no reason whatsoever to believe Bertram would have lashed out violently at anyone."

"Obviously, when Mr. Hargreaves became aware of the irregularity in provenance, he wanted to set it right," I said. "Did he tell you what measures he intended to take?"

"We never discussed it. He died before we could."

Colin was silent.

I drew in a deep breath, held it for a moment, and blew it out. "Right. First, I would like to state outright my sincere belief that you, Mrs. Hargreaves, had nothing to do with Lord Deeley's murder. You're far too sensible to hold a grudge for twenty years and then exact revenge."

"I should hope so," Mrs. Hargreaves said. "To suggest otherwise is ludicrous. Now, then, I have something pertinent to the case to tell you. Bertram's tisane was delivered today, by a local boy. He told me it comes from an apothecary in Luxor. I called into the establishment this morning. Bertram had a standing order with them for the past seven years. As to why he chose to tell everyone it came from Constantinople, I could not say. It's an insensible thing to have done."

"We might not always understand what drives them at first glance, but people rarely do things that are truly insensible," I said.

"I don't agree with that sentiment at all," Kat said. "Most people of my acquaintance behave in ways that are wholly insensible. It's charming."

I found this hard to believe, the charming part, at any rate. "We know he was intent on keeping the tisane only for himself," I said. "Did the apothecary tell you anything about the ingredients or intended purpose of the concoction? Was it outrageously expensive?"

"Expensive, yes, but not outrageously so, not for a person of Deeley's wealth," Mrs. Hargreaves said. "As for ingredients, I have the list. It seems wholly innocuous, but purports to support one's health in a manner that will extend one's life. It was not a standard tisane. The apothecary developed it specially for Bertram."

"So he was looking for a Fountain of

Youth?" I asked.

"As do many men his age," Mrs. Hargreaves said. "Clearly he was satisfied with the results or he wouldn't have kept buying it."

"Perhaps I should look into it," Kat said. "It's never too early to think about preserving one's appearance."

"This was more about vitality than looks," Mrs. Hargreaves said. "The apothecary explained that European visitors often request custom formulations. It's all the rage, apparently. The lure of exotic medicine and ancient recipes, or something of that sort. Vague promises of dramatic results backed up by nothing. Bertram asked that brahmi, the leaves of the ginkgo tree, and something called ashwagandha be included in his preparation. All of these are supposed to provide myriad benefits that enhance one's physical well-being."

"Are any of them particularly expensive?" I asked.

"No, but the fourth ingredient upon which he insisted was gold powder, which explains the rather steep price."

"Gold powder?" Colin sounded incredulous. "Deeley never struck me as the sort of chap who would fall for that kind of fairy tale."

"It is used in Indian medicine, I believe, as are brahmi and ashwagandha."

"Which leads me to wonder that he claimed the tisane came from Constantinople," I said. "India would have made more sense. Why the lie?"

"Constantinople sounds far more exotic," Kat said. "It's not part of the wretched British Empire."

"Perhaps it was meant to make stronger his insistence that no one else use it," Mrs. Hargreaves said. "Bertram had a generous nature. He would have felt odd about refusing to share the tisane. Pretending that it came from outside the Empire and was difficult to get would have prevented his guests from pushing the issue."

"And we're to believe he didn't want to share it because of the price?" I asked. "Surely it doesn't cost more than many of the wines he serves his guests, let alone his whisky."

"The apothecary warned him that the ingredients are quite powerful," she said. "One could not necessarily predict how a random individual might react to them. It's likely he was trying to avoid causing anyone adverse effects."

"So he did consider it a medicine," I said, "and he believed drinking a precious metal would benefit his health. He wasn't the first man seduced by the supposed powers of gold."

"Rich men believe what they want," Colin said. "My question is why did he want to believe in the power of this tisane?"

"Well that's simple enough to answer," Mrs. Hargreaves said. "His father died relatively young. He didn't want to suffer the same fate."

"What was his condition?" I asked.

"It seemed to me that he'd long been generally unwell," she said. "It wasn't any one specific thing. Some people have a tendency toward ill health. Bertram's father was one of them."

"Even in his youth?" I asked.

"That, I couldn't say. I only know he had his struggles later in life. I can understand Bertram wanting to avoid a similar fate. It's why he always made a point of keeping physically fit. *Mens sana in corpore sano* and all that."

"Inappropriate though it may sound, his attempt at remaining virile might have been inspired by his affection for you, Grandmama," Kat said. Mrs. Hargreaves sniffed but did not reply.

"Regardless, Lord Deeley concocted — with the assistance of the apothecary — a tisane he thought would protect him from the ravages of old age," I said. "He did seem the picture of health."

"Indeed," Colin said. "No one would ever have considered him infirm. Perhaps we're wrong to dismiss the tisane's powers and should ask the apothecary to start sending it to us."

"He'd be delighted at the income it would provide," Mrs. Hargreaves said. "He told me that he gets frequent requests for gold powder. It seems we haven't come all that far from medieval alchemists."

"I'd argue they were more sensible," I said. "One can immediately grasp the appeal of being able to make gold. Wanting to consume it, however, is much dodgier." My mind was reeling, but I could not afford to lose focus. I excused myself and went off in search of Jones, whom I needed to question about the typewriter. He came to me in Lord Deeley's study.

"Do please sit down," I said, installing myself behind the desk.

"I'm more comfortable standing, if it's all the same to you, madam."

"Of course. I understand there is a typewriting machine at the estate in Cornwall. Do you know how often it is used?"

"Lord Deeley bought it for his steward,

thinking it would make him more efficient. The man never took to it, though. It is I who uses it more than anyone. It's a rather spectacular thing. Far quicker than writing things by hand, once one becomes accustomed to it."

"That machine was used to write the letters we've found in this house," I said. "All of them. Who else had access to it?"

The butler paled and swallowed hard. "Anyone, I suppose. It's not as if the steward's office was off limits to the household."

"So Lord Deeley's guests might have used it?"

He brightened a bit at the suggestion. "It is possible, madam, but I can't say with confidence that any of them did."

I did not press him on the subject, but I would have to consider how readily he admitted to using it himself. If he were responsible for his master's death, this fit neatly into the pattern of concocting evidence that was at once potentially ruinous and at the same time too heavy-handed and obvious.

"There's one other thing, and it's most serious," I said. "There are rumors that Lord Deeley was involved in the death of Nicholas Hargreaves, who was killed in a carriage accident. I don't believe there is any truth to the gossip and would very much like to find evidence that could put the stories to bed, once and for all."

"I am most shocked," Jones said. "I've never heard a word about this, not here, not in England. Naturally, I will do whatever I can to help."

"Lord Deeley kept a journal. Was that long a habit of his?"

"Yes, madam. He keeps the completed volumes in his library in Cornwall."

"Not somewhere more private?" I asked.

"No, madam. He felt rather strongly that the record of his life offered insight into the history of the era in which he lived and, as such, was important enough to be considered of public interest. He'd often talked of publishing them, although not the ones pertaining to his archaeological activities."

"Could you have anything that includes these dates" — I wrote a range that covered a year before and after Mr. Hargreaves's death on a piece of paper and handed it to the butler — "sent here as quickly as possible? Personal journals and records of his excavations."

"Of course, madam. I shall send a telegram to the housekeeper at once."

I thanked him and breathed a sigh, not quite of relief — it was too soon for that —

but comforting all the same. I desperately wanted to prove Mr. Hargreaves had not been murdered, not only to spare Colin and his mother further pain, but also to convince myself that Mrs. Hargreaves had no motive for murder. Most of me — nearly all, in fact — believed she had nothing to do with it, but I could not deny that my opinion was molded, at least in part, by a desire that she be innocent. Wanting is not getting. I could not let myself stand in the way of the truth.

When Kamose returned home after his eight days in the Valley, I did not need to tell him what had happened while he was gone. Pentu had taken care of that, intercepting Kamose on his way home and sparing no effort to cast himself as the hero of the piece. It irritated me, more than it should have. I still didn't trust the man. It probably didn't help that both my parents, as well as Bek and my husband, wouldn't stop lauding him. He'd ingratiated himself with my family, just as he'd done with Sanura's when he first moved to the village.

"That's not a fair accusation, Meryt," Kamose said, after sitting through my rant on the subject. "Sanura's father took Pentu under his wing. Pentu was not imposing on him. And it made sense — they're both stonecutters. Dedi chose to mentor him."

"I don't claim I'm being reasonable," I said, "but I'm still convinced Pentu and Sanura are behind everything happening to us."

"Why?" Kamose asked. "How do they benefit? I can see that Sanura might take pleasure in tormenting you, but she could achieve the same effect in much easier ways. Gossip and goading would be just as effective so far as she's concerned. Tearing you down socially is the sort of thing I'd expect from her. It would make her feel good and I'm certain it would increase her standing with her friends. As for Pentu, he's like a brother to her, so he would do anything she asked, but, again, why? What could they hope to accomplish?"

"You imply that they're rational," I said. "I don't believe Sanura is any longer. I think she's going mad."

"Have you told Bek this?"

"No."

"Presumably because you know you don't have the evidence to support your claim. She was somewhat unhinged in one conversation. That's hardly proof of madness."

I didn't argue with him. What was the point? Instead, I went to my workshop and started a new piece. Not one of my father's ushabtis. I selected a chunk of limestone from my materials and picked up a hammer and chisel. I worked feverishly, only half aware of what I was doing. Limestone isn't too hard, so the work moved quickly, and soon I had revealed the basic form the sculpture would take. The face was human — a woman, bewigged and beautiful — the body that of a cobra. My hands seemed to work without direction as I focused on the details. Her eyes. Her lips. The scales on her coiled body. This was Meretseger, the Peak of the West, Lady of the Sky, She Who Loves Silence: the cobra goddess who watched over the royal necropolis and Pa Demi. She was patron to all of the workers in the village and quick to show mercy. When necessary, she would lash out viciously against those bent on harm.

Ra's barque had disappeared into bright streaks of red in the sky by the time I had the basic form of the sculpture complete. I had not stopped all day, even to eat. Kamose knew my habits. He brought jugs of water, silently placing them on my workbench, but did not disturb me.

I stayed up all night, ignoring Kamose's pleas that I eat, that I come to bed. I finished just as the sun was beginning to rise. I ate a handful of figs and drank as much water as I could. And then, without waking my husband, I slipped out of the house, taking three statues with me: Meretseger as well as those of Ptah and Thoth that had been stolen and returned. I set off for the mountain, to my cave. That was where they belonged, where they would be safe. I had gone no more than a dozen or so paces when I saw Pentu, his face etched with worry, watching me.

"I'm going with you," he said. "I've seen the danger and I now know from whence it comes. I can no longer consider Sanura a friend. She is evil."

LUXOR, 1904
35

The next morning, we received another lengthy letter from the boys. Tom reported he was hard at work on his novel chronicling the adventures of the pharaoh Thomasmose. Richard was reading the Icelandic sagas. Henry was still insisting they were coming to Egypt. He included details that revealed an unsettling knowledge of train and ship timetables. Frankly, it was a relief after reading that to go back to thinking about murder. I penned a note to the Inspector of Monuments for Upper Egypt, an Englishman called Howard Carter, asking to set up a meeting. I wanted to speak with him about illegal excavations at Deir el Medina. That done, I went to Per Ma'at, having decided to turn my attention to the dead man's collection of antiquities, to see if anything in his collection bore the hieroglyphic signature of the ushabti Mr. McLeod found at Deir el Medina.

Jones volunteered to assist me. We looked at every object in the house but uncovered nothing marked *my way is good.* Jones then suggested that we consult the inventory Lord Deeley kept. Listed within were eight pieces described as stamped with the hieroglyphs in question: a set of five ushabtis and statues of the gods Ptah, Thoth, and Meretseger. We combed through the house again, but they were not to be found. There were so many ushabtis we could not determine where the missing ones belonged, but when we entered his master's bedroom, dark concern crept across Jones's face.

"I'm horrified that I didn't notice this earlier. I have not taken note of the contents of the room since his death, but it's obvious to me now that things are gone. On one bedside table was a grouping of statues — I believe them to be the statues of the gods mentioned in the inventory and am certain they were there the day he died. On the other was a set of canopic jars."

"What about the jars?" I asked.

"I can't say I noticed them," Jones said. "I serve — served — both as Lord Deeley's valet and his butler. I first came into the household as a footman, long ago. After his father's death, Lord Deeley asked me to serve as his valet. He hired a new chap when

I rose to the role of butler, but after some years, that individual left for another position and Lord Deeley asked if I would take on those duties as well. It would not be an onerous burden as I have the household supremely well organized, so I did not object. As such, it was I who helped him dress that morning. He had left a pair of cuff links on the table with the sculptures, and I fetched them so he could wear them that day."

"Were the sculptures still there when he returned from his ride?" I asked.

"I'm afraid I could not say with any confidence. It was only due to the cuff links that I took notice of them in the morning."

I asked him to summon the maid who had cleaned the room that day. She was a petite woman still in the first flush of youth, with dark liquid eyes and hair so black it was almost blue. She couldn't positively remember either the statues or the jars being in the room on Lord Deeley's final morning but thought it likely she would have noticed their absence.

"They were not there the next morning, of that I am sure," she said. "I assumed the police had taken them. Or that one of Lord Deeley's friends had, to have them at his funeral. They are most powerful gods, you know, even if they are ancient."

"But surely no one believes in them now," I said.

The maid shrugged. "I see no wisdom in rejecting the aid of any god who might offer it. I am open to all avenues of help, especially when it comes to securing a comfortable place in the afterlife."

I did not argue; I could remember thinking along similar lines not so long ago. I didn't believe the items were removed for funerary purposes, but it was possible that someone took them thinking they could be sold for a decent amount. Most people without a knowledge of archaeology or the antiquities market assume that anything ancient would fetch a tidy price.

If they'd been stolen, it was most likely after Lord Deeley was already dead. If I was lucky, the thief would have sold them to a dealer in Luxor.

That evening, Mr. McLeod called on us at the *Timsah*. He had located the burial chamber of his tomb, and it appeared to be intact. Though not filled with the gold objects a royal burial would include, there was no question that this was an astonishing and significant find.

"This will tell us so much about the lives

of the craftsmen in the village." He was buzzing with palpable excitement. "It will take ages to remove everything, but now I shan't have trouble securing funding. The painting is extraordinary, and you can still see the marks in the dust where someone swept before sealing the tomb. It's beyond anything I could have hoped for."

We celebrated with champagne and, when the moment was right, told him about the objects that had vanished from Lord Deeley's collection. Mr. McLeod immediately started to pen a list of dealers with dubious scruples, those who would be unconcerned about the provenance of the objects they acquired. Selim, who had brought the wine, heard us discussing this and cautioned that we would get nowhere by swooping in and asking direct questions. That was considered impolite. First, we had to admire the wares in the shop. Then, we must inquire after the health of the owner and the health of his family. An exchange of banal flattery would follow. After that, we might be offered a cup of tea, which Selim counseled us to accept. Only after that had been drunk, he said, we could begin — gently — probing about the sculptures.

I was grateful for his advice. The pronounced cultural differences between our countries were numerous, and I had no interest in offending anyone's sensibilities. To do so would be not only rude, but also entirely counterproductive. Colin and I set off the next morning, and we followed Selim's guidance to the letter. This resulted in the consumption of an inordinate amount of tea, but very little else. No one admitted to having seen, let alone purchased, Lord Deeley's missing sculptures or canopic jars. I'd hoped to be done in time to meet with Mr. Carter at two o'clock, but it was not to be. By half one, we had visited only two-thirds of the establishments. I left Colin to continue and went to the Karnak Hotel for my appointment.

Mr. Carter was waiting for me on the hotel's terrace. He was a charming — albeit awkward — man, probably slightly younger than I, intelligent and eager, happy to assist in any way he could. He was the sort of individual who had little interest in society, a quality that endeared him to me at once. I had brought Mr. McLeod's ushabti, explained where it had been found, and then told him about the similarly marked pieces formerly in Colin's father's collection as well as those now missing from Lord Deeley's collection.

"Yes, it's fascinating, truly," he said,

examining the ushabti. "Egyptians didn't sign their work. I've never seen a case like this before. I could imagine the animal sculptures your father-in-law owned are an aberration, but it's very odd to find ushabtis bearing the same mark."

"I realize Mr. Hargreaves acquired his pieces long before you were an inspector, but hoped you might be able to recall rumors, stories — anything, really — about illegal digging at Deir el Medina."

"There's far too much of that everywhere in Egypt," he said. "You're thinking sometime around 1883? That's right about when Lord Deeley had his falling-out with the Egyptologists working in Luxor. There was an incident — I checked the date after I received your note — in December of 1882. My counterpart was called to Deir el Medina after people had noticed signs of illegal activity in an area covered in debris from long ago rockslides. He didn't find much and nothing came on the market that suggested the thieves had, either. The activity stopped after that. It's entirely possible that these pieces you mention are connected to whatever had been going on there. As for the ushabti McLeod found, my guess would be that whoever was digging had discovered the chapel and was using it to store artifacts.

When he heard the inspector planned to investigate — they always find out in advance, no matter how hard we try to keep it quiet — he collected his goods and covered his tracks, but left this little fellow behind."

"No one had any idea who was digging there?" I asked.

"Ironically, many of the archaeologists working in Luxor — this was before my time, you understand — believed Lord Deeley had been poking around Deir el Medina, but they couldn't prove it. That's part of the reason everyone turned on him when he sold a friend objects of dubious provenance. I presume they were your father-in-law's sculptures."

"I suspect you're right. Were there ever any formal accusations against Lord Deeley?"

"No, not at all," he said. "A gentleman of his standing, especially in those days, would not have been held to high academic standards. We try to do better now, but it's a constant struggle. The desert is endless, Lady Emily, and I can only be in once place at a time."

Just then, a striking lady dressed in trousers and a flattering long jacket, with a pith helmet atop her jet-black hair, hailed Mr. Carter as she stepped onto the terrace. She carried a parasol and had a belt around her waist from which hung an array of useful tools. Mr. Carter introduced us, and for a blissful half hour, we conversed about Egypt (she preferred Luxor Temple to Karnak) and archaeology and the fact that she, too, had been harassed by overzealous reporters from the *Daily Yell*. Apparently, Mr. Mallaby didn't ordinarily cover Egypt, and it sounded as if his colleague who did was even more troublesome. It gave me some comfort to know our plight could be worse. We chatted until I saw Colin approaching the hotel and excused myself, eager to see if he had managed to track down the missing antiquities.

Alas, he had not. We walked back to the boat, where Mr. Mallaby was hovering by the dock. He shouted questions louder and louder as we crossed our gangplank, but I turned to speak to him only when we were standing on the deck.

"You'll find no sources for your libelous articles here," I said, "and when the murder is solved, you can be sure you will receive no comments from any of us."

"The truth outs, Lady Emily," he said. "Perhaps you should be asking yourself why you're so bent on protecting people of such dubious morals. Where there's smoke, there's fire, and I've never seen more smoke than that gathering around Troubridge, Granard, and your mother-in-law. If you think Mrs. Hargreaves is innocent, you'd better encourage her to talk to me. I can help rehabilitate her reputation, but only if I know the truth."

We did not respond to this inanity, but instead went into the saloon on the boat, where he could no longer bother us. There, a message was waiting for Colin. He opened it to read, and looked at me, his eyes serious.

"It's from Hasan. His brother will meet you tomorrow, first thing in the morning. I'll send for Mother and Kat. They can stay on board tonight, so you can leave from here, away from the prying eyes of Lady Wilona and the rest. I'll arrange for horses and will follow you at a safe distance."

"Ziad did not kill Lord Deeley," I said. "We'll be in no danger."

"I don't suspect him, but I can't prove his innocence," Colin said. "Furthermore, the murderer may be watching. I'll not risk your safety."

I knew better than to argue; he was using that tone. Furthermore, his work ensured that he was well equipped to trail us without being seen. Confident though I am in my abilities, I do not object to being looked after, at least not entirely. There is a difference between capable and foolish, and I'd learned not to reject help in a vain attempt to make myself appear stronger. There is power in knowing one's limits.

Hasan's message wasn't the only thing waiting for us. I had a letter from Sisley Weldon's sister, so full of revelation it boggled my mind. Mr. Troubridge was Miriam's father, and Sisley had never loved another man. When she found herself pregnant, she sought advice from her lover's best friend, Lord Deeley. He told her in no uncertain terms that Mr. Troubridge would not want the child. I let Colin read it but decided to wait until after tomorrow's meeting with Ziad to decide how to handle it. In addition, a response arrived to the telegram I'd sent to Lord Deeley's housekeeper in Cornwall. She confirmed that there was a typewriter on the estate, kept in the steward's office. The sample she sent of the machine's type was a perfect match for the letters we'd found at Per Ma'at.

Mrs. Hargreaves and Kat arrived at the *Timsah* in time for dinner. They would send word to Per Ma'at that they were staying on the boat because they were too tired to return to the house. None of us would sleep much that night, not with the anticipation of the next day's activities hovering over us.

PA DEMI, REGNAL YEAR TWO
36

Pentu was the last person I wanted to come to the cave with me, but I had to admit he was the only one who took my concerns about Sanura seriously. Maybe I could trust him. At any rate, I couldn't physically stop him from following me, so I didn't bother to try. We trudged across the desert toward the base of the mountain and started up the winding path.

"I'm worried about you, worried about what she might do." He sounded entirely sincere. "Your husband is letting you down. I won't make the same mistake."

I didn't like him criticizing Kamose. It was one thing for me to be irritated with him. Pentu making accusations was something entirely different. "Wives get to say things friends don't."

He smiled and mumbled an apology. He looked more attractive when he showed a little humility. Not that he'd ever be handsome. It was just that he wasn't wholly repulsive. Maybe my father was right about him improving as you got to know him. We climbed up and up, just as Ra's barque was rising in the sky. Finally, we reached the spot where I guided us off the path toward the cave.

"You'd never know this was here," Pentu said as we approached the entrance. "How did you find it?"

"I was on top of the mountain when a storm started. I thought I was doomed. The lightning was like nothing I'd ever seen. I tried to make my way down, but darkness fell and the rain was coming so hard, I couldn't find the path. I prayed to Meretseger, the goddess of the mountain. She led me here."

"You come here to pray?" he asked.

I nodded. We stepped inside. I placed the statues I'd brought into the niche carved into the wall, raised my hands on either side of my head, and prayed. Pentu might have been praying, too. I was too caught up in my own words to notice his. That changed, however, when I felt his arm around my waist. He was right behind me. I could feel his breath on my neck.

"This is nice, being here together," he whispered. "I've wanted you for a long time,

Meryt. You didn't make it easy, did you, but I've always liked a bit of a fight."

I tried to spin around and free myself from him, but he only pulled me closer, so I decided to try to laugh it off instead. "Don't be ridiculous. I'm not the fighting sort. When do you go back to the Valley?"

"Oh, Meryt, don't." His lips brushed my shoulders and I felt his thick tongue on my skin. I started to retch. He flung me down onto the ground and kicked me in the gut. "There's a time for all things. I thought the time for fighting was done, but if you want more, I'm game. Is that how you like it? I wouldn't have guessed."

"Leave, right now, and I won't tell anyone what you've done."

Now he laughed. "Meryt, Meryt, what makes you think anyone would listen to you? I'm your friend. Your parents are grateful for the protection I've given you. Even your beloved Kamose is happy to have me in his house. He trusts me. Trusts me so much that he didn't object when I had to spend the night."

"You slept on the roof. I didn't."

"You came up there to lie with me. Or so I'll tell Kamose." He grabbed a handful of my hair and tugged it, hard. "And then there was the afternoon when you needed me to carry alabaster for you. I took you in your silly little workshop."

"None of that happened and you know it better than anyone."

"I do, don't I? That's the delight of it. I know it. You know it. No one else does. They will only know what I tell them."

"Kamose would never believe you."

"Kamose is as jealous as the next husband, and the penalty for adultery is steep. Do you really want to risk it? Come, we will enjoy each other in this precious cave, the place where the goddess of the mountain led you. Don't you see? She brought you here so that today, we could be here together. We will take our pleasure, now, and again. Whenever either of us desires it. No one will be the wiser."

"I will never desire it. You disgust me."

"I like that, too. A little fight, but not too much." He touched my face; I flinched and pulled away.

"Don't touch me," I said.

He laughed again. "I will do what I want. Who are you to stop me? Do as I say, and I will tell no one. Deny me what I want and I will go to your husband."

"You would be punished, too."

He shrugged. "The penalty I would face is not so harsh as yours would be. I'm willing to take the risk. Are you?"

"Stop it, Pentu."

It was Sanura. I don't know how she knew where we were. She followed us, I guess. I hadn't noticed.

"I won't stand by and let you do this to her, too," she said.

"What are you going to do?" He stepped away from me and in one swift movement struck her on the head, so hard that she flew into the rock wall. "You can't stop me. It's an affront that you'd even suggest it." He hit her again, and again. Blood from the resulting gashes streamed down her face. I struggled to my feet and looked around for something I could use as a weapon. There was nothing but my statues and a small pottery brazier. Pentu wasn't paying me any attention. He was totally focused on Sanura. "I expect better from you, girl. We've enjoyed each other. Don't ruin it now." She'd fallen to the ground and wasn't moving. He kicked her, hard, in the lower back. She moaned.

I didn't know what to do. I rushed at his back, leapt up, flinging my legs around his waist and my arms around his neck, pulling as hard as I could. Sanura opened her eyes. Somehow she managed to move, rising to her feet and kicking Pentu in the groin. He moaned and crouched down. I kept the pressure on his neck, even as my hands and arms started to shake from the strain. Sanura pushed her fingers into his eyes. He screamed, but then he stopped and went limp.

"I think he's dead," I said.

Sanura staggered out of the cave. I didn't blame her for fleeing. I released my grip on Pentu's neck and laid him on his back so that I could listen for the sound of his heart. It was still beating. I needed to run, too. He stirred. His eyes were bloody, but he opened them. He grabbed me by the arm.

That was when I realized Sanura hadn't fled. She'd gone for a weapon. She flew back into the cave, holding a rock bigger than her head high above her. She rushed toward Pentu and slammed it down. His skull split with a sickening sound and she collapsed onto the ground.

"I knew he meant to kill me as soon as he started hitting my face. He was always careful before not to leave marks where anyone else could see them. Once I was married, he couldn't hit me anymore, but he knew he could control me by threatening to tell Bek we were lovers." She closed her eyes and grimaced. Even I could see her injuries were severe. Blood poured from her ears and her skin was gray and cold to the touch. "I can't live through this, Meryt. I don't want to. My time is over. I never wanted to betray your brother. It started long before then. Pentu came to me, just like he came to you, after making sure everyone who loved me trusted him. He threatened me, just like he threatened you, but I didn't have the strength to fight back, not until today."

"I will run and get the Wise Woman," I said. "She will help you. You'll survive, I —"

She half choked, blood coming from her mouth. "We both know that's not possible. I don't want to. My time is over. I'm ready to be done with this life." Her eyes rolled back in her head and she struggled to speak. "Make this my tomb. Bek will decorate it. You will furnish it. No one will ever know what he's done. Promise me, promise me Bek will never know."

"I promise."

"I wanted to warn you, but I didn't know how. First, I hated you too much. You had everything I didn't. A simple life, with no pain or complication. And then I was jealous. Jealous that Pentu wanted you, even though I didn't want him, not at all. How does that make sense? I knew what he would do to you, though, and even though I despised you, I realized I couldn't let that happen. By the time I tried to warn you, it was too late. You hated me, too. My efforts were too little and too scattered. I thought when I told you to destroy your sculptures because they had magic in them and warned you to keep away from him at the same time, it would lead you to see how serious the situation was. It wasn't the right approach. I'm not good with people. I never have been. I didn't know what to do."

Tears ran hot on my cheeks. She should have told me what Pentu was doing to her; she should have told someone. But who? Would any of us have believed her? She was right. I hated her, too, and in doing so made it possible for Pentu to keep hurting her. Why did we shut each other out? Why did we not recognize that we could be allies? Why did we let jealousy consume us?

"He used me to help torment you. I did drug the wine you and Bek drank at my house. I returned the statues he had stolen to your doorstep. He wanted you afraid and vulnerable. It was wrong of me, but I was desperate to have him transfer his attentions to someone else."

"It doesn't matter anymore," I said. "He can't hurt you ever again."

"Hold my hand." I did as she asked and

411

sat there, forever, or so it felt, and then she stopped breathing. Then it didn't feel like forever anymore. It felt like not nearly long enough. Sobs consumed me. I collapsed onto her, weeping, not noticing that outside, a storm had started, as strong as the one that came the day the goddess of the mountain first led me to this cave. I would stay there, with her body and Pentu's, until the storm stopped. What would happen then?

Luxor, 1904

37

I was up before the sun rose and can't say for certain I'd slept at all. Mrs. Hargreaves, Kat, and I mounted the horses awaiting us. Hasan had given Colin a map for us to follow, but we hardly needed it. I'd had visions of a rendezvous far out in the desert, but Ziad had arranged to meet us in a shockingly public place: the mortuary temple of the great female pharaoh Hatshepsut at Deir el Bahri on the west bank of the Nile, only about five and a half miles from Luxor. Sometimes hiding in plain sight is the wisest choice. Ziad instructed me to wear a red flower on my jacket so that he could recognize us.

The ride was extremely pleasant. The morning air was still cool, and the horses, though not as splendid as Lord Deeley's Arabians, were equal to the task. We soon left the verdant strip along the river and crossed into the desert, after which we had to traverse only a short distance before the colonnaded terraces of the temple came into view, strong horizontal lines against the towering limestone cliffs rising behind them. Here, there were no towering pylons, no jumble of structures, no clutter, only an imposing simplicity. The ancients called the site Djeser-djeseru — the Sublime of the Sublimes — and the name was more than appropriate. To my mind, there was no more impressive building to be found anywhere in Egypt. Almost the moment we left our horses in the donkey park, a stooped man in a dingy gallabiya approached us. He had a dark turban wrapped around his head and a scarf pulled around his neck and the bottom of his face.

"You have hired the services of a guide, no? I am he. Mr. Hargreaves told me to wait for you here. I would have met you at your boat so that you would have no trouble finding the site, but it seems I need not have worried, as you have arrived."

Obviously, this was Ziad, doing his best to look elderly and infirm instead of youthful and vigorous. He led us into the Lower Court of the temple, which was lined with two colonnades, each with a double row of columns.

"You Europeans describe the pharaohs'

temples as funerary, but that is not an apt description," he said. "The ancients referred to them as temples of millions of years. Yes, they were used as part of the funeral, but they also were the places where the pharaohs' closeness to the gods was solidified, ensuring they would reign over the heavens as they had the earth. Hatshepsut built this one. She ruled first with her half brother and husband, Thutmose II. She was the God's Wife of Amun. Upon his death, she became regent for his young son — her stepson; pharaohs rarely limited themselves to a single wife or a mere handful of concubines — but sometime thereafter declared herself pharaoh, and led Egypt into a prosperous and peaceful period."

"No small feat for a woman in the fifteenth century BC," I said.

Ziad nodded. "Pharaohs are divine. The gods gave her the strength to achieve what she did."

The temple complex was spectacular, with three levels of columned terraces reached via wide, sloping ramps. The pale cliffs loomed behind it all, a not-so-subtle reminder that man's creations did not surpass those of the gods. I turned around and looked back toward the east and the Nile, where the sun was still low in the sky. The air seemed almost to shimmer. Ziad led us through the Central Court to the Birth Colonnade, whose square columns supported its still-intact roof. Painted scenes on the walls told the story of Amun taking the form of Thutmose I and coming to the pharaoh's wife. The result, of course, was Hatshepsut, the daughter of a god, a woman so divine that her gender would not stand in the way of her rule. Even so, throughout the temple, someone — probably unhappy that she'd made herself pharaoh — had hacked away images of her face.

Ziad did not let us linger and pulled us into a small, quiet recess between the Birth Colonnade and a nearby vestibule. "We will not have this place to ourselves for long," he said, lowering the scarf and revealing an exquisitely handsome face, "but there is no better location for us to speak without being overheard. I have only done what Effendi Deeley asked of me. It is no decision of mine, he alone could make it."

"I'm afraid I'm not sure what you mean," I said.

"If the man wants to be mummified, who am I to stop him? You English are strange creatures. It is not for me to judge."

"Mummified?" Kat asked. "That's fantastic! What a thing to do. I might follow his example. Can you think of anything more phenomenal?"

Had I been less shocked by what Ziad had revealed, I might have responded to Kat. As it was, I couldn't think about anything beyond Lord Deeley's request. "He wanted to be mummified?"

"Yes, Lady Emily, it was always so. I have studied the ancient art and agreed to do the work for him. It is no crime! He was very clear that this was to be done only after he was dead — I took no part in his murder. I did not leave Per Ma'at because I was guilty or afraid, but because I had to make preparations. Only later did I learn I was suspected of killing my master."

My head was spinning. "Lord Deeley was buried in the Foreigners' Cemetery in Luxor."

Ziad grinned. "Only temporarily, as he planned. I removed the body from its grave the night of his burial. There was no moon, you recall. It made my work easier. I reburied the coffin and brought Effendi Deeley to the workshop I have set up in a cave in the desert. After the required seventy days, I will place his mummy and his grave goods in the tomb he selected."

"Lord Deeley's body is in a cave in the desert?" Mrs. Hargreaves looked dangerously pale, but I knew she would not let herself faint. We both of us despised swooning females.

"Yes, yes, of course, madam, I am following all the procedures exactly. There is no need to worry."

I tried to figuratively step back from the situation. No doubt, numerous people had odd requests for their burials. Sir Richard Burton, who tried — but did not succeed — to find the source of the Nile, was buried in London in a stone tomb designed to look like a Bedouin tent. I believe camel bells were strung from the ceiling inside. If Lord Deeley wished to be mummified, that was his prerogative. Except . . .

"Why the false burial?" I asked. "Why not let his wishes be known?"

"Effendi Deeley was very clear. Just like the pharaohs, he wanted no one to know the location of his tomb so that he would not be disturbed. He looked forward to a peaceful afterlife."

"Where is the tomb?" Mrs. Hargreaves asked.

"Now, madam, you know I cannot tell you that. It would go against Effendi Deeley's wishes."

"Effendi Deeley was murdered," Kat said, "so his wishes may have to be ignored."

"I see no reason for that," Ziad said. "He is already dead. The location of his body will not reveal the identity of his killer."

"You mentioned grave goods," I said. "What, specifically, do they include?"

"There are canopic jars, of course, for his organs — not the heart, which must stay in his body to be weighed against the feather of Ma'at. There are five ushabtis to serve him in the afterlife. There is a copy of the *Book of Coming Forth by Day,* which contains all the spells he will require. Some furniture, so that he will be comfortable. Clothing made from the finest linen. Games for his entertainment. Many objects, Lady Emily, too many to name individually. Effendi Deeley collected them himself. He didn't want new things, but ancient ones. Except for the clothing. Ancient linen he could not find readily available. Most of the things have been in place waiting for some time except the canopic jars and a few other objects. Those he brought to me the day he died."

"The day he died?" I asked.

"Yes, he had arranged to meet me."

"When did he make the arrangement?"

Ziad shrugged. "A few days earlier, I don't remember. He did this every year after he arrived in Luxor. He would bring me more things for his tomb. This year, we visited the site together."

"You didn't do that normally?" I asked.

"No, only this time."

"Did he bring to you three statues of ancient gods, Ptah, Thoth, and Meret-seger?" I asked.

"Yes, along with canopic jars and his ushab-tis. He does not worship those gods, but he told me they came from the site he chose for his tomb, as did his ushabtis. I argued he should have more than five, but he was adamant that he wanted only the ones he found in what will become his tomb."

It had to be at Deir el Medina, where Mr. McLeod had found a single ushabti, signed, like Lord Deeley's was, *my way is good.* "Is the tomb part of an ancient necropolis?" I asked.

Ziad grinned. "No, Lady Emily, he did not want it somewhere so easy to find. Otherwise, what good would it be?" We heard voices approaching. "Is there anything else you want from me?"

"We want to know who killed Lord Dee-ley," Mrs. Hargreaves said. "Can you offer any illumination on the subject?"

"Some questions, madam, are not meant to be answered. Would you like to finish our tour of this magnificent temple, or must you return to the river?"

420

Evidently, this, too, was a question not meant to be answered. He disappeared into the shadows before we could reply. We searched but found no sign of him anywhere at Deir el Bahri. I paused on the ramp rising from the Central Court to the Upper Court. The sun was beating down on us from the porcelain blue sky.

"I think I'm beginning to understand," I said.

"How so?" Kat asked, looking ready to scream from frustration. Mrs. Hargreaves was silent and ashen. "I'm more confused than ever."

"In the end, a murder always makes sense. So much about this one doesn't — or didn't — at least not until I looked at it from just the right perspective. I believe I finally have that perspective."

Colin, who had followed us to Hatshepsut's magnificent temple, did not show himself until we were back at the *Timsah.* I left his mother and Kat to tell him what had happened while I composed a series of telegrams. When I received the expected replies, I read them but kept the contents to myself. I wasn't sharing my thoughts with anyone, not even Colin. They were too raw, too ill-formed. Now, though, I knew the only way to finally sort through them was to say them out loud to all of Lord Deeley's guests. I couldn't explain every detail — that would come only if I managed to get them out of the others. They held pieces of the puzzle that must be revealed. But they weren't the only ones. I sent messengers to summon Mr. McLeod and Mr. Mallaby to Per Ma'at. We arrived there shortly after them. I gathered everyone — along with the loyal Jones — in the dining room at the house, seating them around the table where we'd shared our host's fateful last meal.

"This case has been the strangest I've ever been part of," I said. "So many pieces seem at odds with one another. Lord Deeley died from poison after a feast he had meticulously planned for his friends. Soon afterwards, we came to learn that many of these friends — Mr. Granard, Mr. Troubridge, and Mrs. Hargreaves in particular — had cause to be angry with him. Possibly, angry enough to want him dead."

Mr. Granard rose from his chair, banging a fist on the table. "I say, Hargreaves, if you think I shall quietly take your wife flinging baseless accusations —"

"Sit down, Granard," Colin said. "I've yet to hear an accusation."

"You've not heard one because I'm not

making one," I said. "Mr. McLeod and Lady Wilona had motives as well, but they were weak. I thought the murderer was doing his best —"

"Or her best," Kat interrupted.

"Quite." I continued. "Doing his — or her — best to cover his own tracks. If everyone had a motive, why notice his — or hers — in particular? Yet, two of those motives were all but worthless. Mr. McLeod would have appreciated funding from his friend, but he wasn't left altogether in a lurch. He still had a year to find it elsewhere. As for Lady Wilona, her friends are no strangers to her financial plight."

"It is utterly outrageous that you would slander me so," Lady Wilona began. I did not let her finish.

"Lady Wilona is not a woman without sense. Mortifying though help from Lord Deeley might seem, it was far preferable to the alternative, and hence, not a motive for murder. Lord Deeley's death did not help her — it harmed her. There will be no more financial aid coming from him. At least not directly," I said. "We all know how colorful the newspaper reports concerning the murder at Per Ma'at have been. That is to be expected in the circumstances, at least to a point, but one reporter in particular, you,

Mr. Mallaby, had obviously found a willing source among us, someone ready to reveal every available detail about Lord Deeley's guests. Do you care to share the person's identity?"

"A reporter doesn't unmask his sources, Lady Emily," Mr. Mallaby said. "He would never get another one if he did."

"As I suffer from no such obstacles, I'll do the honors." I walked toward Lady Wilona. "It was a gift, wasn't it, to find a reporter on hand, ready to pay you for information, just when your benefactor's death threatened your comfort?"

She sputtered but could not form a coherent word.

"Mr. Mallaby, how did you come to find yourself in Luxor?" I asked. "I learned this afternoon from a lady of unimpeachable character that you are not the *Daily Yell*'s usual correspondent in this part of the world."

"No, I'm not." He shifted uncomfortably and tugged at his tie. "My editor received a letter — an anonymous letter — nearly three weeks before the murder, stating that an ancient curse was about to doom Lord Deeley and his guests. My colleague, Kevin O'Connell, was the one who would ordinarily cover such events —"

"Events?" Colin interrupted. "Fictions, more like."

"Call them what you will. The letter suggested that if I were sent instead, a source would present herself. It also included various details that would induce the person in question to speak to me."

Lady Wilona's face had turned an alarming shade of crimson. Her cheeks puffed. Her torso shook. I almost started to fear for her health. "I have been used abominably! I was told that my insights into my friend's death would help flush out his killer. I was careful to draw no attention to what I was doing. That's why I pretended to be poisoned. It gave me the perfect excuse for taking tea outside of the house. Mr. Mallaby and I met at the Luxor Hotel so I might keep him abreast of developments."

That she believed the drama of her fake poisoning was discreet beggared all belief. We all looked astonished at the suggestion. She continued.

"For such a valuable service, I would naturally be compensated. The man from Scotland Yard assured me this was as it should be."

"What man from Scotland Yard?" Colin asked.

"The one who wrote to me, explaining the

situation."

"Do you still have the letter?" he asked.

"No, I destroyed it, as I'd been instructed. There was nothing phony about it. It was written on the finest paper."

"Heavy linen, with an engraved bee at the top, typed not handwritten?" I asked.

"That matches the description of the letter I received telling me about Lady Wilona," Mr. Mallaby said.

"And the ones I found," Kat said.

"It's also the same stationery used by the killer to write the letter ostensibly sent to Mr. Granard," I said. "The letter was placed in his wife's book the day Lord Deeley died, probably around the same time the apricot pits were left in Mr. Troubridge's wardrobe. It was the apricot pits more than anything else that troubled me. They were such an odd thing to find, yet they were essential, were they not? We also found an old diary that contained a picture of Sisley Weldon and her daughter. A picture that wouldn't have drawn our notice if we hadn't already been told to suspect him of something nefarious, which is exactly what the apricot pits were meant to do."

Kat's mouth dropped open. "I never meant to —"

I stopped Kat. "I'm not accusing you of

426

anything. Think on it, though. Anyone searching Mr. Troubridge's room would have come across the diary and the photograph. What of it? It's no crime to keep a memento of a past relationship. But the killer needed our attention drawn to that relationship. Why? So that we'd learn the truth about the aftermath of it. Sisley Weldon was a financially unstable unmarried mother. Unable to support herself and her child, she gave the baby away, and then, unable to live with her despair, she killed herself. Sisley Weldon was the only woman Mr. Troubridge has ever loved, the only woman he would ever consider marrying. He'd always wanted a child. Unfortunately, he never told her that, which made her easy to manipulate."

"There now, where are you going with this?" Mr. Troubridge said. "No one manipulated Sisley. Her death was a tragedy, a tragedy that could have been avoided if I hadn't been such a bloody fool."

"Could it have been avoided?" I asked. "Lord Deeley stepped in and offered financial support for the child, ensuring she would grow up in comfortable circumstances, but he specified that she must never know anything about her biological parents."

"How do you know this?" Mr. Troubridge asked.

"I've had a letter from Miss Weldon's sister," I said. I passed it to him. "She wrote that Lord Deeley asked Sisley to give her two pictures: one of her and the baby, as well as another of Sisley with you, Mr. Troubridge. She complied. They were the ones we found in your journal. She also wrote that she knew without doubt that Sisley never loved any man but you. She is certain Marian is your daughter."

"And we are meant to believe that Caspian has known so all along, aren't we?" Kat asked.

"Precisely," I said. "It gives him a reason to want his friend dead. Which brings us next to my mother-in-law, who also has a motive for murder. Or so it seemed. The letter Kat found tucked into her nightclothes — typewritten on the same stationery we're all so familiar with — suggested that Lord Deeley was driving the carriage that struck down Nicholas Hargreaves, leaving him fatally injured. What stronger motive could one have? If Lord Deeley had killed her beloved husband, surely Mrs. Hargreaves would want revenge. This is where our killer went a bit awry, reaching too far. Yes, Mr. Hargreaves was hit by a vehicle. He fell into a coma from which he never recovered. There was no need to discuss it further. We English prefer to pack away unpleasant things from which nothing good can ever come, a practice that is not wholly unreasonable."

"I can't agree with that," Kat said, crinkling her nose.

"Mr. Hargreaves was already unconscious when the doctor reached him, but his wife was at his side before that. Mrs. Hargreaves admitted to me that her husband briefly regained consciousness before he died. I suspect he told her what happened. He knew who had hit him: a local man, one of his own tenant farmers who was driving on dark, icy roads to go home to his family. His wagon skidded and struck his landlord. He saw at once that the injured man would not survive. Horrified by what he'd done and terrified of the consequences, he fled. No one had seen him. Mr. Hargreaves bore him no ill will — he knew it was an accident. He didn't want the man punished or shamed. Mrs. Hargreaves agreed to keep the secret. So you see, she has no motive for murder." This was all speculation on my part, fueled by my mother-in-law's reaction to the possibility that her friend had been involved. She never seemed upset enough by it. It was as if she knew without doubt it wasn't true. I hoped she would now admit this.

"What does this have to do with anything?" Mrs. Hargreaves asked. "This is a private matter, handled by me at Nicholas's direction."

"So I'm correct, am I?" She nodded. "You spoke to the man responsible, didn't you? Neither you nor your husband would have wanted him to live with the guilt."

"The way the road curved, he couldn't have seen Nicholas until it was too late, and the wagon slid on the ice," she said. "It was no one's fault."

"Did you ever speak of the incident to anyone other than the man in question?"

"Bertram knew," she said, her voice a bare whisper. "He knew everything. He remembered John Thomas's wife, who had worked as a maid in his house in Cornwall. She's the one who asked Nicholas to come see her ill husband that awful night. Bertram went to her asking questions. He wanted to find whoever was responsible — he was furious on my behalf, angry while I grieved. I couldn't let him mount an investigation that could have ruined everything. I was determined to keep my promise to Nicholas that the man would not suffer as a result of the accident."

"Once again, a motive for murder vanishes," I said. "But what hasn't vanished? There's more to the stories of each of these friendships. You helped me begin to see the way, Mr. Granard, when you admitted to me that it was you who told the prime minister about your Oxford prank that went horribly wrong. You confessed and got a cabinet position, but your partner in the hijinks was not so lucky. Lord Deeley was never named a minister, despite years of dedicated service to the party."

"That's hardly my fault," Mr. Granard said. "He could have admitted to what we'd done as easily as I had."

"Why didn't he?" I asked.

"How should I know?"

"I suspect that you didn't go to the prime minister without first speaking to your friend. To have done otherwise would have been a betrayal, and you consider yourself a man of honor. Surely you at least proposed the idea to him? Perhaps you suggested that confessing would put you both in a stronger position, as you wouldn't have to live in constant fear of the scandal coming out and sinking your careers?"

"We may have discussed it in principle, but we never addressed it directly," Mr.

Granard said. "It was clear to me that he had no interest in bringing it up. He was confident no one else ever would."

"Yet you weren't so confident, were you, Mr. Granard? You feared scandal." I turned to Mr. Troubridge before the other gentleman replied. "You, sir, are no stranger to such things."

"I've never claimed otherwise," he said.

"Lord Deeley stood by you when the rest of society abandoned you," I said. "He valued your friendship because you amused him."

"That's right. I'm not the sort of gent good for much else," he said.

"The ladies find you the most amusing of all, don't they?"

"There now, I won't have that sort of thing discussed in mixed company."

"I heartily agree," Lady Wilona said as most of the others around the table made noises of assent. "It isn't appropriate in the least."

"And cyanide poisoning is?" I asked. Everyone settled and fell quiet again. "I suspect that Lord Deeley wasn't altogether honorable in his handling of the situation with Miss Weldon. I didn't understand why she went to him when she found herself with child, but according to her sister, she

432

knew he was your closest friend. Afraid to confront you and face rejection, she tested the waters with Lord Deeley first. He pounced on the opportunity to take advantage of the situation. He confirmed her worst fears. He told her you never wanted children and that she'd been a pleasant diversion, but nothing more. You weren't the marrying kind. Miss Weldon plunged into despair. She gave up the baby and killed herself, while he swooped in and financed the child's upbringing."

"That's a horrible thing to say." Mr. Troubridge looked stricken. "If he did any of that, then he never should have called himself my friend. He —"

"What might have caused him to consider himself something other than your friend?" I asked. "Could it have had something to do with his late wife? Lady Deeley, I understand, was rather fond of you."

"Lady Deeley was an invalid who had hardly any joy in her life," Mr. Troubridge said. "I flirted to entertain her, that's all."

"It went further than a flirtation, didn't it?" I asked. "I remember what you told me. That Lady Deeley would have been one of the great beauties of her generation if she hadn't been ill. That she was lonely. That you offered her comfort. That it was *heart-*

breakingly obvious when she was coming close to death. *Heartbreakingly.* I think the comfort you offered her went beyond the bounds of friendship."

Mr. Troubridge's face was the color I imagined one would find on the visage of a sickly crocodile. "She deserved a little happiness. I won't be made to feel bad on that count."

"You had an affair, an affair that Lord Deeley knew nothing about until after his wife's death. That's why he had such a difficult time coping with his loss."

"Yes, but the affair was short-lived. How could I deny her? She was miserable most of the time and Deeley had never been particularly interested in her. I still don't understand why he married her. We never intended for him to find out, but someone —"

"I witnessed things and I told him," Jones said. He'd refused to sit at the table and was standing behind Colin. "He had my absolute loyalty. When it became clear her end was coming, he became rather morbid and started remembering their marriage as something it had never been. I didn't want him to hold false beliefs."

This shocked me. Truly, Jones was devoted to his master, but hadn't this revelation

434

caused unnecessary pain? I had learned of the affair from Miss Weldon's sister. Her letter explained that Lord Deeley had told Sisley about the illicit relationship. Even though it had occurred before she knew Mr. Troubridge, she had not thought him capable of such betrayal. The revelation had devastated her and made it all the easier for her to believe everything he told her about Mr. Troubridge. She threw him over because she believed there was no hope for her and her baby. "No, I imagine you don't understand why he married her," I said. "Perhaps you could illuminate us on the subject, Mrs. Hargreaves?"

"Why would I have anything to say on the matter?" she asked. "It's nothing to do with me."

"It's quite a lot to do with you, actually," I said. "Of all the evidence providing motives for Lord Deeley's murder, that concerning you is the most muddled. We have the story of your husband's death accompanied by earnest journal entries written by Lord Deeley. There's no doubt he wrote those entries. They're in his handwriting. He admits his long-standing love for you. He screws up the courage to confess his great sin, which we are to presume was running your husband down with his carriage.

He writes that you have found your way toward forgiving him. He writes that, at long last, you return his feelings. This is all nonsense, of course. You've never felt anything for him but friendship, and that friendship endured for decades. It had its wobbles, though, didn't it? Particularly on your first trip to Egypt, when you met the man you married."

"That's common knowledge," Mrs. Hargreaves said. "What of it?"

"There's little more distressing than having one's heart broken," I said. "What experience is more emotionally powerful? Countless crimes stem from revenge spurred by lost love."

"I didn't murder Bertram."

"I'm not suggesting you did," I said. "In fact, I'm not suggesting that anyone sitting at this table killed him. The person responsible for his death is not in this house."

I hated my role in everything that happened, but never more so than when I told Bek his wife was dead. My father offered to do it, but I knew it should be my task. I felt almost as responsible for it as Pentu. My brother took in the news quietly. He nodded and then turned and walked out of the room to the steps that led to his roof.

For a while, there was no peace to be found in the village. Everyone was quick to say they'd known there was something wrong with Pentu. Which is worse? Claiming so after evil deeds are done, or standing by quietly until the truth comes to light? I didn't know. For two months, I couldn't bring myself to sculpt. I wouldn't even go into my workshop. Finally, after Sanura's funeral — we buried her in the cave, as she asked — my father told me that if I didn't get back to making his ushabtis, he'd give the job to someone else.

So I finished them. Well, started them. The six I'd already completed I put in a simple wooden box and carried up to the cave on the mountain. I left them there, along with the three statues I'd brought that fateful day. Ptah, Thoth, and Meretseger stood in their niche, on top of the box of ushabtis. And then I began a new set for my father. They were technically better — expertly carved, beautifully painted — but I would always consider the original ones more powerful. Too powerful, even.

As the year drew to a close, I found myself pregnant again. I had no expectations for the child, assuming it, like all the others before, would either die in my womb or soon after emerging from it. But she didn't. She was strong from the moment of her birth, strong and beautiful. We called her Sanura. Bek adored her. No one could have been a more doting uncle.

Three years later, he married again, finally allowing himself to find new happiness, and we all went on with our lives. Things matter so much, but at the same time, not at all. Who will care in a thousand years? No one will know our names. No one will know our stories. No one will know the courage Sanura showed that day in my little cave, the cave where her mummy lies for eternity, protected by Meretseger, She Who Loves Silence.

"If the person who killed Deeley isn't in this house, why in the name of all that is decent have you summoned us here?" Mr. Granard said. "Personally, I find it distasteful in the extreme to be once again around the table where he died. I suppose one could justify it if it were meant to stoke the murderer's guilt to the point where he confesses, but if you're not expecting that, what are you doing, Lady Emily?"

"Lord Deeley presented himself as a man who never held a grudge," I said. "Nearly all of you have assured me of this. Why was that so important to him? The gentleman doth protest too much, methinks. He certainly held a long grudge against the Egyptologists in Luxor. That is abundantly clear. Was Lord Deeley a cricketer, Mr. Troubridge? I assume you are, as you travel with a copy of the laws of the sport."

"I believe he was in his youth, yes," Mr.

Troubridge said. "Does it matter?"

"Cricket is a long game, with matches spanning multiple days, is that right?"

"Yes."

"So it requires patience and strategy," I said. "Just the qualities necessary when planning slow revenge. The meal we consumed around this table was phenomenal, the sort of thing one would expect at a celebration at Windsor Castle. Had it not ended so badly, we all might have considered it among the finest of our lives. Yet it wasn't the sort of thing Lord Deeley normally served to the guests he invited to Per Ma'at. He preferred to serve dishes better suited to the hot climate. Why the change this year? Some have suggested it was an attempt to impress Mrs. Hargreaves. Apparently he knew she was fond of consommé à la Monaco and raspberry soufflés glacés. Do you believe, Mrs. Hargreaves, that the dinner menu was a delicate attention directed to you?"

"Heavens, no," she said. "Yes, I enjoy consommé à la Monaco and raspberry soufflés glacés, but not more than any number of other dishes. They were favorites of Bertram's."

"Precisely," I said. "Just as was every single dish served to us that evening. I have confirmation via telegram from the cook at his house in Cornwall."

"What are you driving at?" Dr. Rockley asked. "I'm beyond confused."

"Lord Deeley was not murdered," I said. "He planned an elaborate suicide and had two reasons for doing so. First, to escape the symptoms of a terrible, progressive disease. Second, to exact revenge on the people he felt had caused the most pain in his life."

Now there was no murmur buzzing around the table, only the sounds of loud outrage. Colin looked at me with shock in his eyes, but that shock turned to admiration almost at once. He had faith that I could back up this seemingly outrageous claim. "Let's settle down and listen to what Emily has to say."

"You all know Lord Deeley's father passed away relatively young. What you may not know, however, is that gentleman — like his own father — suffered from a hereditary disease, the early symptoms of which include clumsiness, depression, and mood swings. As it progresses, the patient loses the ability to control his muscles. He has difficulty speaking and swallowing. He suffers from tremors and seizures. Death usually comes as a result of no longer being able to swallow or from injuries caused by a fall, but suicide is another common outcome. Who could condemn a person for wanting to escape such a dreadful fate?"

"Here now, Deeley wasn't ill," Mr. Granard said.

"Quite right," Lady Wilona agreed.

"He was a bit moody," Mrs. Granard said. "We all saw that. He snapped at that poor serving boy on the boat more times than I can count when there was no cause to do so."

"He did seem a bit low when he called on me in France," Mrs. Hargreaves said. "That's part of the reason I agreed to come here."

"He stumbled rather often on the boat, now that I think about it," Dr. Rockley said. "I'm mortified that I didn't question him about it. He laughed it off, saying he always had trouble getting his sea legs. River legs, I suppose."

"It would explain why when he went for a ride that last day, he chose a donkey instead of one of his fine steeds," Mr. McLeod said.

"You knew he went for a ride?" I asked. "Why did you never mention this?"

"I didn't think it mattered," the archaeologist said. "It's not as if I spoke to him. I saw him and a servant halfway up the mountain path near Deir el Medina. He was on a donkey, the servant was walking alongside."

"This is all a lot of rot," Dr. Rockley said. "If Lord Deeley were contending with a serious illness, he would have told me. He hired me to provide medical care."

"He hired you to reassure us and the authorities that he was in the rudest of good health," I said. "His symptoms weren't yet unmanageable. Yes, with hindsight we can say he was moody and clumsy, but only in hindsight. No one noticed any problems as they were happening. Only Lord Deeley could. He had seen this disease kill his grandfather and then his father. He had no intention of suffering the same slow decline. He decided to kill himself before the symptoms destroyed his quality of life."

"Forgive me, but you are reaching, Lady Emily," Dr. Rockley said. "I assure you that if he were in the grips of any such disease, I would have noticed."

I lifted up my next telegram. "This is from Dr. Claydon, Lord Deeley's longtime personal physician. It confirms that he, like his father and grandfather before him, suffered from an aggravated form of chorea for which there is no cure. Furthermore, it acknowledges that in the past five months or so, Lord Deeley started seeing an increase in symptoms he knew would get progressively worse. He did not want to live to see that happen."

"That's why he wanted me to act as valet. He didn't want anyone else in a position to see him so intimately." Jones, who had been standing, now took a seat. "I didn't question his motives. Why should I? I never dreamed they could be so nefarious."

"Nefarious indeed," Miss Evans said. I'd all but forgotten she was there. "Why did he want his death to look like murder?"

"Mr. Granard, Mr. Troubridge, and Mrs. Hargreaves all hurt him, deeply. Far from never holding a grudge, Lord Deeley clung to his resentment for each of them," I said. "We can't know precisely what drove him, but it is clear that he wanted the authorities to consider them suspects in his death. He arranged for a reporter to have access to his home and his guests, no doubt to ensure that, whatever happened, all of their reputations would suffer immeasurably. He had to know one of them would be held responsible and hanged for the crime, which he must have considered adequate justice for the wrongs done to him. Lord Deeley was going to die regardless. Perhaps, in his mind, the tragedy of his situation would be mitigated by taking his life in a manner of his own choosing and doing so in a way that would exact revenge on those who had hurt him."

"The powerless do crave control," Lady Wilona said. She, of everyone present, knew that all too well.

"It doesn't justify sending an innocent person to the gallows!" Mr. Troubridge was tugging at his collar, no doubt imagining the feeling of the hangman's noose.

"It most certainly does not," Mr. Granard said.

All the color had drained from Mrs. Hargreaves's face. "We were all unkind to him. We toyed with his feelings, his political fortunes, his life, but we hardly took notice of what we'd done. You, Mr. Granard, chose to believe you were being honorable when you destroyed his political chances. Mr. Troubridge, you assumed that he had too little interest in his wife to care where she placed her affection. I took for granted that he would be content with friendship and never considered his true emotions. We deserve censure."

"But not execution," Mr. McLeod said. "That's taking things rather to an extreme."

"I'm familiar with the sort of chorea to which Lady Emily refers," Dr. Rockley said. "It has severe effects on the mind. Lord

446

Deeley evidently had already lost the ability to think rationally. But how did you come to see it, Lady Emily?"

"It started with the tisane," I said. "I never understood why he made such a fuss about it. He guarded it so fiercely, like a man who was depending on it for everything. Which, in a way, he was. He knew that modern medicine could offer no hope for his condition, but he hoped — desperately — that he could find relief in the older ways. He would try anything."

"When nothing works, what other option does one have?" Dr. Rockley asked.

"Precisely. The evidence popping up all over the house confounded me at first," I said, "until it started to become clear that the killer — whom we all assumed to be a murderer — had deliberately planted it to cast aspersions on nearly everyone. Then I realized that it could have been planted the morning of his death. He sent you all off for shopping and lunch in Luxor, but stayed behind, supposedly in his room, until he went off for his ride. He had ample opportunity to put one letter in Mrs. Granard's Sherlock Holmes, another under the chessboard, another in Mrs. Hargreaves's armoire, and the photographs and apricot pits in Mr. Troubridge's room. In fact, a maid saw him going into Mr. Troubridge's room with a dish of fresh apricots. He was very careful not to be caught doing anything that might appear odd. It was trickier getting Mr. Hargreaves's ledger — which Lord Deeley took from the British Museum — onto the *Timsah*, but he managed that earlier in the day, when he met us at the dock in Luxor. He came aboard to greet us and must have slipped it onto the bookshelf in the boat's saloon. He went down there on the pretense of seeing if flowers he claimed to have sent had been delivered. We suspected nothing. The simplest part of his plan was dealing with his own diary. He could have written the entries pertaining to Mrs. Hargreaves anytime and left the bookmark deliberately placed to point us in the right direction."

"How do you know he took the ledger from the British Museum?" Miss Evans asked. "I should have thought any number of people might have."

"You can't access these sorts of records without first asking permission of the keeper," I said. "I have a telegram from that man, stating that Lord Deeley asked to see all the records concerning Mrs. Hargreaves's donations to the museum the week before he set off for Egypt. No one requested them before or since. The objects weren't of particular interest to scholars."

"I still don't understand how you came to suspect suicide," Mrs. Hargreaves said.

"It wasn't until we spoke to Ziad," I said. Now, I explained to the others Lord Deeley's true plans for his burial; they were all suitably horrified save Miss Evans, who pointed out that the tenth Duke of Hamilton had requested the same treatment and apparently was buried in an ancient sarcophagus.

"He was much taken with the work of Mr. Thomas Joseph Pettigrew, who was an expert at unwrapping mummies in the first half of the last century," she said. "He hosted parties so others could watch. I suppose it was deliciously morbid. My grandmother's sister worked in his household. That's how I know about the duke." No one said anything for a moment. I paused, then continued, ignoring her comment.

"Ziad met with Lord Deeley the day of his death — he was the servant you saw, Mr. McLeod, walking beside his master's donkey near Deir el Medina. He gave Ziad the final objects to be included with his burial goods: his canopic jars, ushabtis, and the three statues of the gods. All of these were things that he'd kept in his bedroom, precious objects he'd found in the place he planned to be buried, objects he would not part with until almost the moment of his death. He had to get them to Ziad before he died, so that they could be put to their intended use. Ziad thought nothing of it, because he did not have any reason to suspect Lord Deeley particularly treasured those items. He assumed it was like every other year when Lord Deeley brought more grave goods for his tomb. The only difference was this time, Lord Deeley wanted to visit the tomb. Why? Because it was his last chance to make sure everything was in order. Satisfied that it was, he returned home, drank a scotch, waited for his guests to return from Luxor, and proceeded with his plan."

Jones nodded. "Ziad talked about the ancient religion often. He seemed rather taken with it. I always thought it stemmed from his being superstitious and having an interest in the antiquities in the house, but it must have been more. Lord Deeley turned to him for help because of that knowledge."

"It's a compelling story, Lady Emily, but can you prove any of it?" Mr. Troubridge asked.

"Lord Deeley made sure to leave no confession," I said, "but I would argue that yes, my proof is incontrovertible, backed up with evidence provided by all of you, his servants, and, perhaps most significantly, his personal physician. You each had a piece of the story, but until it was taken all together, it didn't make sense."

"Now it does." Mr. Granard was staring down at the table.

"There is one final thing." I held up a last letter. "All of the letters planted in Per Ma'at were written with the same typewriter. People rarely realize that the way a specific machine strikes is as unique as an individual's handwriting. I asked the housekeeper in Cornwall to send me samples of typing from any typewriters in the house, not because I suspected Lord Deeley of any underhanded actions at the time, but because I thought there might be someone in Cornwall angry enough at him to turn to murder. There was only one typewriter on the estate, used by Lord Deeley's steward, kept in the man's office. The letters are a perfect match for those on the missives meant to cast suspicion on Lord Deeley's friends. He typed them himself."

"It's hard to believe," Mr. Granard said. "I'm dreadfully sorry for my part in all of it. I don't like to think I played any role in driving a dear friend — for that's what he was, no matter what happened between us — to suicide."

"I wouldn't say you played a role in that." Colin's voice was low, but authoritative. "He chose suicide knowing how the disease would savage him. He could have achieved the same result without having attempted to destroy the lives of three of his friends in the process. It's important to separate the two things."

"Will the police be brought in again?" Mr. Troubridge asked.

"I will inform them of what has transpired," Colin said. "Ziad will be cleared of all suspicion and the matter will be settled, once and for all."

"Pity Deeley didn't get what he wanted in the end," Mr. Troubridge said. "Not that I regret avoiding the hangman. It's just a bit sad, isn't it, that something that so consumed him came to naught?"

"I can't agree," Mrs. Granard said. "Revenge is futile. Even if he had succeeded, what good would it have done? He would already have been dead and not seen the effects of his plan. It was badly conceived and badly done. I shan't hold it against him as there is reason to believe he was not in full control of his faculties."

"It would have been better if he'd never

tried," Mrs. Hargreaves said. "None of us will ever be able to remember all his good qualities. He's ruined that forever."

"I think you'll find that in time, you'll be able to reconcile the good with the bad," I said. "We're all more complicated than perhaps we'd like to think. No one is all good or all bad."

There was little left to say. We sat around the table, quiet, for what felt like an interminable period of time, the silence broken at last by Lady Wilona.

"I want to see his tomb," she said. "His real tomb. I don't care what he believed about the afterlife. We're not going to steal his grave goods or . . ." Her voice trailed for a moment. "We won't demand that the mummification be stopped. What would be the point?"

No one argued against her.

"I'd like to see the tomb, too," Mrs. Hargreaves said.

There was a general consensus on the subject. Mr. Granard was particularly firm.

"You must demand that this Ziad fellow take us there," he said. "Enough of this bowing to absurd ideas about the afterlife."

"They're not absurd," Mr. McLeod said. "At least they apparently weren't to Lord Deeley, and Ziad gave his word that he would not reveal the location of the tomb. It would be wrong to force him to. I know the hills around Deir el Medina better than most. I'm confident I can find the site, but will do so only if you all promise to leave Ziad out of it. He's suffered enough. Furthermore, there will be no stories written about this for the newspapers, Mr. Mallaby. Let Lord Deeley rest in peace."

What was there to do but agree? Mr. McLeod was right that we ought not force Ziad to go back on a promise to his respected employer, regardless of how ridiculous any of us thought it to be. The next morning, my husband and I would set off with him, in search of a modern tomb.

Before he returned to the boat, Colin went to the police to take care of all the administrative details of the case. No one objected to reclassifying Lord Deeley's death as suicide except, perhaps, Mr. Mallaby and his colleagues. No doubt they would conjure up some way to keep the story of the curse alive, even if they wouldn't know anything about the tomb. Mr. Mallaby had promised to never write a word about it, in exchange for Mr. McLeod promising him two exclusives: one, on the intact tomb he'd found at Deir el Medina, the second to come should he ever find a tomb brimming with golden treasure.

The sun had just started to rise from the horizon when we set off for Deir el Medina the next day. We scoured every inch of the mountain that towered over the ruins of the village, the four of us searching in different directions. It was nearly four o'clock before Mr. McLeod called out.

"Look, here, this seems to be something!"

We clamored to join him on a narrow outcropping barely visible even once one knew where it was. It led to a low opening in the side of the hill. He lit a lantern and then ducked in first; I followed immediately after. The flickering light revealed a small cave, crammed with burial goods, just as Ziad had said, with a simple stone sarcophagus in the center. The ushabtis were in a wooden box nearby. The canopic jars were nowhere to be seen. They would remain in Ziad's ersatz workshop with Lord Deeley's body until the mummification process was complete. A niche carved into the wall held the statues of Ptah, Thoth, and Meretseger that had once stood on Lord Deeley's bedside table. They were signed *my way is good.*

"It's as if they have returned home," I

said, standing in front of them. Each vibrated with personality.

"Possibly, but it's just as likely they were found somewhere else," Mr. McLeod said. "When excavators don't keep proper records, there's no way of knowing."

"No, I can't agree," I said, "not about these sculptures. They belong here. I can feel it."

"Far be it from me to argue with a lady's intuition. To do so never gets a chap anywhere." He stood next to me and studied them. When he continued, his voice was stilted. "You know, I think you might be right. I admit I was humoring you, but now . . . there is something about them, isn't there? It's as if there's a spirit in them. They look almost alive. And at home. Yes, they do belong here. Our sculptor, whose way is good, was onto something, wasn't he?"

"She." I smiled. "I'm convinced they were made by a woman."

"Of course they were," he said. "Now I am humoring you again, Lady Emily. We will never know anything about whoever carved these wonderful pieces. That does not, however, take anything away from the wonder of them."

"There's another coffin," Colin said, hold-

456

ing up his lamp in a dark recess in the back of the cave.

It was ancient, fashioned from wood, and beautifully decorated. Mr. McLeod pulled a brush from his pocket and gently removed the dust from it. "It's a woman," he said. "We could guess that from the size, but don't have to as her name is spelled out here. She was called Sanura." He pointed to a group of hieroglyphs.

"And now that you've spoken her name, she lives again," I said. "Isn't that what the ancient Egyptians believed?"

"More or less." He looked puzzled. "I don't understand why she's buried here. Surely Deeley didn't mean to share his tomb . . ."

"Why not?" I asked. "Surely she was here first? It would have been ungentlemanly to evict her from her eternal resting place."

"Perhaps he accepted that she belonged here," Colin said, "along with her grave goods, goods they will now share. Dashed odd, though."

Mr. McLeod shuddered. "Insensible though it may be, I agree. She belongs here. I can feel it."

"She must never be moved," I said. "Even Lord Deeley could see that. Otherwise, he'd have put her on display in Per Ma'at. I wouldn't have thought the dead could have power over a man like him."

"I wouldn't go that far," Mr. McLeod said. "The coffin isn't nearly spectacular enough for his collection. It's a beautiful example, though. You're correct that we can't disturb her, much though I'd love to open the lid. Sanura will be allowed to rest, undisturbed."

The following day, Mr. McLeod took Lord Deeley's guests to his tomb. Colin and I did not accompany them, staying on the *Timsah* instead. Lord Deeley's journals had arrived from Cornwall that morning. While I no longer needed to search for evidence that he had not harmed Nicholas Hargreaves, I was still interested in his excavations. His notes on the subject were rather limited, evidently because his digs were unauthorized and he didn't want a clear record. However, he had spent the winter of 1881–1882 exploring the hills around Deir el Medina. He used a magnificently decorated chapel for storage, just as Howard Carter had suspected, and was forced to remove the objects he'd collected when he learned the authorities had become aware of his activity. He lamented not having had time to remove sections of the painted walls and having lost one of a set of six ushabtis. He recorded mentioning the *my way is good* signature to one unnamed Egyptologist and having been met with derision. The man insisted any pieces so marked must be forgeries but was never given the opportunity to examine them. Both Mr. McLeod and Mr. Carter assured us they were authentic. I was glad to have the matter settled.

"Now, at last, we can properly explore the area, but how best to begin?" I asked. We were sitting on the deck, my Baedeker's and a map open on the table between us. "Do we go straight to the tombs in the Valley of the Kings or explore the mortuary temples first? And what about Abu Simbel?"

"I propose that we send Kat and my mother off on their own," Colin said, taking my hand and gazing into my eyes. "I'm happy to visit any and all sites you propose, but let's go alone, so that, at last, we can succumb to the endless romance of the Nile. We need not rush. I can hire another boat."

I was already imagining every detail. A delicious warmth coursed through me. "We could start by —"

I heard a voice that sent chills down my spine. I stopped cold and looked at my husband. He, too, sat frozen.

"Mama, Papa, we're here! We've arrived at last! I thought a duke would do a better job of expediting our trip, but I've only recently been told that some of them are more useless than others." It was Henry, charging along the dock. Richard and Tom — the latter wearing a decent reproduction of a pharaoh's striped helmet — followed a few steps behind. Further back, I spotted my dear friend Jeremy Sheffield, Duke of Bainbridge, walking next to an enormous box punched full of what looked like air holes that was being carried by four burly servants.

"I've brought a crocodile," Henry said, mounting our gangplank. "Dukes are good for something, it seems, even the useless ones. I can't believe you've never told us His Grace has a private menagerie at one of his houses. It's unforgiveable, Mama, truly. I've a lead for Cedric — that's what I've named him — so he can walk along the banks of the Nile with me. Won't it be grand?"

Grand was not the word I would have chosen. So much for the endless romance of the Nile. We would have no privacy, regardless of the number of boats Colin hired. The enthusiasm evident on the boys' faces made it impossible to wholly regret their arrival. Colin squeezed my hand. I knew what he was thinking. We would come back, alone. For now, though, I had to turn my focus to something more urgent. The servants had lowered the box and opened it, allowing the creature — on his lead — to step outside. I hadn't the slightest notion of how to care for a captive crocodile, but something in Cedric's yellow eyes told me he wasn't satisfied with Jeremy's accommodations. Could crocodiles have exacting standards? I suspected I would find out soon enough.

ACKNOWLEDGMENTS

Myriad thanks to . . .

Charles Spicer, the best editor in the business.

My wonderful team at Minotaur: Sarah Grill, Andy Martin, Terry McGarry, Sarah Melnyk, Danielle Prielipp, and David Rostein. Special thanks to Omar Chapa for drawing such perfect hieroglyphs.

Anne Hawkins, agent extraordinaire.

Barbara Peters, whose insights into Egypt — not to mention into mysteries — are unparalleled.

Lindsay Ocal, a wonderful, resourceful, and sharp reader who tracked down the best possible Egyptian grammar for Emily to study.

Cara Sargent, who taught me Middle Egyptian at Yale.

Brett Battles, Rob Browne, Bill Cameron, Christina Chen, Jon Clinch, Jane Grant, Nick Hawkins, Elizabeth Letts, Lara Matthys, Carrie Medders, Erica Ruth Neubauer, Missy Rightley, Renee Rosen, and Lauren Willig. Love you all.

Alexander, Katie, and Jess.

My parents.

Andrew, my North Star.

BIBLIOGRAPHY

Aldred, Cyril. *The Egyptians.* 1961. 3rd ed., London: Thames & Hudson, 1998.

Allen, James P. *The Debate Between a Man and His Soul: A Masterpiece of Ancient Egyptian Literature.* Leiden: Brill, 2011.

———. *Middle Egyptian : An Introduction to the Language and Culture of Hieroglyphs.* Cambridge: Cambridge University Press, 2000.

Baedeker, Karl, ed. *Egypt: Handbook for Travellers.* 5th ed., Leipsic: Baedeker, 1902.

Creasman, Pearce Paul, ed. *Archaeological Research in the Valley of the Kings and Ancient Thebes: Papers Presented in Honor of Richard H. Wilkinson.* Tucson: University of Arizona Egyptian Expedition, 2013.

Humphreys, Andrew. *Grand Hotels of Egypt in the Golden Age of Travel.* Cairo: American University in Cairo Press, 2015.

465

———. *On the Nile in the Golden Age of Travel.* Cairo: American University in Cairo Press, 2016.

McDowell, A. G. *Village Life in Ancient Egypt: Laundry Lists and Love Songs.* Oxford: Clarendon, 2001.

Mertz, Barbara. *Red Land, Black Land: Daily Life in Ancient Egypt.* 1966. 2nd ed., New York: William Morrow, 2008.

———. *Temples, Tombs & Hieroglyphs: A Popular History of Ancient Egypt.* 1964. 2nd ed., New York: William Morrow, 2007.

Meskell, Lynn. "An Archaeology of Social Relations in an Egyptian Village." *Journal of Archaeological Method and Theory* 5, no. 3 (September 1998): 209–43.

———. "Archaeologies of Life and Death." *American Journal of Archaeology* 103, no. 2 (1999): 181–99.

———. "Intimate Archaeologies: The Case of Kha and Merit." *World Archaeology* 29, no. 3 (February 1998): 363–79.

———. *Private Life in New Kingdom Egypt.* Princeton, N.J.: Princeton University Press, 2002.

Robins, Gay. *Women in Ancient Egypt.* Cambridge, Mass.: Harvard University Press, 1993.

Simpson, William Kelly, ed. *The Literature*

of Ancient Egypt: An Anthology of Stories, Instructions, and Poetry. New Haven, Conn.: Yale University Press, 2003.

Wilkinson, Toby. *Lives of the Ancient Egyptians.* London: Thames & Hudson, 2019.

———. *A World Beneath the Sands: The Golden Age of Archaeology.* New York: W. W. Norton, 2020.

Wilkinson, Toby, and Julian Platt. *Aristocrats and Archaeologists: An Edwardian Journey on the Nile.* Cairo: American University in Cairo Press, 2017.

Wilson-Yang, K. M., and George Burns. "The Stability of the Tomb of Nefertari 1904–1987." *Studies in Conservation* 34, no. 4 (November 1989): 153.

AUTHOR'S NOTE

Before I started writing this novel, I reread all of Agatha Christie's Poirot stories. It's impossible to think of Egypt and mysteries without giving Agatha Christie's iconic detective his due. Yet it wasn't *Death on the Nile* that inspired my story. I won't say which book did — so as not to spoil the end for anyone who hasn't read it — but my idea started to form as I realized I was wrong when I tried to guess the identity of the murderer. Christie was a master of misdirection.

Like many others, I first encountered the world of ancient Egypt at the "Treasures of King Tutankhamun" exhibit that toured the world in the 1970s. I was only a small child, but the art, the language, and the history transfixed me. I still have my ticket, yellow with an image of the boy king's spectacular funeral mask. There's something endlessly fascinating about the civilization. Its appeal is universal, going back thousands of years. The pyramids awed even ancient tourists.

The Middle Egyptian word for "father" is transliterated as *jt(j)*. While we can't be precisely sure how the vowels — unwritten in the language — would have sounded, current research suggests the word would be pronounced *eetee*. This is what I have Meryt call her father. Apologies to those who have far greater knowledge of the subject if I've made a grievous error.

I'm indebted to Glenn Janes for permission to use his wonderful translation of the shabti spell. The toast Lord Deeley gives before his last dinner is taken from "Practical Egyptian Magical Spells," presented at the 1998 Oriental Institute Annual Dinner by Robert K. Ritner. It's excerpted from *Grace Before a Meal from Edfu,* retranslated from A. M. Blackman, "The King of Egypt's Grace Before Meat," *Journal of Egyptian Archaeology* 31 (1945): 57–73. The translation of the poem Meryt puts on the statue she gives Sanura is from William Kelly Simpson's *The Literature of Ancient Egypt: An Anthology of Stories, Instructions, and Poetry.*

The pranks that inspired Mr. Granard's odious activities at Oxford are based on the antics of a group of seventeenth-century students, which are reported on in a Christ Church College Oxford blog post, "Student Pranks," from September 1, 2018. These students included Alexander Morison, a "person of notorious and incorrigible debauchery," who was accused of "loud and uncivil clamours and hooting" as well as "debauching with a gentleman commoner."

Alexander, the Tenth Duke of Hamilton, had an extensive collection of Egyptian antiquities. One of the objects he displayed in Hamilton Palace was a sarcophagus that originally belonged to a woman called Iretiru who'd been buried in Saqqara during the Ptolemaic period. The duke apparently liked lying in it, but discovered it was a bit small for him, so he had bits of the inside carved out so that he could be buried in it. After his death in 1852, his body was mummified by Thomas Joseph Pettigrew. It was still too big for the coffin. Depending on who you believe, either the mummy's legs were broken or its feet cut off to make it fit.

In 1906 Italian archaeologist Ernesto Schiaparelli discovered an intact tomb in Deir el Medina. Built separately from its chapel, it belonged to Kha, chief workman during the Eighteenth Dynasty, and his wife, Merit. The treasures inside were extraordinary, providing enormous insight into life — and burial practices — in the village. I hope Mr. McLeod's excavations were as fruitful.

Howard Carter started working in Egypt when he was seventeen. In 1905 he was embroiled in controversy after siding with Egyptian guards at Saqqara who clashed violently with a group of French tourists. He refused to apologize and resigned his position with the Antiquities Service. After Carter supported himself for several years as an artist, the Fifth Earl of Carnarvon hired him to take charge of the excavations the earl sponsored. In 1922 Carter discovered the tomb of Tutankhamun.

I know many of my readers will catch the myriad references to Elizabeth Peters's Amelia Peabody series in this novel. I couldn't send Emily to Egypt without letting her encounter my favorite detective.

ABOUT THE AUTHOR

Tasha Alexander, the daughter of two philosophy professors, studied English literature and medieval history at the University of Notre Dame. She and her husband, novelist Andrew Grant, live on a ranch in southeastern Wyoming.